A FORTUNATE MURDER

A NOVEL BY TAMMY SHARP

A
FORTUNATE
MURDER

A NOVEL BY TAMMY SHARP

ISBN # 978-1-68593-188-9

Additional copies of this book are available from the Author.

Also available on Amazon

 WISE PUBLICATIONS

CUSTOM BOOK MANUFACTURING SINCE 1982

809 East Napoleon St., Sulphur, Louisiana 70663

337-527-8308 | wisepublications@yahoo.com

Visit our online Bookstore! **www.wisepublications.biz**

FOR MY FAMILY

Thank you for protecting and providing for me,
even when I didn't deserve it.

Warning: If you've ever been abused (who hasn't?) the following may be a wild ride for you. I pray you've been granted a good seat and good mojo.

"The lust for comfort murders the passions of the soul."

—-Khalil Gibran

1

THURSDAY, FEBRUARY 2, 2017

"If you look for truth, you may find comfort in the end; if you look for comfort you will not get either comfort or truth...only in the end, despair."

—C.S. Lewis

I scooted forward on the cold courtroom bench, trying to get more comfortable. If I sat on the edge of the bench, my feet could reach the floor, but I had to hunch over to write, which was intolerable.

Tilted slightly, the bench sucked me back. If I succumbed, my feet wouldn't reach the floor. Fine. For about 5 minutes, then I'd be out of comfortable positions. I wanted to rearrange myself, but couldn't figure how without disturbing someone else. While I waited for something to change, I looked at my hands. So far this morning, since getting my assignment, I had resisted the urge to chew on my fingernails. Anxiety drummed deeply but remained incoherent. My nails had not looked so good in a long time. Almost polish-worthy. The cuticles were still jagged. And my thumbs, ridiculously short nails in a bed of broken skin, would always remain a hot mess. They ached to be gnawed. I tucked them away into my fists, smashing them until I heard them give a satisfying crack.

you'll give yourself arthritis

My Pawpaw's eyes smiled at me.

like Nanew

He had thought fondly of her. She bewildered him, frustrated him, completed him. But we never talked about it.

I did not want her swollen knuckles and said so then.

stop popping them

But nothing else seemed to satisfy. At the age of 10, maybe earlier, I was addicted to satisfaction.

earlier

much

I heard shuffling and looked around me. Everyone was standing. My eyes swung to the doors left of the judge's bench looking for the distraction. Wearing orange coveralls and walking into the courtroom to the defendant's chair, was my oldest and best friend Caci. Her hair, dark brown at the roots, orangish on the ends, sprang out from her head in many directions.

Medusa

In my mind I saw her yawning sleepily, throwing her pillow at me as she stomped off to the bathroom.

just tryna survive

She'd kept it dyed ash blonde ever since she got permission in seventh grade. It was a striking contrast to her dark skin and eyes. She hated her curls, but I thought they were her best feature, wild, unpredictable and fun. Like Caci. Now, it looked as if she hadn't paid her hair much attention in a while. Her face, no make-up, was ashen. The courtroom, too bright, revealed deep creases, made deeper by gauntness and darting, bruised eyes. Her cheeks were sunken.

When I looked at her and not who she used to be, the sores made me suck in my breath. It looked as if a windshield had shattered in front of her, leaving behind dozens of tiny, now scabbed over, cuts speckled across her face and arms. Her mouth seemed to work of its own accord, in spasms. I couldn't predict it.

My throat ached. I felt a wave of nausea.

Caci's court-appointed lawyer was standing, shoulders hunched, at the table beside her. Caci was jiggling one of her shackled legs. If her mother were here she'd put her hand on that jouncing knee to stop it from rattling her shackles. Was she a flight risk? The big bailiff had a gun. Had Caci jumped on somebody? I almost hoped she had.

heck yeah

Her lawyer looked as if he were trying to remember something, flipping through his pad, handwriting scrawled across the pages. His desperation bothered me like a familiar itch. By now I was sitting on the edge of the bench, back straight, trying not to fidget. I looked at my hands, pressing my nails and fingertips into one another as hard as I could and wondered how he'd become a lawyer with that sort of anxiety.

I glanced up in time to see Caci look over her shoulder and spot me. There was surprise, then a shot of joy I felt like a current, then jittery despair. She didn't look away. Her eyes widened, and her mouth tightened. Then she led my eyes toward the door in time to see Ty Stewart, of all people, breeze in. My stomach gave a sickening, familiar lurch, and I felt the tip of my most attractive fingernail slide over the edge of my bottom teeth, painfully.

His suit was gorgeous and looked very expensive. His shirt also looked brand new, so white it almost glowed.

mama's boy

do not

bite that

I took my fingernail away from my mouth. A scene from an old movie with Brian Dennehy as a lawyer or D.A., I couldn't remember, played out in my mind.

he keeps a new shirt in his desk drawer

still in its package

snide, arrogant, changing a soiled shirt for a new, snowy white one

made you want to slap him

as if he were fooling us right to our face

as if the new white shirt covered his issue

Ty had shaved his head. The shadow of his receding hairline told me why. I breathed in and out several times, calming myself, and put my hand completely down. The baldness, of course, accentuated all his other features: a perfect tan, bright blue eyes and blindingly white teeth.

He had been skinny with braces and a full head of hair in junior high, and later, skinny with perfect teeth and perfect hair in high school. Now he was a handsome, trendy lawyer dressed in designer duds and probably wearing the best smelling cologne in the world. I bet he also drove a Corvette. Or maybe a Porsche. I wasn't sure if Bethel lawyers made that much money. Only small construction companies made those kinds of bucks in small, stagnant towns. And that they made elsewhere. Like Robbie Lynn's father—*Ohhhh, noooo, it's Mr. Bill* and Ty's father, Edward, Mr. Ed—*a horse is a horse of course of course.*

I shook my head

kilroy

he wasn't as tall a man as his father—*of course*—neither was he too skinny

"All rise," the bailiff stepped forward as Mr. Ed, the judge, trotted into the room. Caci glanced back at me over her shoulder, and then the judge drew her attention as he sat with a flourish, poised well above everyone else and looking through his bifocals and down his nose. He was a large man, very tall and rotund. His face was red enough that I wondered about his blood pressure. He had a full head of white, untamed hair, a white mustache and white, bushy eyebrows to match.

After maneuverings and short, unintelligible speeches by both lawyers, I was stunned when he banged the gavel, setting Caci's bond at $1 million. Her lawyer looked just as stunned, but Caci seemed unfazed, as if a million bond was no more shocking than a murdered father or murder charges. Her slight frame seemed to deny it all as I watched the bailiff escort her in her noisy shackles from the courtroom.

When she was gone, I walked over to speak to Ty out of politeness.

"Moriah Jordan," Ty said, watching me approach and smiling in a way that made me want to check behind me. He had changed. A lot. For one, he was handsome. His frame and face had filled out. While he wasn't as tall a man as his father of course neither was he too skinny anymore. His muscular frame taxed his suit ever so slightly, drawing the eyes. Up close, his bright blue eyes, perfect teeth and deep tan were even more attractive. That my stomach dipped at the way he said my name as his eyes swept me, was unexpected. He reached out to give me a side hug, which stirred anxiety in my gut.

"Robbie Lynn will be so excited to know you're home," he said with a croon in his voice, making my skin tingle with alarm.

I hadn't made any effort to contact Robbie Lynn when I came home. When Mama told me about their engagement, I was glad I hadn't.

"Where in the world have you been the last few years?" he continued, releasing me and looking down at me as if I were a long lost friend of whom he'd been very fond. He folded his arms and leaned back on the table, crossing his leather loafers. He wasn't wearing socks. I wondered if becoming a lawyer included charm classes. I stumbled into the politeness of adulthood as much as I could. "Freelancing," I said with a shrug.

"And now you're home?" I did not like that he was asking the questions, but I had none of my own ready. "For good? I guess you can write from anywhere these days." He seemed as if he had all day to visit.

or flirt

of course

His father, the judge, had left the bench, and the courtroom was clearing.

"For a while, anyway," I said, wanting to get away.

"I'm sorry to hear about your mom. That must be hard." I supposed empathy classes were part of law school, too.

I shrugged again. "Thank you. She's fine for now." What I didn't say and would never to anyone, especially Ty, was I didn't trust her very much to make sound decisions. And there was no one else.

"Well maybe we'll all get lucky and you'll decide to stick around. *The Times* could use some polishing."

His polite words took me by surprise again so I mumbled "Thanks."

Then, in self defense said, "A million bond seems kind of steep." He smiled, but his eyes were not soft, as if he knew he hadn't fooled me. "Now let's not be overly dramatic, Mojo," which he knew would cause me to bristle. But I just let him explain things to me.

"First, it's not at all uncommon in a situation like this, as you well know, I'm certain. And you also know I can't talk about it," he said.

there he is

prissy lil thang we all remember

is this his first rodeo

He stood from the table, as if he were done entertaining me, as if he had no time for someone who would ask him to break any rules, and turned to gather his things.

"It's always worth a shot," I said. But he didn't see my smile, so I kept jabbing. "It's a cozy courtroom scene, too. Just like old times. You, your dad. Caci, her dad. Robbie Lynn's dad."

He turned back to me, his eyes glittering, and searched my face. Then, as if he didn't find anything of interest, he shrugged. "Well," he said. "It's a small town. We're all bound to bump into each other professionally."

I crinkled my eyebrows at his understatement.

"We all have to do our jobs, Mojo," he said, sneering a little like old times. "Even if we don't like it. Even if it involves the murder of a dear friend by his meth-addicted daughter."

By now he'd turned away to finish snapping his briefcase closed.

"Alleged, you mean." He acknowledged me but barely nodded. "And as long as it's fair," I said, shrugging. I saw his jaw tighten but didn't hang around for him to say anything back. "See you later, Ty-Baby," I said, twiddling my fingers at him like his mama, beating him not only to the exit, but to the revival of our less pleasant nicknames.

I felt him watching me as I left.

Being the news editor in a small town also included being the news reporter, a graphic designer, the webmaster and sometimes the receptionist. When I got back to the office from the arraignment, Hank, the publisher, wouldn't listen to me about recusing myself.

"Suck it up," he'd said, shrugging. "Them's the breaks in a small town."

Furious, but helpless, I clocked out when I left his office and went to my car. I couldn't really afford to lose my job. I'd been home a month, employed a week and, since Mama had been doing so much better, had also just moved into a little house. Like three days after getting the job. Stroke or not, I could not live with my mama, but I had to be as close as possible. And that meant renting, which meant I needed an income. I tapped out a vague message to Hank about not expecting me back in, as I had some personal business and meetings in the evening. He had agreed to a flexible schedule in lieu of more money.

I needed to go see Caci.

I didn't know if she was capable of killing Mr. Rob.

I'd tried to call her before I arrived home, before I knew anything, but didn't get an answer.

secret secret

Then Mama had filled me in same as she had with Robbie Lynn, almost in the same breath, as if to prove she'd always been right about those girls. I let her. I hadn't spoken to either in over a decade, and I had enough to worry with, I told myself, with Mama and trying to find a job and a place to live without taking on Caci and her issues. And then she was arrested for murdering her father.

The 12-foot fencing around the detention center was topped with spiraling razor wire that winked in the sun. Concrete picnic tables were situated at various spots in the yard. I was surprised at how easy it was to see her. I had only to say: "Acacia Molejo" to the receptionist before I found myself sitting across from her, plexiglass between us in the stale, hollow visiting room. We were alone. Up close, she was thinner than I'd ever seen her. The scabs on her face stood out like tiny gashes. She was twitchy and had a hard time making eye contact. Her symptoms were plain to see, but not as pronounced as I'd read they could be. She still had all her teeth, though she was grinding them and working her jaw in a way that alarmed me. I wondered how meth had changed her inside.

"It took you long enough," she said into the receiver and then gave a little laugh and seemed to shrug. I couldn't tell if it was a twitch or if she was really shrugging.

"I wasn't gonna leave my mama and my job to come hunt you down. Besides, I tried calling. You never called me back." My tone held a simmering anger I hadn't realized was there.

"Whatever," she said, this time lifting her left shoulder in a solid shrug. Her gauntness was surreal. I rolled my eyes at her, not caring if I hurt her feelings, wanting to hurt her.

"What do you need?" I was fighting the urge to leave her to her misery. How could she choose this? But earlier, in the courtroom, she had used our old language to ask me to come. There had been a time when words had not been necessary between us.

"I need you to check on Micah. Mama has him. He has basketball every Saturday at the gym. This Saturday is his birthday. Just go put your eyes on him and let me know. Mama's pretty mad at me. She won't bring him to see him."

"Yeah I can do that." It sounded thin. Caci's mother would take care of the boy.

"Micah and Daddy were buddies," she said in a broken whisper that cut me. "He was a good grandfather." I knew she wasn't a murderer, and she didn't deserve to go to jail for something someone else had done.

"Caci what happened?" I blurted. She shifted her eyes. I felt tears in mine. I wiped at them, and she did the same, viciously, then covered her eyes with her hand. Then she took a deep breath and looked up. I bit my lip and tried to look reassuring.

"This is such a mess, Mojo. God. I'm an awful mess," she said, her eyes imploring me for something I didn't understand.

She looked down at the table top in front of her. I tried to think of something to say. Her hand shook before she clenched her fingers together in a fist and said my name, making me look up at her face again. She was staring at me.

"Remember our sleepovers at Robbie Lynn's?"

I almost snorted out loud, and I saw her lips tighten, a minute shoulder jerk, as if she were also holding in a laugh, but no, it looked like relief. For a moment I was back sneaking a smoke from her mom's pack while Caci watched, trying not to laugh. "Yeah, I remember."

"I wish we could go back," she said. She was staring at me hard. "Remember the Pirate Project?"

"Yeah. Jean Lafitte," I said, thinking also of Ty and my worst memory. "Contraband Days," I said.

Robbie Lynn's mother took us to the festival in Lake Charles in the spring of our seventh grade year, both as a reward for winning the regional social studies fair in our division and so we could do more research for the state competition. We had spent three whole weekends together either in Lake Charles or at Robbie Lynn's house, working on the project and having the time of our lives. Or at least that's how it felt to me. They had been fun-filled, extravagant weekends, as Robbie Lynn's mother always seemed to have an endless supply of money and never grew tired of carting us around and spending it. But I think it must have also been the beginning of the end for Caci and me.

The night before we were supposed to go down to Lake Charles for the festival, Robbie Lynn's parents had a backyard pool party. I rode with Caci and her parents over to Robbie Lynn's, and we all walked around back to the pool. There were already people there, very few of whom I knew. Mr. Rob seemed to know all of them.

Robbie Lynn was lounging in a deck chair in a red two piece and making gaga eyes at Ty. Next to her, also in a lounger, was Lana Dowd. Ty had eyes only for Lana, who also had on a red two piece, but filled out more. Ty was ignoring Robbie Lynn, and Lana was ignoring them both. I was thankful that he hadn't noticed me at all.

Ty was always quick to make fun of someone. I was his target most of the time. An ordeal at the restaurant only a few weeks before had seemed to give him an endless supply of ammunition.

Caci, Robbie Lynn and I had gotten together at the restaurant on a day it was closed to spread our things out in the dining room to work on the Pirate Project. At some point, Ty had shown up with Mr. Ed and Mr. Bill. They had all secluded themselves in Mr. Rob's office, while Ty stayed in the dining room with us. Robbie Lynn became immediately useless as most of her babble became directed at Ty. But Ty was ignoring us all, playing a handheld video game.

Then we heard a delivery truck pull up, which was not uncommon. For some reason, Caci got very quiet and still. I was asking their opinion about the display board. No one answered me, so I looked up. Robbie Lynn had abandoned us to talk at Ty, who was doing a superb job of not noticing her. Caci was staring at the door to the kitchen. I looked over in time to see her older cousin, Memo, walk through. I saw him look at Caci, and I saw the look on Caci's face, which I didn't understand.

The next thing I remember I was standing near the kitchen door breathing hard. A bitter metallic taste was in my mouth. I felt wetness on my thighs and realized I had peed on myself. I looked around and the three fathers were standing side by side, crouched and facing me, their hands extended toward me, as if warding off a wild animal, but also trying to corral it. They were standing between me and Memo, facing me. I realized they saw me as a threat. I couldn't see Memo clearly, but I heard him cussing as he slipped through the kitchen door. "She bit me!" he yelled in his thick Hispanic accent.

"Just calm down, Mojo," Mr. Rob said, his voice full of pity and understanding.

"What the hell!" Mr. Ed said, his head bobbing as he looked at me. His face was blood red, and I thought he might have a heart attack right there. Mr. Bill was also looking at me, his lips curled in distaste.

Then I felt Caci's hand slip into mine.

"He scared her," she said to her father.

I didn't know what she was talking about, but I didn't say anything.

"That's no reason to bite a man hard enough to draw blood, like a savage little animal," Mr. Ed said.

I heard Ty snigger and looked over at him. He rolled his eyes at me and sneered, looking pointedly at my wet pants.

"Gross!" he said. "She's got blood on her mouth. And I didn't see him do anything. He was just walking past and she went crazy on him, like a little drama queen. Like a rabid bunny."

I reached up and wiped my mouth. My hand came away smeared with blood which made me sick. I bent over and puked. It splattered on the floor, causing everyone except Caci to take a step back. Caci just patted me on the back and held my hair.

Terrified, I was crying before I even stood back up. Caci's empathy on top of the terror was more than I could bear. Robbie Lynn came forward and with Caci ushered me to the bathroom where they helped me clean up.

Caci began babbling as soon as the door shut. She let go of me and started digging around in a nearby cart. "He's always trying to scare us," she said, still digging. "I hate him. I'm glad you bit him and I'm glad he's bleeding. I hope he bleeds to death." She finally straightened with a make-up bag in her hands. She switched her babble to make-up then, to all of our relief.

Robbie Lynn, had begun dispensing paper towels and handing

them to me as I wiped my face, my eyes, rinsed my mouth and blew my nose repeatedly. Her eyes were wide as she listened, but she didn't say anything. Before long her father came to the door and told her it was time for them to leave.

Caci and I stayed in the bathroom until we were sure Mr. Ed and Ty were also gone. She didn't say much else about what had happened. Instead, we spent the next hour experimenting with makeup. Both of us wanted to forget what had happened.

From that point on, Ty called me Rab, short for "rabid." Sometimes he called me "Bunny." When he called me Rab, if Robbie Lynn was nearby, she'd slap playfully at his arm as if he'd made a cute joke and change the subject.

At the pool party that day, Caci and I both hung back, especially with Lana there. We all three hated her flawless, snobby guts.

"Girls, did you bring your swimsuits? Robbie Lynn! Your friends are here! Why don't you take them upstairs to put their stuff away and to change?" said Mrs. Helen, Robbie Lynn's mom.

Upstairs Robbie Lynn gushed about Ty, while Caci and I rolled our eyes at each other. We got all the way back down to the pool before I remembered sunscreen. So I turned to go back inside, falling in behind the three fathers who detoured into what looked like Mr. Bill's office at the bottom of the stairs.

Upstairs, I dabbed sunscreen on my face, then jogged back downstairs to do the rest poolside, but the sunscreen slipped out of my hand, hit the carpeted stairs with a muffled thud and bounced and skittered underneath a table right next to Mr. Bill's office. It went all the way up against the wall behind the table. I passed by the opened office door and got down on my hands and knees to reach the sunscreen.

"You don't want to do that, Rob," I heard Edward say. He sounded annoyed, commanding, his red, blustery face, I imagined, like it had been the day I bit Memo.

Mr. Rob, who spoke with a heavy accent, said something I didn't understand.

"You're going to ruin everything." That was Mr. Bill.

Then Mr. Rob said something else. Then very plainly I heard him say, "He's out of control." He was louder. Upset.

"How about I have him brought in and questioned?" said Mr. Ed. "That might cool him off. He's just a thug who's too big for his britches." His voice had taken on a soothing tone. "Just keep playing along. Let's not be idiots."

"It's not that much more money," Mr. Bill said. "What's the big deal? I'm sure she'll be fine."

"We'll help you figure it out," Mr. Ed said. "Don't worry. Go ahead and do what he's asking. We'll cover for you. Just in case. We don't want anything to happen to your mother. And like Bill said, it's just a little more, not a lot. Maybe he won't ask again. We'll see if we can't get him picked up for something."

At that point I was afraid that they would see me and think I was eavesdropping, which I was, so I grabbed my sunscreen and slipped back out to the pool.

"Caci, how's your grandma?" I asked her. It was her turn to be surprised. And then a morose look came over her face.

"She died about a week before all this. We didn't even get a chance to see her before she passed. And we didn't get to go back to Mexico for the funeral. Daddy was pretty upset over it."

"I'm sorry," I said. "What were you gonna say about the festival?" I asked.

"Oh, just that being at Robbie Lynn's was my favorite," Caci said, her eyes taking on a deep intensity as she looked at me. "I especially loved her closet. She always had the best stuff in her closet," she said, enunciating oddly.

I stared back at her and Caci's eyes widened at me. Robbie Lynn had always been way more girly than either of us. Spending time with Robbie Lynn almost always included a shopping trip of some kind.

My first shopping trip with Robbie Lynn, her mother and Caci had been an eye opener. That same weekend, at the mall in Lake Charles, Robbie Lynn had made a beeline for a popular clothes shop and had gathered up five or ten outfits in her arms and headed for the dressing room while her mother browsed unconcerned.

Caci, too, had an armful of clothes. I followed behind them to the dressing room.

"Why don't you get something to try on, Mojo?" Robbie Lynn asked as she slipped into the dressing room. I shrugged. I had $50 Mama had given me for the weekend. I didn't see the point of trying on anything if I couldn't buy it. Turns out, I never spent the $50 that weekend, or any other weekend I spent with them, as Mrs. Helen paid for everything.

"Mojo, why don't you have anything to try on?" Mrs. Helen said from behind me. "Come here. What size are you? Do you like this?" She held up a pair of jeans. The price tag said they cost $100.

"Um," I said, mortified. I couldn't even buy a pair of socks in this store. But Mrs. Helen put the jeans in my arms.

"Go on," she said, pulling a couple of blouses and a hoodie off the rack as she urged me to the dressing room. "Hurry up, I need to get over to the department store." Once in the dressing room, I couldn't resist trying them on. I loved them all and would have jumped at the chance to take them home. But I sure couldn't buy them; it was well over $300. I left them in the dressing room when I was done.

Robbie Lynn, Caci and Mrs. Helen were all at the cash register when I came out. I was shocked to see that Robbie Lynn was buying almost everything that she'd tried on, almost $500 worth of clothing. Mrs. Helen pulled out a wad of cash to pay for it.

"Mojo you didn't like anything you tried on? I'll pay for it, honey." She looked at me expectantly.

"No, ma'am," I said. "It's ok. None of it really fit," I lied.

"Well, ok, but are you sure? I don't want you to not get something."

"I'm sure."

"Caci, what about you?"

"Yes, ma'am," Caci said, putting her haul on the counter. "But Daddy gave me money." Then she, too, pulled out a wad of cash.

In the department store, Mrs. Helen filled two buggies with items, all of which she paid cash for. She even made a dash through the girl's department and picked a few things out for me just because she didn't want me to leave empty-handed. I was astounded. I had never seen so much money all in one place and was a little scared we might get robbed. But no one else seemed concerned. My two best friends seemed to have an endless supply of money. I wasn't sure how those things worked, but I figured it was because they both had fathers that took care of them. When we got back to Robbie Lynn's house late that night, she stuffed all her new clothes into her closet. Neither Caci nor I would have been caught dead in any of her clothes. Too much pink and purple for us.

But Caci had not been talking about Robbie Lynn's clothes. That weekend had also been the weekend we had all three started smoking, calling the cigarettes contraband. We'd swiped a whole carton from Robbie Lynn's mother, who chain smoked and bought in bulk. Then we'd hidden the cigarettes in Robbie Lynn's closet, along with a fifth of vodka Caci had swiped from the restaurant.

Caci's intense gaze never wavered, causing my heart to start a slow thud in my chest.

"You know I never kicked the habit. I could eat a cigarette right about now," she said. "Did you quit?"

"Yeah. Five thousand times before it took," I said. My head was buzzing, like the first nicotine rush after giving in again. It was difficult to concentrate on what Caci was saying.

"Cigarettes are contraband here." She was looking at me, but it felt like she was at the end of a tunnel, reminding me of the telephone game we used to play. I couldn't be sure that I was really hearing what she was saying to me. There was too much between us, too much space, too many people.

"Well now would be a good time to quit a lot of stuff, Caci," I said, knowing my answer sounded canned, but knowing too she was the only one who would hear it that way.

"Yeah," she said. "Contraband gonna do me in." She seemed to be done with the messages.

secret secret I've got a secret

I knew what she wanted me to do. But she was still looking at me intently. "Remember that day at the restaurant when we were little and the food truck came? Not the day in seventh grade," she amended quickly, referring to the time I bit Memo, which she knew I didn't like to talk about.

But I didn't remember.

"What? I got nothing," I said.

She narrowed her eyes at me, as if she knew I was holding out on her. "That was like the best day of our lives." She had a tone I couldn't read.

I shrugged, done with the game. She knew I hated it when I couldn't remember. Not only did I not remember that day, I didn't remember Caci ever bringing it up before. "Got me, Case. If it was such a good day, then tell me what happened."

She watched me carefully, then shook her head and sighed. "I don't think I'd be here if I had a memory like yours."

She looked behind her at the clock on the wall. "Can I get you to do me one more favor?"

"I'll try," I said, miffed at being dismissed, at her holding out on me, but also glad the conversation was nearing an end with no more emotional pitfalls to navigate.

"Can you go by First Baptist and talk to the preacher for me?"

Again she took me by surprise. Caci had never been religious. "Sure. What do you want me to tell him?"

"Just ask him to pray me out of this awful mess." Then she hung up the receiver on her side, still looking at me even as the guard escorted her out. At the door, she lifted her hand to her mouth, swiping her index finger and middle finger over her lips.

It was our old sign for a smoke, for escape, to get away, smoke a cigarette like we saw our mothers do, to huddle up and hatch a plan.

As I got into my car in the parking lot the words "awful mess" echoed in my brain, reminding me of a Diamond Rio song. I was trying it out in my head, recalling the lyrics, and remembering again, with something akin to bliss or joy, and like a refrain, that the man behind the coffee cup was the one I wanted to marry.

When I got to addiction my mind rebelled, so I forgot about the mess Caci was still in, despite everything, and went back to my old, familiar mantra of "LA Woman," singing the simple refrain, letting it carry me back into town, away from the detention center, the razor wire, brick and fence holding my best friend captive, and back, on purpose, into the fray.

2

*"...the trouble is, humans do have a knack of choosing precisely
those things that are worst for them."*

—Albus Dumbledore, Harry Potter and the Sorcerer's Stone

By the time I got to the office Friday morning, Hank had already fielded half a dozen calls from concerned officials about my visit with Caci. Theresa, our receptionist, had intercepted me at the time clock and told me he wanted to see me the minute I came in.

"Didn't your mama ever tell you that whatever you do will beat you home in Bethel?" he asked when I sat down across from him in his office. His chubby face was a little pale, and he was perspiring. He used a handkerchief to wipe the sweat off.

"You know the judge has threatened to bar you from the courtroom," he said, glaring at me. "And both attorneys would be delighted."

I snorted. "The prosecutor is the judge's son," I pointed out. "The murder victim was also the judge's buddy and business associate. How is that fair and impartial?"

"Well I guess that evens things out," he said, not letting up on the glare. "It is what it is, but the prosecutor is sure not visiting the accused in jail."

"I didn't visit her as your reporter. I am her friend before anything else," I said. "I've tried to tell you that I should be recused from the story. I'm sorry if you were blindsided."

Hank threw up his hands in disgust and cussed. "Well let me be very clear. You either need a job or you don't. Do not visit her again or you will be unemployed. You are an observer, not a participant in this story.

Report what you see and hear. All copy goes through me. You can be friends again after the trial."

The mindlessness of that last remark infuriated me. Caci was staring at life in prison at best, the death penalty at worst. Though the last execution in Louisiana had been in 2010, the fear was by no means absent. I guess Hank could see finally by the look on my face how much this was getting to me. He sighed and ran his hand through his sparse hair, looking away from me.

"Look, there are things going on here that you don't know about. Hell, I don't even know about." He put air quotation marks around the word "know."

That got my attention. "What do you mean?"

"It's just a feeling. A deep gut feeling I've had for a long time. I've never had the time to really pursue it. I can't make it to all the meetings or do any investigating if I also run the paper. Suffice it to say that things are not what they seem. There are some questionable things going on, and I need someone who is discerning and not prone to getting in trouble to help me figure it out."

He was being mysterious, which irritated me. "I thought that was you. Maybe I was wrong."

"Just tell me what you suspect. Whom do you suspect? Of what, exactly?" I needed details.

"No. I need to see if you find the trail I'm on."

This time it was me throwing up my hands. "Hank I'm no investigator! I'm a feature writer for crying out loud. I don't even know how the law process works, assuming it's law enforcement you think is crooked. I don't even know enough to ask the right questions. And I'm emotionally involved. I can't be objective."

"It's not rocket science," he said. "You're smart. You can learn. You can put two and two together, and I'm betting you have good instincts," he said. "Most of the time. Plus, I can answer your questions about how things work and make sure you're being as objective as possible."

"Give me some hints." I hated not knowing something almost as much as I hated getting in trouble and being scolded.

"No. Just pay attention. And stay away from the detention center. Now go away."

Outwardly, I huffed at being dismissed, but got up and left his office. He was right behind me and shut his door as I stepped through.

Inwardly, I was mortified, angry, befuddled and even more paranoid now. But basically we were back where we started, except now, apparently, on threat of being unemployed, I could not be Caci's friend. And now there was some kind of mystery I was supposed to unravel with absolutely no leads. More fodder for the anxiety gnawing at my stomach.

I couldn't afford to be unemployed. If Hank thought something was fishy, I could already tell him I believed it. My gut told me Caci was being framed, and Ty, probably Edward too, and maybe Robbie Lynn's daddy, had something to do with it all. I resisted the urge to throw my stapler at Hank's door and instead grabbed my bag and left the office to drive around aimlessly, while I thought things through.

It was a little chilly but otherwise a nice day. The sun was shining and daffodils were blooming in people's yards, a sure sign that winter was almost over.

I mulled over my conversation with Caci, while at the same time trying to block out Hank's assignment. But thoughts crowded in.

manipulator

bunny trail

rabid

I set the radio and swung onto the nearby interstate so I could cruise and think. Interstate 10 between Bethel and Lake Charles would be deserted this time of day. It was surrounded by farmland, with the Calcasieu River thrown in. It was a pretty drive, isolated and fast. Perfect for a good think.

I need to visit Robbie Lynn.

and Ty

heck no his turf.

I switched gears back to work.

sheriff's office

BPD

are they the ones Hank thinks are crooked?

God, if it's him.

shut up about him, really

What about Hank's gut?

Gut!

The word echoed from a junior high incident, I was sure. I ignored it, following the path of logic: given my conversation with Hank this morning, I knew the subject of Caci would likely come up, and I would likely be scolded. Again. To top it off, contacting the sheriff's office was not high on my list for another reason. My point of contact, the chief detective, probably hated my guts from high school.

gah

Guts

moving home was a bad idea

Hank had a great system for getting copy for the paper. Having been a one or two-man show for a while, he'd developed ways to get information quickly and had trained the community to send him tips and information. Some arrest reports, the juiciest from the point of view of the arresting entity, as well as minutes to public meetings, the basic fodder of any small town newspaper, were emailed to him. Citizens emailed photos of their kids and pets and community events, which were excellent filler. He also spent a lot of time on the phone, tracking down details and asking questions. With the advent of the internet, most everything had moved online, but the old timers still enjoyed the paper copy, so everything we did went into both the weekly edition and the online edition.

"But it's not my druthers," Hank had told me of his information gathering system during the job interview. "It works in a pinch and as long as nothing is really going on. But nothing can replace having a reporter there. And that's what you'll be doing. You'll go to the public meetings. Go look at the police blotters, go to the events. Look for the things they're leaving out of their press releases. Listen. Ask questions. Learn to read people. Wonder what's really going on. You'll have to learn to take pictures. And you'll write what you see and hear. Five hundred words at a time."

It was watchdog journalism, pure and simple and lonely, a little pathetic, but good. And necessary, but rarely, in most small places.

Hank had seemed certain, more certain than a naturally suspicious person, that something was going on in Bethel.

stop chewing your fingers

stop cracking your knuckles

stop get still, now

be. still.

she wasn't talking to you.

Then who?

I typically took people at face value and believed what they told me. I didn't have much choice, given that my own memory was so unreliable. There was a reason no one had ever hired me as a hard news reporter and a reason I'd never sought the job out. I was terrible at spotting lies and cover-ups and evil intentions, mostly because I was so caught up in making sure others didn't catch me in lies and cover-ups and conclude I had evil intentions.

I do

shut up

nobody asked you

It's chaos

let's quit

full of tricks

silly rabbit

can't leave Caci

Or Mama

move in together

terrible idea

awful

work at wally world

be nice to idiots

put stuff on shelves

Clean

I hate that too

people enjoy it

name one

Caci

that's how she found that little rabbit hole in Robbie Lynn's closet

My phone buzzed in my back pocket alerting me to my next task. Lafitte Parish has two villages, three towns and a city, each of which had monthly or biweekly public meetings. Then there were the parish government meetings, school board, library board, chamber of commerce, main street board and various club meetings, such as Lions, Pilot, Kiwanis and Rotary. I had put each organization's regular meetings into my calendar so I wouldn't forget. After I'd made a schedule for attending meetings, I tackled the various law enforcement agencies. There was one in each town, village and the city. The city of Bethel ran independently, with its own jail. The outlying towns and villages, and all the unincorporated areas, depended on the sheriff's office, either for a jail and back up, or for full-fledged law enforcement.

The sheriff's office and city police had too many arrests on a weekly basis to worry with calling me, though they were not above issuing press releases when it suited them, especially during election season, Hank had told me, or when they had a big bust. The sheriff was an elected official. The chief of police at the Bethel Police Department, however, was appointed. I assumed that the mayor, Robbie Lynn's dad, was the head honcho of Bethel. I wasn't very sure at all about the pecking order in city government. However, establishing contact with the two primary law enforcement agencies was on my to-do list next.

I chose the easy way and to visit the Bethel Police Department first. The police station was in the middle of the city in a square brick building painted an incongruous pale pink with green trim.

The receptionist on the second floor was less than polite.

"Help you?" she asked, staring at her computer screen. She didn't even flick her eyes at me, as I peered into the office from the hallway. I was standing behind a locked door with a window in it. An attic fan suddenly whirred to life in the ceiling above me.

"I'm here to see Chief Harrison," I said over the fan.

"Appointment?" I could barely hear the woman over the fan.

"No ma'am. I was hoping for just a quick word."

"He prefers appointments. Name."

I stared at her blankly, not hearing a question in the woman's dull, monotone voice that was barely audible over the fan.

"Honey what's your name?" The receptionist finally looked at me expectantly.

"Oh! Moriah Jordan. I can't hear you over the fan!" This time I yelled, giving in to the frustration caused by the woman's less than helpful attitude and the noise of the fan.

The receptionist's gaze took on a disapproving slant but she stood up, knocked briefly on the closed office door just behind her desk and stuck her head through the door. Then her whole body disappeared and the door snicked shut behind her. I looked around the office. It was a little shabby. The city had seen better days.

The chief's door suddenly opened, and the woman slid back into her chair. A buzzer sounded at the door to my right. The woman never looked up, never said a word. I twisted the doorknob, pushed, and the door swung in, allowing me into her domain.

She flicked her wrist toward the chief's door, never taking her eyes off her computer screen. I glanced back at her screen as I passed behind her. She was playing solitaire. I tapped on the office door, which swung open, so I stepped in and shut the door. The chief was sitting at his desk, hands clasped on the desktop in front of him. He didn't stand.

"Mojo," he said.

I was surprised he knew my name, let alone my nickname. I had only ever known him from a distance. As far as I knew, he'd always been chief of police in Bethel. He was a solid twenty years older.

"Have a seat." He was all business as he indicated the chair opposite him.

"Probably not a good idea to visit inmates," he said. He was a large man, with droopy blue eyes and a pock-marked face. He looked sleepy.

I was feeling like a rookie after my conversation with Hank that morning. In fact I felt like a fraud. I had no idea how murder investigations went or the protocol for the police, the legal system or the reporters covering the story. And now, on top of all that ignorance, I was supposed to be on the lookout for crooked officials. I smiled at the chief, ignoring his remark, and launched into my spiel, hoping for the best.

"I'm just here to touch base with you. If you need coverage or have press releases you can reach me at this number." I handed him my card, which I had hastily printed out last week while I waited for the more professional looking ones to arrive.

"I'll also be checking the arrest reports on a regular basis. Do you have contact information you can share if I have questions?" I kept my smile in place, more for my sake than his.

"You can call Sue," he said.

"Sue?"

"My secretary," he nodded toward the dragon lady outside his office.

Awesome

"Is she always so nice and laid back?"

My question surprised a smile out of him. "She's just protecting her boss," he said with a faint grin.

"A big guy like you ought to be able to protect himself," I said, giving him a teasing glance.

I was shocked at his flush and "awe shucks" expression.

ha!

he thinks you're flirting

crap. shut. up. Mojo.

"Well, let's just say she takes her job seriously," he said.

I refrained from rolling my eyes and mentioning solitaire.

"Ok well, as I said, I only wanted to touch base with you." I stood up to leave, hoping I seemed more professional than I felt.

"Uh, about Caci," he said.

"Yes?" I turned back to him with what I hoped he thought was an open and welcoming smile, but not very personal.

why does he care?

"I know y'all were best friends growing up. But a lot has happened since y'all were kids."

I felt a chill.

he knows something

what

how

"You don't really know her anymore," he said. "Probably be better if you let justice take its course."

"I don't have any intention of interfering with justice, Chief," I said.

"That's good to hear."

I waited a half second before swinging back around to the door. I left with a big smile and a "thank you so much" that would have done my Nannew proud it was so sincerely southern. I even gave Sue a smile and a "'bye now!" with a twiddle of my fingers.

All the while my mind was buzzing.

what does he care?

how does he know Caci so well?

the visit was recorded, idiot.

but why does city police get to view it?

Caci's was a parish matter.

I must have forgotten something.

At the sheriff's office, I thought I was about to have a repeat experience. I poked my head into the office of the sheriff's chief detective, his spokesperson and the authority on any investigation, including Roberto's murder. An older blond woman sitting at a desk writing on a legal pad looked up at me.

"Help you?" she asked.

"I'm here to see Detective Matthews," I said, walking the rest of the way into the room and standing awkwardly at the desk. The room was small, and there was nowhere to sit. A doorway to the woman's left was half opened. The woman peered at me over her reading glasses. Then she smiled at me, putting me at ease. She held up her finger to me looking toward the half-open door like we were about to share an experience.

"Lii-inc," she called with a sing-song lilt to her voice.

Then from behind the door, in an oddly familiar tune I couldn't place came a tenor voice singing:

"Gloria..."

She looked at me and suppressed a giggle.

I recognized his voice.

"You have a vis-i-tor!" Gloria sang back.

"Send 'em i-iin," floated out of his office, this time mocking his secretary's tone, except instead of going up on the last note, he dropped his voice to a deep, impressive bass.

She looked back at me, winked and nodded toward the door.

"You can go on in," she said in a stage whisper.

I was already moving toward the door, anxious to get the meeting over with and a little off kilter from the odd exchange.

he sings

I tapped on the door with my fingertips before pushing it further open and sticking my head in.

"Hello?" I said, looking around the inside. His desk was to the left of the door, and behind him a window. The office was only slightly bigger than his secretary's and just as tidy. It looked out on a squadron of police cars in the station parking lot. The only disarray were the several piles of papers littering the desk. Another chair was against the far wall along with a filing cabinet and a coat rack that had a sheriff's issue jacket and a cowboy hat on it.

Linc was staring at his computer screen, his back to the door. He turned as I came fully into the room, and his mouth opened a bit and then snapped shut. He stood up and came around the desk hurriedly, meeting me at the door, which he eased shut.

"Well if it isn't Mojo Risin'," he said in such a low, familiar tone it brought goosebumps to my arms. "I've been wondering when you were gonna drop by." He was standing close and looking down at me, a smile playing at the corner of his mouth. He smelled really good. The top of my head only came to his chest, so I had to crain up to see his face.

For a second his eyelashes, which were ridiculously long, distracted me. Then his words seeped in and I took a step back in surprise, saying the first thing that popped into my head. "You have? But why?"

"New reporters always come to see me, for one. And most especially if their best friend is in my jail on murder charges." He reached around my waist and put his hand at the small of my back, guiding me toward the empty chair which he placed on one side of his desk for me. That was something that had always irritated me about him, his way of touching me and moving my body where he wanted.

"Oh. Yeah. That's exactly why I'm here," I said, feeling distracted by his touch, stupid and angry all at the same time.

"They don't call me chief detective for nothing," he said, tapping his temple and winking down at me as I sat. He continued around the edge of his desk to sit in his chair on the other side.

"So how'd your visit go?" he asked in a parental tone, leaning toward me on his elbows. His direct gaze was disconcerting, making it difficult to concentrate on his words. I looked away.

Then I looked back. Hank had told me that everyone knew, but he hadn't told me how they knew, though I was pretty certain it was standard to record a murder suspect's visits. I decided to play a little more dumb. "My visit? How the heck does everybody know I visited Caci?"

"Mojo all visits at the DC are monitored. Plus it's an open murder investigation. Of course we watch her. And who visits her."

"You mean you watched me after I left too?"

He just looked at me and smiled. "Well, not me personally," he finally said. "What do you mean 'everybody'?" he asked.

"I just left Chief Harrison's office and he knew. Hank said he got a handful of calls from people. Like before quitting time on Thursday and more this morning. I'm surprised he didn't call me at home last night to chew me out."

His eyebrows had lifted in surprise when I mentioned Harrison.

"That would be the judge and each attorney who called, for sure. Maybe the DA. I felt compelled to notify them. And Harrison, too, huh? That's interesting. Caci's ex-husband."

"Her what?"

"Ohhhh. You didn't know that? Yeah they ran off to Vegas a year ago and got married."

"Oh my God, he's like twenty years older than we are."

"Twenty-five."

My mouth dropped open. "What the heck was she thinking?"

"I would bet she was thinking something like 'easy street.'"

At my look he went on. "Come on, he's the chief of police. I was pretty surprised that he married her, not the other way around. She's pretty deep into meth and has been for awhile."

"How deep?" I asked. I really had no idea except what I'd assumed, based on my visit.

"Well, we'd arrested her at least twice before they got married."

I felt the walls closing in on me. "For what?"

"Identity theft," he said quietly. "Drunk and disorderly."

"Was she convicted?"

"No," he shook his head. "Her parents dropped the charges, both times."

Again, I was shocked.

"What happened with Harrison?"

"That's curious," he said. "I still can't figure out why he married her. I mean he doesn't strike me as a knight on a white horse. But they ended up annulling it. I know Rob was furious about it."

"Why would he care who she married?"

He shrugged. "Maybe he had a Mexican prince picked out for her," he said. Was he joking?

I tried not to show how much what he'd told me disturbed me, that Caci's addiction had progressed to the point that she was committing crimes. Had been committing crimes well before her father's murder. And why had she married Harrison and then just as quickly annulled it? Harrision was so far opposite of her type that it was comical to think of them together. He was so old. And fat.

Then another thought struck me.

"What about Micah?"

"What about him?"

"Does he belong to Harrison?"

"That's a negative as far as I know. Micah came along well before Harrison and Caci were an item."

"Hmmm," I said, doing the math on his age. "What were things like when he was born?"

"She had probably started to use by then," he said. "She moved back in with Rob and Maria after she found out she was pregnant. I'm not sure she knows who Micah's father is. That may have been what made her want to try and get clean. But after he was born she started going downhill again. She got in trouble. They kicked her out, but let her keep her job at the restaurant. I guess she knew Micah was better off with them, because she left him there."

"I guess meth really changes a person," I said, the hopelessness I'd felt in the courtroom when I first saw Caci had come back in an overwhelming wave. How could she ever overcome this?

"You better believe it," he said. "It is evil stuff in a lot of ways. I've seen it ruin a lot of lives. It's everywhere." He was very serious and his face became so intent it made me uncomfortable.

My emotions were getting dangerously unpredictable, making me want to step away from everything. I also had a vague feeling of unrest from the way he had greeted me. I guess I had vainly expected he would start with something else, like "What have you been up to?" Or "Where you been?" Or maybe even "Do you remember me?" instead of growling my name and giving me goosebumps.

I shook those thoughts and the horror of Caci's situation off as best I could and got back to his original question.

"The visit went ok. But I guess you and half the town already know that. I wasn't there as a reporter, but as her friend."

"That's gonna be a tough tightrope to walk," he said.

"No kidding," I said. "Hank won't let me off the hook."

"He ain't got nobody else," Linc shrugged, still looking at me. "Small town troubles," he said.

"It's a regular theme."

"Happens in the sheriff's office too. For instance, I'm Micah's basketball coach."

"Oh yeah? They don't tell you how to handle all these blurry relationship lines in school."

"They do not," he agreed.

"Has Maria been bringing him to practice and games?"

"Absolutely. He wouldn't miss one. He's a good kid. He'll be ok."

"Thanks," I said. "I appreciate that."

He nodded and gave me a deliberate look. "It's probably not a good idea that you visit her anymore."

"I'm getting that," I said.

"I thought her lawyer was gonna pop a vein. He said he was gonna call the judge and get you barred from the courtroom. And the DA kind of agrees with him." He shrugged. "You know it's probably best for Caci, anyway."

He was quiet for a minute, as if trying to determine whether he should go on. Then he took a breath and said, "I gotta warn you, even if she beats the murder charge, meth addicts don't have any friends for a reason. She's not the same person you knew in high school."

I mulled his words as best I could with him staring at me. I did not want anything Caci confided to me to be something that could incriminate her later. And she was in a precarious situation. The temptation to reach out to me might be more than she could resist; therefore I shouldn't give her an opportunity to confide in me. I agreed with that. Plus, if she was able to somehow get out, there was the meth addiction. If she could steal her parents' identity to feed her addiction, she would no doubt do the same or worse to me. Part of me agreed with that. Another part of me refused, but I nodded anyway. "Do you think she did it?"

"Meth addicts can be unpredictable, violent, especially when they think they aren't getting what they need. Caci had a history of going to Rob when she needed money. And he and Maria both were reaching the end of their rope with her. Everyone knew that. But that's all circumstantial," he said. "And off the record," he added.

"What can you tell me on the record?"

"We're looking at a lot of different scenarios," he said. I rolled my eyes at him.

"You can't give me any specifics?" I knew he couldn't and he wouldn't, but I had to ask.

"Not right now," he said. "But you'll be the fifteenth person I call if we make another arrest." He winked. I couldn't help but laugh.

"It's good to know where I stand in the pecking order," I said.

"I can't argue with that."

I wondered briefly if he was referring to our past relationship, but I brushed it off. I didn't want to go there, I reminded myself.

"So the real reason I'm here is just to touch base for the future," I said.

"Yep, I figured," he said, leaning back in his chair. "Want some coffee?"

"No, thanks," I said. I was already jittery enough.

"So, whatcha been doing the last ten years?"

I shrugged, oddly relieved he'd finally asked that question. "Not hard news, that's for sure," I said, avoiding anything personal. "I'm used to feature writing, and that's really what I prefer. No discerning of motives and double meanings, no figuring out processes and protocols. No wondering about who is telling the truth. To be honest, I'm a little out of my depth with law enforcement and court cases."

"Come on, where's the fun in that? Intrigue, politics, corruption, conspiracies. Drama." He stopped, looking at me, but not unkindly. "I thought that's what reporters thrived on. There's more of that kind of stuff in Bethel than meets the eye."

I felt myself blushing.

"No, I don't care for a lot of drama," I said, quietly.

"I didn't..." he started, but I interrupted him.

"Anyway, it's a learning process," I looked back up at him. "It's not what I'm used to and not what I prefer, but if I want to be near Mom..." I trailed off, shrugging.

"You'll figure it out," he said, dismissing my concerns, his voice softer. "I'll give you a crash course. How is your mom?"

"She's good. Recovering. I stayed with her a couple of weeks right after the stroke, and then moved to my own place. She's able to function pretty well. Some of her friends help me keep an eye on her."

"Are you home for good?"

I shrugged. "I don't know. I'm all she's got," I said. "We'll see. She may tell me to get lost when she's completely recovered. Or she may not completely recover." I paused.

"Well I doubt she'd tell you to get lost. I bet she's thrilled to have you home," he smiled, making his eyes crinkle. He reached inside his desk drawer and pulled out a card. "It's got my cell written on the back," he said, handing it to me. "Have you met Melvin?"

I shook my head, no.

"You got time for a little tour? I'll take you around and introduce you to people you'll need to know, show you the blotter, that kind of thing?"

"Sure," I said, taken aback by his helpfulness.

"The sheriff likes to keep things smooth. If you ever have any questions about investigations, I'm your man. Other stuff, like administration, personnel, policy, that all goes through Melvin. He's chief deputy. If you can't get either of us, then Aletha, the sheriff's secretary, or Gloria, can help you. Sometimes we can't or won't always answer our cells. Depends on the situation."

Won't? I wondered, then, since he was being so helpful, said it out loud.

He stood up and moved around his desk. "You know," he said. "Sometimes we might be in the middle of chasing bad guys. Doesn't happen nearly often enough though," he said wistfully. "Small town. I wouldn't say the crime rate is low, it's just not always detectable. Little excitement." He shrugged.

"What do you mean?"

"Well, we've got our typical blue collar crime. You know, break-ins, thefts. It wasn't a big deal a decade or two ago. But it's definitely increasing with the meth problem. Trends across the nation indicate it's gonna get a lot worse. In bigger cities, the meth problem crosses social lines. It might be low lifes selling it, but it's the higher ups funding it. If it's going on in bigger cities, I have no doubt it's going on here. It's easy money."

He held the door open for me. "Come on, I'll show you around."

I followed him through to his secretary's office. He paused at her desk. She smiled up at him. "Yes? Can I help you?"

"No ma'am," he said, flashing her a brilliant smile and plucking one of her business cards out of a holder to hand to me. "We just need one of these."

She smiled at me. "Call me anytime, honey," then she winked. "I know all his secrets."

"Behave Gloria," he said, as he led me into the hallway where he ducked into another, larger room with a few people, mostly women, sitting at desks working. Then we turned into yet another room with a long table in it, a camera at one end of the room and a counter with a large open book on it. Linc put his hand on the book.

"So this is booking. All arrests come through here, get their picture taken and the charges written in this book. I peered at the open pages, which were filled with a variety of handwriting and ink colors. Linc flipped through the book to an earlier date, ran his finger down the page until he landed on something, then motioned me to come in closer. It was the record of Caci's arrest.

"See? It has the date of the arrest, the charges, the arresting officer."

"But it's not a murder charge," I said, bewildered. The book had "DUI; Driving w/o license; and Schedule II Possession," written in for the charges.

"Right. That didn't come until later." He ran his finger down the column again and pointed to another entry with her name. "Once she was questioned, It came out about her father and she was subsequently charged with that."

"You mean she confessed."

"I most definitely did not say that," he said softly, looking intently at me.

"Well, Linc, what are you saying?"

He blinked. "Just giving you a run down of how things work," he said, his tone now brisk. "After booking, the arresting officer writes a report."

I raised my eyebrows. "I'd like to see that," I said.

"Well, you can't until it's all settled. It's privileged until after the trial," he said.

"What? Why? It should be public knowledge." I really wanted to see that arrest report.

"Eventually, it is. But think about it, Mojo. Would it really be a fair trial if the public could see the arrest report and any potential jurors could form opinions before the trial?"

I acknowledged his point. Then asked another question.

"Do all law enforcement agencies have the same process?"

"It varies from state to state, depending on that state's laws. But it's all basically the same."

"So city arrests have the same basic process?"

"Yep," he said. "Same process."

That was a relief. At least now I had some knowledge to take with me when I went back to the city.

Linc was watching me, so I composed my face and asked another question. "So who all gets copies of those reports? All the lawyers, right?"

"Well sure, but they have to do their own legwork. We keep a copy and send a copy to the courthouse. The lawyers have to ask for it."

As he talked, he walked and I followed. He stopped at an office with its door ajar and tapped on the door. "Hey Melvin," he said. An older man looked up from his desk. He was probably pushing sixty, with thinning gray hair and a florid face. "I'd like you to meet Moriah Jordan. She's the new editor over at the *Times*," Linc said.

Melvin stood up and we reached over his desk to shake hands. "Good to meet you," he said. "Melvin Wallace," he added, by way of introduction.

"Nice to meet you Mr. Wallace," I said.

"Oh call me Melvin," he said. "He reached over and plucked a business card out of its tray and handed it to me.

"Thanks," I said.

"I guess Linc's been giving you the rundown? Got you all straightened out about who to call and all that?"

I nodded.

"Good, good," he said, looking at Linc, then back down to his papers, his already pink face deepening to a shade of magenta.

"We'll get out of your way, now Melvin. Just wanted to introduce you," Linc said, grabbing for the doorknob and sending me signals with his eyes that we should leave.

"Nice meeting you," I said over my shoulder as Linc shut the door and ushered me down the hall.

I gave him a puzzled look.

"Melvin is painfully shy," he whispered, emphasizing the "painfully" by drawing it out and rolling his head comically. "He was about to implode."

"Poor fella," I said, feeling a flash of solidarity with Melvin.

When I left the sheriff's office, I headed back out to the interstate for more thinking. Within minutes, I became aware of a black truck that came up behind me very fast, and rode my bumper. My thoughts, which had been clamoring for attention, ceased. I was going 75. My heart thrummed and my skin felt prickly. There were no other cars around. I tapped on my brakes. He didn't back off at all. If anything he may have gotten closer. I gave my windshield a spray of water and let the wipers swish back and forth a few times, so water would hit his windshield.

useless

The driver, whose outline I could see faintly, despite the tinted windshield, was unfazed. The dark hulking figure caused my gut to clench in fear.

Without warning, the truck whipped over into the lane beside me and held steady at the same speed as me, but in my blind spot. I considered braking, my foot jerked off the accelerator. I was too afraid to hit the brakes, too afraid not to. As clearly as if it had been spoken, I felt the threat from whomever was in the black truck flood through me. A sickening sense of deja vu wisped around me like mist. We were approaching a bridge. I glanced over in time to see the driver had inched up even with me. I saw the glint of a gun. I heard the shot, instinctively braked, swerved. The drunk bumps rattled me, and then something else, some other horrific sound screeched before my car plunged into the ravine on the edge of the woods flipping what felt like several times before coming to a stop. The windshield had shattered and the car seemed to have shrunk. Everything was still. Water was seeping in around me, near my head, but how could that be?

upside down

lots of water

get out

get out

get out

I tried to unclasp the seat belt, but it was locked or I wasn't strong enough.

airbag

water

I saw a gun

he's coming back

is that feet?

It's blurry.

that's blood in your eyes

Finally I was able to undo the seatbelt; it wasn't a big fall since the car roof was smashed. I had to rearrange myself to get out the windshield because the door was unrecognizable. I was studying this predicament from outside the car as best I could with blood obscuring my vision, and feeling a little woozy, too, when I heard something. It took great effort to move my eyes to the sound, which seemed to be coming at me from a distance.

"Ma'am! Ma'am? Are you ok?" A blurry older man appeared at the top of the hill, peering down at me.

"Ma'am the ambulance is on the way. Just hold on. How badly are you hurt?"

I couldn't form any words, and then everything went black.

The next thing I remember is Linc's face close to mine.

He was so close I could see the black stubble of his goatee. Not even a centimeter long, but the whiskers still gave him a dark, mysterious look. He wasn't looking at me. He was looking at my head and frowning. I put my finger on his chin so I could feel the scratch of his beard. This caused him to look at me. "Hey, choir boy," I said.

"Hey goofy," he said, his face only inches from mine, but he was already looking away, at me, still, but not my face.

He looked a little pale. A drop of sweat rolled down his temple and plopped on my cheek, like a tear, and, then, remembering Lana, I pulled my hand away from his chin. His hands were outside my vision, somewhere above me, holding something to my head. I reached up.

"I got it," he said, glancing back down at me with a reassuring smile. "Just relax."

Without moving his hands, which were holding something to my head, he swiped the side of his face with his shoulder. He was wearing a navy blue tshirt, with the Lafitte Sheriff's Office logo on the pocket. The sleeve, now damp from absorbing the sweat on his face, stretched as he moved his arm, revealing smooth skin over the bulge of his bicep. He had already switched his attention back to my head.

nice tan

dizzy

shut your eyes

"Another head injury." I opened my eyes again and found him looking at me. Studying me. After a second or two he seemed satisfied and looked back at my head. "But at least not another coma. Not even unconscious this time." He smiled and seemed relieved.

"I'm sorry," I said, without really knowing why I was apologizing. "Is it bad?" I rolled my eyes up as if I could see what was going on, but that made my stomach churn so I shut them again. Then I became aware of another man, I guessed a paramedic, and opened them again, this time looking past Linc. Yes, I was inside an ambulance, on a gurney. Linc pulled the bandage away and the paramedic peered at my wound.

"Naw, looks like a bad cut is all," the paramedic said. "Head injuries bleed a lot. Still need to take you in to get checked out. Maybe a couple stitches." He took the bandage from Linc, pressed it back against my head and put my hand up against it. "Can you hold it?"

I nodded.

"Definitely she needs to be checked," Linc said to the paramedic. He had been leaning over me. Now he pulled away. "What the heck happened? And where did you learn to talk like that?"

"What do you mean?"

"You were cussing like a sailor when I got here," he said. "Something about an idiot driver in a big black truck. Much more colorful language though."

I just stared at him.

"Do you remember?"

"What are you doing here?" I redirected him, because I did not remember.

"Hello? Sheriff's office. It's my job. And don't change the subject." But he wasn't looking at me. He was squatting inside the ambulance now, next to me, one knee pulled up. He had pulled a notebook out of his back pocket and flipped to a clean sheet.

I watched him, and wondered. The sheriff's office didn't typically handle car accidents on the interstate highways, did they? That was for the state police. And even if the sheriff's office did, wouldn't a car accident fall to a deputy?

"Where is the state trooper?" I asked.

He looked around. "On his way. I just spoke to him. The nearest one is about 30 miles out. So you got me until he gets here. Now. Tell me. What happened?" He looked at me intently, all business.

I told him about the black truck, the choice between concrete parapet or ditch. He wrote while I spoke. I did not mention the gun.

"Did you happen to notice make and model? License plate?" He asked.

"It was a big black truck with tinted windows," I said, "but not so tinted I couldn't see the shape of the driver. It was definitely a man. A big man. And the truck too. Like it was so big I would have to jump to get inside. You know, like high off the ground."

"Well that narrows it down to half the rednecks in Lafitte Parish," he said. "Thankfully the other half drive big red trucks."

"Sorry," I said. "I was kind of busy trying to stay alive."

"Of course you were," he said, looking at me again. "And you did a fine job. Barely a scratch," he winked at me, and my heart did a slow flip.

daaaang it

he could be in on it

he is not

prove it

"And now you gotta go get that scratch taken care of." He looked at the paramedic. "X-rays, too, right?"

The paramedic nodded.

"Good. This isn't her first head injury," Linc said. Then he patted my hand, and my heart did another flop, making me think of my dog Hebert, who thought nothing of offering up his most vulnerable spots to me.

Except I was no poor dog needing affection, despite the way my heart was acting.

"I'll be by later to check on you," he said, as if I belonged to him or something, before he hopped out of the ambulance and shut the door.

"Oh don't worry. It's fine," I said belatedly. And then I blacked out mostly until Monday afternoon.

3

"The most important kind of freedom is to be what you really are…There can't be any large-scale revolution until there's a personal revolution, on an individual level. It's got to happen inside first."

—Jim Morrison

I am sitting at a desk with a man standing over me. I can feel something odd on my head, and reach up. It is a bandage.

Then I fly through my mental checklist.

familiar place, my job

familiar person, Hank

upset? angry? expectant

he wants to know something

I got nothing.

But I'm staring at my screen, a story I'm working on, because my fingers are on the keyboard.

"I'm sorry…?" I give my head a shake, as if I'd been concentrating on the screen and look up at him questioningly.

"I said, what do you have for page one?"

I scan my article before looking up, careful to be deliberate. It looks like I'm almost done with a piece about the police jury's bid to keep a property tax in place to fund a new sheriff's office. I give him the gist.

"Almost done," I say. "I just have to wrap it up and proofread." I glance at the clock and realize why he's so intent. Our deadline is approaching and the story still has to go on the page.

"Do you have artwork? I got a big hole on the front page," he said.

"No art, unless you want Eugene's mug," I say, shrugging. Eugene is the jury president and would love to be on the front page. Hank rolls his eyes.

The story is about a government meeting concerning a building that doesn't exist yet.

no photo ops

linc

An image of his t-shirt-clad arms floats through my head. Maybe we could get a volunteer to be handcuffed. Or I could probably just make it so there is the suggestion of someone in handcuffs, focusing instead on Linc's face. Or his arms.

"I'll think of something," Hank mumbles, interrupting my fantasy as he turns back to his desk. He is the publisher, but also takes great pride in laying the paper out. He likes to think his true calling is graphic design.

he hates confrontation

he'd rather not

I'd rather not

Just before he sits down, he turns back to me. "You probably need to go home and take care of that head, anyway," he said.

I finger the bandage as I proofread the story. Then I hit send, pull out my phone and take a look at the calendar which says work is almost over and the night is devoid of plans.

I say goodbye to Hank and go out to my car. It's dark; low clouds make the late winter afternoon even darker. Then I remember the accident. My car was totaled. But I have keys in my hands, so I press the unlock button on the key fob. Lights on a large black truck blink, and my heart stops. It looks just like the truck that ran me off the road. What was it Linc had said?

Half the rednecks in Lafitte Parish drive big black trucks. The other half drive big red trucks.

I just stare at it as I walk over. It is a working man's truck. I see now that this truck is a very dark gray, not black. Had the truck on Friday been black? Was I certain? I shake my head and tentatively reach out for the door handle. Why did I have the keys to this truck? Surely it wasn't a rental. Rentals were little compact cars, not gas guzzlers.

I know my car was totaled in the accident. I remember the crumpled, unfamiliar door. I open the door to the truck and have to climb, it's so high off the ground. But it makes me feel safe. When the insurance check comes, I decide right then to replace my car with a big truck like this, except with running boards, so I don't have to leap into it.

My phone buzzes with an incoming text.

"How's the truck"

It's from Linc.

"Big," I text back. "Headed home now. Did I thank you?"

I open the glove compartment and look for the registration. Sure enough, it has his name on it. My mind leaps forward, trying to fill in the blanks. A police type radio was installed in the dash of the truck.

a scanner

I need one

He had been the first responding officer on the accident scene. He had helped bandage me, questioned me and then said he'd check on me later just before the ambulance took me to the hospital. I must have put his number in later, then. And he's such a nice guy he loaned me his truck?

yes

Even though I didn't remember a lot of our previous relationship, I have always known that he's a nice guy. Maybe he had more than one vehicle.

Big, I text back. Headed home now. Did I thank you? I can't remember...

He replies with a thumbs up. I start the truck, which seems to growl, and wait a second to see if he says anything else, but that is all, so I put the truck in gear and ease out of the parking lot, feeling very conspicuous. It is an odd feeling, looking down on traffic. Obviously, Linc had checked in on me at the hospital, possibly brought me home and left me his truck? Then how did he get home?

Lana

I repent quickly of that train of thought and wonder how long I'm supposed to keep his truck. It smells like him. Clean. And there isn't a speck of dust inside. He is a much better car keeper than I am. I am alarmed by the little thrill of anticipation running through me at the idea of seeing him again. When did that happen?

it's been years

I probe through what I can remember. Friday was a big part of it, I decide.

idiot

it's been years

He'd gone to a lot of effort to help me, when he could have just sat at his desk and let me flounder around, trying to figure things out. Much like Caci's ex, Harrison had done. Now there was something to ponder when I wasn't busy. I shook my head and got back to the task at hand: figuring out when I had developed a crush on Linc.

want some coffee

it's not him

I coast to a stop at a red light and look in the rear view. My heart leaps and my scalp tingles. The black truck is two cars back in the same lane, and the shape of the man in the truck sends fear coursing through me. My foot jerks on the brake pedal because my leg is shaking and the truck lurches. I slam on the brake and grip the steering wheel.

I am vaguely aware that the light turns green because the cars in the lane beside me start to pass me. The car behind me honks, and instinctively I step on the gas, but too hard, and the truck leaps forward. Thankfully the car in front of me had already taken off. I take my foot off the gas pedal, indecisive. What if he changes lanes to pass me and he sees me? I speed up and wilt with relief when the truck turns at the next intersection. I am still shaking, weak, and tears are blurring my vision. I swipe at my eyes and a sob escapes.

dry it up

I'm gonna be sick

he's gonna kill us

I am grateful when I pull into my driveway. Hebert, my Akbash, goes on high alert when he sees the truck, and barks madly from beyond the fence which surrounds the back and side yards of my house. The front yard is open to the gravel road that leads to my house from the highway. The gate to the backyard is near the front door of the house. I feel a sense of security at Hebert's reaction to the strange truck. He's a good dog, protective. The shakes have subsided some.

He cocks his head when I get out of the truck, his tail stiff, ears up. "Hebert. What you doin' buddy? Did you have a good day?" I say, as I approach his gate to let him out of the yard and into the house with me. He wags his tail when he recognizes me and puts his front paws on the fence, barking with joy now. "What a good boy you are!" When I open the gate, he sniffs my shoes, my crotch and takes off running for the road.

"Hebert No!" It's been awhile since he's done this, just taken off running, and my heart leaps. There are little farms surrounding us. Farms with chickens and other livestock being watched over by cur dogs and farmers with guns. Dangerous territory for an energetic, curious dog used to living in the city with no knowledge of guns. I grab the leash and trot toward him.

he had a gun

shoulda coulda said

Hebert stops at the truck to give all the tires a good sniff and to replace whatever he smells there with a shot of his own urine. I catch up to him by the time he's sprayed the last tire.

"Come on boy, let's go inside." I snap the leash on him and decide I'll no longer let him out of his yard without being leashed. It's just too risky.

Inside, I unleash him, and he makes a tour of all the rooms, sniffing to see if anything has changed. Being safe at home has helped me calm down considerably. But I avoid thinking too much about the man in the black truck.

not yet

give us a minute

I kick off my shoes, change into yoga pants and a comfy t-shirt, flip on the tv for some background noise and stand staring into the fridge.

I still need to buy groceries. There is a half-gallon of milk, almost empty. A small container of strawberry yogurt, still good. Leftovers from a dinner with Mama in a zip top baggy and now green and fuzzy, which I toss into the garbage. Hebert has made it to the kitchen and is sitting beside me, also staring into the fridge with great expectations. He follows the long arc of the baggy through the air with his nose and gives a little woof as it lands in the trash can. I can tell he is gauging his chances of going for it, not looking directly at me, but ultra aware of my body language.

"Leave it," I say. Then he peers at me with a look of long-suffering. Clearly I don't understand the joys of snuffling through the garbage can for rotten food. I pat myself on the back for getting a house with a shady, fenced back yard for him to hang out in while I'm at work. Teaching him to "leave it" during his puppy stage while living in an apartment during graduate school had been a necessary nightmare.

I turn back to the refrigerator and gaze at the six pack of beer and a half-eaten take-out pizza. I don't remember buying either. Neither had been in the fridge on Thursday night. I'd spent the whole day and most of the night away on Friday because of the wreck. I also didn't have much of a memory of either Saturday or Sunday night. The pizza is a meat lovers.

Maybe Linc brought it after I got out of the hospital Friday night? But would he bring beer too? There was a whole six pack.

heck yeah

Maybe the beer showed up Saturday night. No empties in the trash.

I prefer cheese pizza, but I'm too tired and emotionally spent to try and figure out how it got there, and too hungry to think of anything else for dinner, so I get it out, tear off two slices, pick off the meat, which I put in Hebert's bowl on top of his dog food, and pop the slices into the microwave.

While the microwave runs, I watch Hebert scarf down his food, then let him out into the backyard when he's done. I live in a little house on a dirt road about a mile from my mother's house. We can't see each other from our respective yards, because lots of pine trees are between us, but we're close enough so that I'm available to her if she needs me.

Her stroke in late December had been impeccably timed, really. I was just finishing up work on a series of features about tourist attractions in Charlotte. A new lease on my apartment was looming, and I was starting to feel unsettled, like maybe I needed something more permanent. And Hebert needed a yard. Had needed one all along. I was just sitting down with the want ads to start serious job hunting when the phone rang. It was my mother's doctor. After a brief conversation, I looked up my hometown newspaper on the Internet, sent them my resume and called a moving company to rent a truck. Before I'd even left town, Hank had called and done a quick phone interview, then practically hired me on the spot. But I had deferred, not wanting to take on too much while Mom was recovering.

So I drove home on Christmas Day, my 28th birthday, moved back in with my Mama, and lived the month of January off my savings. The stroke had been mild, but the threat of more to come made me want to stay near. By the end of January, just last week, she had progressed to the point that she could function for the most part on her own. I called Hank on Friday, and he told me to start the following Monday. On that same Friday, I called and rented a house and spent the weekend moving in. I still, in fact, have boxes to unpack. As for Mama, I, a home health nurse, and a few friends plan on taking turns checking on her.

The front door of my cute little house opens into the living room, which has a nice wood heater with a glass door. I can build a fire if I want and watch it burn. It does get cold enough in Louisiana during the winter for a fire, but it never stays cold for very long, which is something I really like about my home state. Though it was still the south, it got considerably colder in North Carolina. Charlotte had been my home since I'd left Bethel. I was always at first amazed when winter hit in Charlotte at just how stinking cold it got. After about a week of walking carefully on icy concrete and driving carefully on icy roads and bundling up every time I wanted to step outside, I was kind of over it. In Louisiana, you don't get used to it being cold. You just tolerate it, because in a week or two, rarely longer, it's gonna get balmy again. Winter is a few passing phases from December through early March. Every once in a while, November and April might get roped in. I much prefer being used to warm weather. However, the wood heater is nice for when it does get chilly. The problem is getting wood. The rental company said the landlord knew someone who would deliver wood for me. I have to remember to get the phone number. I tap this reminder into my phone.

The kitchen is at the back of the house and my favorite room. It has lots of windows and a little area off to the side with a table. I call it the dining room, but its more like a nook. It is a nice spot in the mornings to drink my coffee and eat my breakfast and in the evenings to eat my dinner. The evenings are especially nice because of the sunsets. I can look out on the very peaceful scene of my landlord's hay pasture. It's nothing but a very large expanse of green grass dotted by a few oak trees that look black in the dim light of morning and evening. In the spring and early summer, the grass is ridiculously green. I know this from growing up here. The intense green, I also know, can be attributed to the tons of chicken manure my landlord spreads over it in late winter. Riding my bicycle by the manure pile on warm days had been an olfactory adventure during my childhood.

It's always a fun time for his neighbors, who happen to be his relatives, for about a week in February (just in line with Valentine's Day if memory serves me) when his great big tractor with its front end loader bites into the big black pile of chicken manure that's been curing for several months, sending out invisible, suffocating billows of stink. Yet another reason to keep Hebert on a leash, or he will head straight over to roll in it. I think that the nose hairs of anyone who lives nearby must get singed during that week from the ammonia in the air.

And I guess it's worth it. It makes the pasture something to see in early spring. Like it's blinding it's so green. And I guess the hay is good for someone's cows.

A short hallway leads from the living room to the bathroom and two bedrooms. One of the bedrooms I had intended to use for an office, but it's ended up being a storage room for things I don't know what to do with, which, if I'm completely honest, I knew in my heart would be the way of things. Strange food shows up in my fridge, and sometimes odd items show up, too. Once, in graduate school when I was working on my thesis and stressed out, I woke up one morning and found a snorkeling kit on the dining room table. It looked brand new, but was no longer in the packaging. It was also wet, a perfect match to the dripping swim suit hanging in the shower.

don't ask

don't tell

Strange things showing up—*in the place where everything is hidden* —as if they belong to me and I have need of them is something that I thought was normal up until I was about 10. I haven't ever told anyone about that.

in the place where everything is hidden

as if they belong to me and I have need of them is something that I thought was normal up until I was about 10.

I haven't ever told anyone about that.

if you have to ask, you'll never know

I call it the Room of Requirement and leave it at that. Some things are better left undelved. I had a similar room in my apartment. I never went in there except for a quick glance and to put things there that showed up.

if you have to ask, you'll never know

When I got ready to move out at the end of December, I woke up and that room was all packed up and ready to go. All I had to do was load it on the truck. Same thing last week. I had unloaded all the boxes over the weekend, putting those for the Room of Requirement just inside the door, and focusing my energy on unpacking kitchen, bathroom and bedroom boxes. But on Thursday morning the room was unpacked, if you can call spreading the items all over the room unpacking. The empty boxes were stacked outside next to the garbage can.

I realize suddenly that I'd had a blackout the night Mr. Rob was murdered. The microwave dings, and I get my pizza and a beer and head for the back porch, letting that thought sink in. The sun is just beginning to set, but this new realization makes it difficult to enjoy. I haven't felt this ungrounded since I left home for college.

I sought to make myself cleverer

more important

ran away

My senior year in high school had been really tough. The blackouts were driving me crazy back then. Somehow, though, I had held it together long enough to apply for college, get packed and drive halfway across the country. And something happened during that long drive that seemed to settle me down. The blackouts became more and more distant the more time I was away from home. By the time I was done with graduate school, they had seemed to become almost nonexistent. Almost.

I still had the Room of Requirement.

But as soon as the call from Mama's doctor came, things had seemed to get stirred up again. I'm not at all sure what to do about it. I've been toying with the idea of seeing a therapist. Mama had me see one in high school. I'd even been hospitalized for several weeks because Mama said I had seemed to go off the deep end. But no one except Caci knew that I had recurring blackouts, though Mama, as far as I knew, was aware that I had blacked out once. The thing is, I don't really want anyone knowing. I don't want to know. The idea lurking behind them seems to grow and threatens to overwhelm me, so I shove it aside, and think about the lost weekend.

Sunday had come back to me. I still did not remember anything past the hospital on Friday night, and all of Saturday was a complete blank. But I remembered going to church with Mama Sunday morning. I wore a floppy hat to hide the big white bandage on my forehead. As far as I know no one noticed. At least no one commented on my injury.

And I got things rolling on two things on my to-do list. I made appointments with Robbie Lynn and the preacher, Brother Emmett. The title felt cultish on my tongue. I had never noticed it until I'd come back home. Brother Emmett is an older man, at least 80, and he has a very kind face and what I would call twinkly eyes behind his bifocals. He has a ready smile and seems very cheerful.

Church is a social affair in Bethel, especially at First Baptist Bethel. Robbie Lynn and Ty's families both attend, as do Linc and his parents, with quite a few other well-established families in the community. But in addition, and the thing that was different from my high school days was that there are a few families who aren't so well off, single parents, widows and widowers, divorcee's, even a few recovering addicts, which spoke well for Brother Emmett who, though not new to the community, was new to the church, I thought. Mama and I had seldom attended when I was in school, as we'd rarely felt welcome. But Mama had begun attending regularly while I was away and had developed quite a few strong friendships with other widows in the church. And she thought highly of Brother Emmett, as did a lot of people.

People mingled in the aisles, stood at their pews and chatted as I took Mama to our seat. When we were settled, I looked around and spied Robbie Lynn with Ty all the way up at the front, talking with another couple. Nearby, their parents, including Judge Edward Spencer, were chatting as well. Robbie Lynn had her back to me. I didn't know how I was going to get her attention. I didn't want to approach her, not with the judge and Ty standing nearby. No sign of Linc or his parents.

In a few minutes, the strains of a hymn began from the pianist up front and people quieted down and took their seats. Then the choir trooped quietly into the choir loft behind the pulpit. Linc was in the back row with several other men. No robes or halos were in sight. He was dressed in a dark blue button down shirt and jeans.

dadgum

riddikulus

expelliarmus

His black hair, cut in a fade, was longer, a little spiky, even tousled, on top. His ghost of a beard, apparently standard during the work week, was cleanly shaved this morning except for his goatee, but it too was trimmed and sharper, looking more like a five o'clock shadow.

We all stood, and the song leader took us through several congregational hymns, some old, some new, with the choir doing the heavy lifting on most of the singing. For the benefit of the congregation, the words to the songs were on a screen above the choir. And all the members of the choir kept their eyes trained above our heads, so I turned and discovered a similar screen for their benefit. When I turned back toward the choir, Linc caught my eye and winked, which caused me to blush.

I studiously avoided looking at him after that. The congregation sat after the last song, but the choir remained standing. The song leader gave some signals to someone behind me, I guessed the person in charge of sound but no way was I turning around again, and as the choir members pulled out song books, recorded music filled the air. The song leader turned to the choir and began conducting.

I was taken aback when a lone voice in the back, Linc's, lifted in a jazzy, upbeat tune about an old church choir. The words were catchy, and the joy in Linc's face and voice were so palpable it made me catch my breath. Then, out of nowhere, a soprano chimed in. I looked around the faces in the choir and spotted Gloria, eyes clenched shut, face and hands raised in what can only be described as ecstasy, as she sang from the depths of her soul.

The choir chimed in, and then Linc answered. There was scattered hand clapping in the congregation; then the song leader turned to encourage it, and the people stood up, clapping and singing along with Linc who was belting it out like a professional.

he chose it

riddikulus

expelliarmus

all you need

I was stunned by the emotions flying through the room. I wanted to laugh and cry at the same time. I wanted to dance. Though I managed to keep myself contained through all of the song, most everyone else in the congregation was letting loose. Even the judge and his son were clapping in time. But I couldn't see their faces, as they were in front of me. As the song came to a close, there was much applause, even a few whistles, and quite a few amens and hallelujahs as the choir left the loft and took their seats in the congregation.

Linc walked past to a spot behind me. Confused by all the emotions that had erupted from him and which had spread like fire to not just me but every person in the room, I refused to look at him. What was this? It felt dangerous. And I was having a hard time identifying another reaction. It felt like jealousy. Was I jealous of him, or of whatever was causing him to feel such joy? With what felt like Herculean effort I clamped down on myself and trained my eyes and ears on Brother Emmett as he took to the pulpit.

Like a good church goer, I opened my Bible and found the passage he announced, and read along. It was a story I had never heard before. King Hezekiah, threatened with invasion by the Assyrian army, had pleaded with God to step in and save his people. And God had done just that. Brother Emmett went on to focus on the aspect of prayer in the story, making three very relevant, alliterative and unfortunately forgettable points about inviting God to intervene in our lives.

"Because Hezekiah asked," he said to the congregation during his closing. "Simply because he asked. What mighty things will God do for you, if you ask?"

By then my mind had wandered back to and all around my motives for attending church. In fact I'd spent most of the sermon trying to figure out how to talk to Robbie Lynn.

Help me get to Robbie Lynn, I thought, and then felt guilty for such an irreverent request.

some joy

wouldn't hurt

easy on the hallelujah

and terror

When the final notes of "Just As I Am" faded, Brother Emmett nodded to Edward Stewart, who came forward and gave the benediction in a booming voice full of thous and wherefores, as if he were reading a legal brief in the King James version. Then the congregation turned to the back doors as one, and I saw Linc's hand touch Lana Dowd's back.

two-timer

it's his way

what? touchy? feely?

solicitous

They were both headed toward the door, but I saw her face clearly. She was blonde and even more angelic than she had been in high school. He bent his head to hear something she said, his hand lingering attentively at the small of her back. I was suddenly very grateful that I had not responded to his wink, which surely had been directed at her, not me—*oh God*—How humiliating that would have been. I was weak with relief that I hadn't done anything to let him know how I felt.

crap

Everyone was filing out to shake Brother Emmett's hand and exchange a few words. I pulled myself together enough when Mama and I approached him to ask if I could come by and see him sometime this week.

"Oh sure! How 'bout Tuesday morning? Say about 9?" He had hold of my hand and was smiling broadly at me.

"Perfect," I said, and stepped aside as he let go of my hand. Then he took Mama's hand, startling her out of the curious look she was giving me. He gazed into her eyes.

"How are you?"

She smiled benignly at him. "I'm good, Emmett." No "brother" for her, I noticed. And then I realized that there was no Mrs. Brother Emmett. Or would it be Sister something or other? I guessed he was a widow.

mama and emmett sittin' in a tree

Mama developed another gear besides her normal plod and had not only breezed past me but was fast approaching a dangerous set of concrete steps. I hurried to catch up, and together we moved out of the foyer and through the glass double doors to stand blinking for a second on the steps in the spring sun.

"It is so bright out here!" she said, digging in her purse for her sunglasses. She was still a little unsteady on her feet, so I stood nearby to make sure she was able to reach the handrail before making her way down the steps. I felt like a puppy at a dog park, with so many distractions flirting around me, and couldn't help but look around to see if I could spot Linc and Lana, but they were nowhere to be seen.

"Mojo!" I looked behind me to see Robbie Lynn just leaving the church. "Mojo, Wait! I can't believe it!"

I smiled as she came toward me, relieved that she was making the first move. I hadn't seen any way to make my way up to her pew from my position near the middle back without drawing attention to myself.

"Robbie Lynn! Oh my God! Hey! Your hair is gorgeous!" I said, genuinely happy to be able to talk to her. Her hair was blonde now, about two shades lighter than when we were in high school. And I was telling the truth; she was utterly gorgeous. She wore a bright pink sleeveless silk dress that hugged her perfect size six curves and accentuated her tan. A black, flowing gauzy cardigan kept the dress church-appropriate. She came toward me, mincing a little in her high heels, with her arms outstretched for a hug. We embraced on the steps and then quickly moved aside as the crowd, including Ty, his parents and Robbie Lynn's parents, kept pouring out of the church. I put my arm around Mama's waist to move her toward the car. Robbie Lynn fell in step beside us, grabbing Mama's other elbow. Behind us, Ty and the parents walked more slowly, obviously keeping their distance, and moved toward their own vehicles. Robbie Lynn chatted as we walked.

"I'm so glad to see you! Gosh I had heard you were back in town, and of course, I knew about the stroke. I'm so, so sorry Mrs. Jordan, but you look great! And Mojo so do you! Oh and have you heard? I'm so excited! Mama and I have been running around like crazy getting ready for the wedding." She held her left hand out for me to admire a huge diamond on her ring finger.

"I had heard, girl!" I took her hand and admired the ring. "It's gorgeous! Congratulations! When's the big day?"

"May 20!" She said, and I immediately made the connection to Caci's trial date, which had been set for June 12. At the time I had wondered why it was so far out. Now it seemed clear. Having a murder trial before the wedding would be too crazy for both the judge and the prosecutor. A month after was way more doable. "We've already got the invitations out. Did ya'll get yours yet? Well it should come next week. We licked til we were blue in the face last week."

I nodded and helped Mama into the passenger seat of her car, having forgotten how hard it was to get a word in when Robbie Lynn was excited. When I shut the door, Robbie put her hand on my arm, looking suddenly stricken. I expected the next words out of her mouth to be about Caci.

"I'm so sorry, Mojo."

"For what?" I put my hand over hers, wondering why she was apologizing for Caci's situation.

"I didn't ask you to be a bridesmaid," she said, throwing me off for a second. "I'm a rotten friend, I know. I haven't been in touch like I should, but I did truly miss you, Mojo. I just figured with the move home and your mom, well, maybe you didn't have time."

She looked so dejected I had to laugh. "Robbie Lynn, you didn't hurt my feelings at all. You know I hate getting dressed up. And it's a two-way street. I didn't keep in touch either."

"Thank God," she said, and hugged me. "But now that you're here, and you're mom seems to be doing so much better, you can totally be a part of the wedding. I insist. Come over Tuesday evening. We're working on the menu and trying to figure out flowers. I could really use the help."

"I would love to come over, but I'm not sure how much help I'll be. I'm awful at stuff like that."

"No, no. It'll be fun," she said. "At least we can catch up!" She glanced over at Ty who was standing beside a silver Mercedes, sunglasses on, facing our general direction, not smiling. "I have to go, but Tuesday night, seven o'clock!" She said over her shoulder as she hurried to Ty and the Mercedes.

With a tiny jolt I realized at least one of my little prayers had been answered. It was much later that I realized Robbie Lynn hadn't mentioned Caci at all.

After my shower Monday night, I wiped the fog off the bathroom mirror, intending to remove my bandage. The white square was startling, accentuating the dark circles under my eyes. I needed a good night's sleep. I wondered about my lost time. Just because I didn't remember, didn't mean I hadn't been doing something. Like the day of the accident. I was sure, from the way Linc talked, that I had been conscious when he arrived on the scene. I just don't remember what I said or what I did from the time the stranger called the ambulance until I was in the ambulance. Apparently cussing was involved.

Add to that last Wednesday night, all of Saturday, the rest of Sunday after church and most of Monday unaccounted for. I just hoped it hadn't been anything outrageous. No one had called to bless me out, so I guessed that was good news.

I usually kept my hair in a messy bun on top of my head, but I had worn it down today. Probably hoping to draw attention away from the bandage. I didn't remember getting dressed that morning and was surprised at my outfit, suede boots I remembered seeing in the Room of Requirement and a floral peasant skirt paired with a pink tank top and a black fitted blazer. Combined with my long straight hair I looked like an odd mixture of cowgirl hippie.

My hair has always kind of overwhelmed me. I could never remember to make appointments, so a cute cut that needed to be maintained was out of the question. Plus it grows very fast. So I just let it grow and resort to pony tails and messy buns and ball caps. When I can't get it in a semi-neat bun anymore, it's time to whack some off, which I've been known to do myself in order to avoid a salon. I am very normal looking; none of my features are remarkable. I have straight teeth, and all of them, a feat some people my age can't claim. But my hazel eyes are my best feature, big, dark with thick eyelashes. I am five feet two. And curvier than I want to be.

"Built like a brick outhouse," Stephen used to say. I never knew if that was a compliment or insult.

Both

"Child bearing hips," Mama used to tease when I started puberty. And that was early. I had been eleven. She had said it then, but not so much later, I guess, because it became apparent that I probably shouldn't have kids with my other problems.

I reached up and carefully pulled the bandage away. It was taped above my left eye. I guessed that my head had been gashed by a piece of flying glass or metal. The bandage was taped tightly and it took some doing to get it off. The gash was about three inches long, from my hairline to my eyebrow. It was ugly and red, with a bruise spreading out in a halo around it. There were five neat stitches, the black thread looking ominous against the dried blood, the bruise, and my pale skin. I had been lucky that whatever cut me hadn't blinded me. I might end up with a scar there, but hopefully it would be faint. I wasn't sure if I should take the bandage off, but did it anyway. But then, seeing the ugly wound, I didn't want to leave it exposed. The bandage was way more attractive. It would be the first thing people noticed about me for the next two weeks, for sure. I decided to let the wound breathe tonight and figure out a way to cover it tomorrow. Maybe another hat or something.

After dabbing on some ointment prescribed by the doctor (no memory of filling it or picking it up but there it was on the counter with the instructions clearly visible), I turned the lights out and cuddled into my bed. Hebert was at my feet and already asleep. But I wasn't so lucky. My various and sundry predicaments whirled around in my brain, like a kaleidoscope, impossible to focus on one thing before it changed into something else. I tried my old trick of listing things out.

First, I had to see Robbie Lynn. I had a feeling that would help a lot where Caci was concerned. I was still a little unsettled that Robbie Lynn hadn't even mentioned Caci when we'd talked at church. But then, I guess she'd probably been warned by Ty. Did he confide in Robbie Lynn? I had a hard time envisioning that. I imagined that Ty kept his own counsel. But what about his father? Did they discuss the case at Sunday dinner? Was that even legal? I didn't know and made a mental note to check on it. If things didn't go Caci's way, I might be able to make noise about proper procedure. I was set to go to Robbie Lynn's tomorrow night. I needed to check out her closet, but it would be interesting to see how conversation developed between the two of us.

Second, I had no car. Well, I had no car of my own. I probably should have headed over to the rental agency when I got off work, but I just didn't have it in me. I would figure out transportation in the morning. Then I'd need to get Linc's truck back to him. The oddness of Linc's truck looking so similar to the black truck that ran me off the road surfaced again. Was I somehow getting the two confused? With all the blackouts, was I imagining that I was run off the road by a big, black truck? Could it have been Linc who ran me off the road? Something inside me recoiled at the thought. But still, he had arrived on the scene so quickly. Had even seemed evasive. I had just left his office.

Why was someone trying to kill me? Something to do with Caci? Why would Linc be involved? Hank's gut?

I wondered about the man who had climbed down the embankment to check on me. Had anyone questioned him? Did he see who ran me off the road? Maybe I should check on that, I thought, and rolled over to switch the light on and grab my phone. My mental list making had created the need for a whole other to-do list. I opened my reminder app and typed in "judge/lawyer relationships" then "accident witness" and lay back against the pillow, my phone still in my hand, light still on.

Third topic of concern was that I was set to see Brother Emmett tomorrow. Not sure why this was important, except Caci had said so. Also in the morning.

Fourth, (I was not listing in order of importance), I kept having blackouts, and my memory of the last few days was like a piece of Swiss cheese. I felt like I was moving toward some sort of mental crisis, but was helpless to stop it. The frustration that went with not being able to remember parts of my life frothed around in my stomach like battery acid. I was no stranger to the feelings boiling around inside me, but that didn't make it any easier. I suspected that the turmoil of Caci's situation, being confused over Linc and just being home, had stirred things up.

Fifth, when I wasn't blacking out, I found myself daydreaming about Linc and how hot he looked in a tight tshirt and jeans. I mean, he had been hot, even as a teenager, but age had definitely sharpened that focus. And he must work out or something because I didn't see any extra on him at all. And he smelled spicy. And oh God, why couldn't I remember being his girlfriend? And how long had he been seeing Lana Dowd? I wanted to scratch her eyes out. And then there was the suspicion. I wasn't entirely sure I could trust him. Those two things alone were more than I could handle.

And sixth, most terrifying of all, I had this sick feeling that I had seen that shape in the black truck before under different circumstances. It had been coming to me in flashes since this afternoon, imagery of that man's shape bending over me, walking away from me, and, then, worst of all, bearing down on me relentlessly.

My head throbbed. It was a long time before I fell asleep.

4

"You have never talked to a mere mortal."

—C.S. Lewis

The next morning the first thing I did was call Hank to tell him I needed to get transportation situated. Then I called my insurance company, who said I could go pick up a car any time. I texted that information to Linc, hoping he wasn't needing his truck back immediately, as I needed to run my errand to see Brother Emmett immediately.

"No worries," he texted back. "I have the bike."

That was good information to have. At least I hadn't taken his only mode of transportation. But I should have known. Linc was a boy scout. Of course he had alternate transportation. The better to rescue damsels in distress. But why did it have to be a bike? I was betting it was a sleek black Harley. That thought made my armpits sweat. Why couldn't his second vehicle be a rusted, beat up minivan? Then I wondered how he'd gotten to church Sunday. Maybe she had picked him up, I thought.

"What if it rains?" I texted.

"I might get wet. And I'll need a ride."

I actually blushed and my stomach did a slow flip at the thought of picking up a wet Linc and driving him where he needed to be. And then I felt a little surge of victory.

No mention of her. It was a struggle not to text him anything other than,

"Absolutely. Thanks again."

"Yep. Lmk when you get your new ride." Then he sent a screenshot of the day's weather forecast. Sunny skies.

While I had my coffee, I googled "judge and lawyer relationships" and discovered just what everyone had been telling me. The judge himself was in the best position to determine whether or not his impartiality was questionable, which itself was questionable I thought, but who was I to argue? Then, I pondered how best to find out if anyone had spoken to the man who may have witnessed my accident. I decided to ask Hank about it.

I went with a baseball cap to cover the wound. It had improved significantly in appearance, so I very gingerly pulled my hair back into a ponytail and covered the whole mess gently with the cap. I hoped no one tugged on it.

he will

It's a hazard

that's why she's wearing it

for attention

I ripped the hat off to work through the inner conflict and studied my head closely, then my closet, concluding outloud that the least stupid thing was to wear the hat. There was peace within, at last, so I climbed in Linc's truck, keeping an eye out for black trucks as I drove to the church. The hat and Linc's truck made me feel protected. Sunshades also helped. I was relieved when I pulled into the church parking lot. I still didn't know what to do if I did see the truck.

ride like the wind

follow it

license plate

As I hopped down, I heard the roar of a Harley.

linc

I looked around and spotted a figure on a bike pull up to the church, right near the office, and park. The helmet came off to reveal a balding head. Then the figure, dressed in jeans, boots and a black T-shirt, stood and dismounted to reveal an elderly paunch.

"Brother Emmett?" He turned with his jolly smile.

"Well good morning young lady! And how are you?"

By then I had reached him and held out my hand, which he took and squeezed gently before letting me go.

"I'm fine! I didn't know you rode."

He looked puzzled. And something else.

what

"Keeps me young," he said, avoiding my eyes.

"And cool, Brother Emmett. A preacher on a Harley must be a great conversation starter."

His eyes twinkled at me. "Yes, but you knew that already," he said.

He swept his arm ahead of us to indicate the church. "Come in!"

I walked toward the outside doors of the church office while he looked for a key on his key ring. It felt like I had a brick in my stomach, a familiar feeling most often connected to what I call blackout fallout. I had run into Brother Emmett during a blackout. I could tell by his demeanor. I had done or said something that contradicted something that I had done or said during a blackout. It made people squirrelly toward me. He found the key, opened the outer door and held it for me while I walked through, feeling like a juvenile in trouble. Then he motioned for me to follow him into his office. Once we were settled inside, him behind a slightly messy desk and me perched on a chair opposite, he looked at me seriously. I felt like I was in the principal's office in junior high school.

"How is your mama?"

I hadn't expected that, but then I remembered the way he'd looked at her Sunday morning, and the pep he'd put in her step.

he ain't just lookin' after sheep

she told him something

"Oh she's fine. Getting better everyday. Maybe a little unsteady on her feet, but physical therapy is working."

"Good to hear!" And he seemed genuinely thrilled. "She does seem better, but I wanted to make sure.

"And how about your head?" he said, pointing to his own forehead. "I heard about your accident."

"Oh, well, it's fine. Just a little tender. How did you..?"

"Linc texted our prayer chain," he said.

"Prayer chain?" An image of little old ladies chained together and praying popped into my head, Gloria, Linc's secretary, in the midst of them singing.

"Yes," Brother Emmett nodded, not offering any other explanation. He didn't seem to think it was needed, so I moved on, making a mental note I could only hope to receive later to ask Linc about it when I saw him next. Then I told him why I had come, about my meeting with Caci, and how she'd asked me to ask him for prayer. He grew silent and still as I talked, not looking at me, but listening deeply.

When I was done he sighed heavily.

"I've been praying for Caci for months," he said. "You know, she came here that night, after the murder."

"What?"

He nodded.

"Why would she do that?" I blurted, then blushed. "I didn't mean…"

"It's ok," he said. "It's a fair question. We have a relationship."

I stopped blinking, and he laughed.

"No, no," he said, seeing my face and letting out a chuckle. "It's through my ministry," he said. "You know, at the bars," he was looking at me so expectantly, I was sure he was referring to something I should know about, so I nodded.

"Tell me more about that," I said carefully, vaguely, watching his face, knowing I was on shifting ground.

"Well," he said. "I chose that life for a while. My boy did too, and it killed him."

I nodded, remembering how Caci had looked, how different she'd become. How grateful I was she wasn't worse.

"It's like war," he said, "only more insidious."

"So me and a few of the men in the church go out to the bars once or twice a month and try to reach some of them." He'd been looking at the top of his desk, lips pursed, but then he looked up at me. "When they get picked up and put in jail, we visit them there too." Then he looked at me intently.

"I'm so glad I ran into you Saturday night and you decided to join us Sunday morning," he said, his eyes piercing mine, as if he could gouge out any desire I might have to become an addict.

"Oh!" I said, mortified. "Well, I was planning on coming anyway, to church, I mean."

He nodded, but didn't offer any more information, and I didn't know what to ask. He didn't take his eyes away, and I resisted the urge to squirm in my seat like a guilty little girl.

I took a shot. "I used to play on a pool team in college," which was the truth. "I do like to stay sharp."

I was relieved when he nodded.

"Well, you were certainly giving them a challenge at the Desperada," he said. "You bested some of the better pool players Saturday night.

"Except Gilroy," he mused, making my blood tingle.

kilroy

And then, as if remembering I was still in the room, "You should be careful, though. That's a rough bar. I'm certain that a motorcycle gang is running drugs there. And you were playing with several of them. And I do mean playing, Mojo."

I swallowed, wondering what I'd been doing.

winning

"Meth is a business in Bethel," he went on. " And business is about supply and demand. These people do not hesitate to create demand, and they always take the easiest way through the people they like least."

As he spoke, his voice rose and intensified and I suddenly saw the difference between a pastor and a preacher.

is he accusing me

listen

Caci

My throat was suddenly dry, and I needed to leave the room. I reached down deep for some remnants of professionalism and moxy. "You're the second person who has told me about the meth problem here," I said. "Would you be interested in doing a story on your ministry?" I asked, realizing as I said it that it was a great idea.

His eyebrows shot up. "Well, that would be interesting. Worth praying about, certainly," he said.

I nodded, about to stand, but his eyes drifted back to his desk, leaving me feeling relieved they were no longer on me, but with no end in sight to the sermon.

"That's where we met," he said.

what

wistfulness

lordy

"The Desperada was Caci's preferred bar," he said. "I was sometimes able to distract her a little if I could catch her before she was too far gone. Not much, but enough that we could talk about some important things, you know. She became a different person when she was on that stuff." He shook his head. "Evil."

I didn't know if he was talking about Caci or meth or both.

"I'm actually supposed to testify in her defense," he added.

"Really?" I wasn't sure what I could ask him. Or what he would tell me.

He looked at me sternly. "This is not for the paper, Mojo," he said. "Strictly for your own peace of mind. I know you and Caci have been friends since you were little bitty. You may be one of the only people left who still loves her enough to help her through this."

"Yes sir."

"That night that Rob was killed, she came busting into the sanctuary while the choir was practicing. It was a Wednesday night. Linc was not here that night, or I'm sure things would have gone quite differently. She looked like she was running from somebody," he said, raising his brows for emphasis. "I was up front and heard the doors clatter when she came in, and when I looked back she was standing at the back of the church looking lost and terrified. So I went back there to talk to her. I thought she was on something.

"Anyway, when I got back there she was shaking and white as a ghost. I made her sit down. She started crying. Obviously hysterical. I gave her some Kleenex. When she had calmed down a little I asked her what had happened.

"She looked me dead in the eye and said, 'He shot my Daddy.' It was very plain. No mistaking. And let me tell you she was too messed up to be acting. Nobody is that good of an actor.

"I asked her who, but then she got hysterical again. I couldn't make out anything she was saying. And then she got an even wilder look in her eyes and said she had to leave, that he would kill her too. And she mentioned Micah, her mother. She was terrified something might happen to them, too. Then she got up and ran out. I called Linc immediately."

"Do you think she did it?"

"No I do not. I think she witnessed it. And I am praying that somehow the police find out who did kill her daddy. Not just for her sake, but her mother and her son's too."

I nodded, grateful that he was in Caci's corner, and grateful for a reason to believe her.

I left the church with relief, but by the time I got back out to the truck, it had dissipated. Nothing was different. I still didn't have any proof that would help Caci. I sat in Linc's truck in the parking lot, fiddling with the dials on the stereo system, which was very nice but mystified me. Then I turned on the police scanner and was instantly captivated by the noise, the idea of knowing where the police were headed, so left it on. I definitely needed one of these. The whole truck was spotless. A package of gum in a small cubby was the only evidence that someone else besides me had been in it. I reached for it.

sugah

free

The windows were tinted very dark.

line toer

Being in the church parking lot in his truck made me feel like I was in a tank.

safe

Shhhhh

big wheels

big guns

stop it

I wondered who else they were looking at for Mr. Rob's murder. Caci obviously recognized the murderer but was afraid to talk. I wondered again about why she'd indicated I should check Robbie Lynn's closet.

Maybe the evidence was there. But why would it be there, of all places? I would find out tonight.

I sighed, started the truck and headed for the newspaper office.

saturday night

count your blessings

I feel the air

name them

getting hot

one by one

I am better than the average person at pool. Stephen and Daddy had taught me how to run the table.

olympic

hot

But as far as I knew I hadn't played pool in years until Saturday night.

I checked my phone journal again after parking at the newspaper office. Nothing.

Then I looked up "prayer chain" on my phone.

"A group of people who pray for needs as they arise. The members are links and requests make their way from one person to another." Not for the first time in my life, I wished out loud that someone would tell me what the heck was going on. On a whim, I searched for the Desperada bar and saw it was only a mile from me. I cranked back up and went to check it out.

It was near the abandoned train depot, a throwback, I guessed, from when the town bustled with trade: lumber and the company stores mostly. The building itself looked desperate, hanging on to the edge of town like a leech, but it was no more familiar to me than the depot itself, which I had never explored.

The sand-colored brick was dirty and stained. The miniscule parking lot was big enough for only three vehicles, as if all but the building itself had been acquired by neighboring businesses. But it only needed parking at the end of the week and at night.

5

In all chaos there is a cosmos,
in all disorder a secret order.

—Carl Jung

When I next wake I am in my bed. It's either daylight or hell beyond me. The bright light hurts, so I keep my eyes closed. My head feels cottony, my mouth decayed. I reach up and feel my bandage. It's gone, but the stitches are still there. I remember that I took the bandage off Monday evening and didn't replace it Tuesday morning, opting instead for a baseball cap. The wound is tender. I'm still and listen. Only my breathing, and then suddenly the dog's, and I feel his heat near me. Smell him. I open my eyes to his tongue lolling in my face.

"Gross. Get back." He whimpers to be let out, and guilt wells up as I roll out of bed, check my phone and head for the back door, Hebert close on my heels.

It is 9:05 a.m. Wednesday, February 8, 2017. I was supposed to have gone to Robbie Lynn's house last night.

I probe my brain and am rewarded with memories of most of yesterday, including driving up to her house in the evening, getting out, going to the door. Robbie's mother let me in and told me she was on the phone upstairs in her room. I went up, knocked on the door, poked my head in. She waved me in. Her bed was covered in silk flowers in different shades of pink and purple. Tulips, freesia, glads, tiny little blooms as small as the tip of my pinky finger and huge blooms as big as my face were piled on her bed. She smiled at me when I walked in, but then adopted that spacey look people get when they're on the phone.

"Ty, we were supposed to shop for tuxes for the groomsmen this weekend." She frowned, a little whine in her voice, and stood with one arm across her middle, supporting the arm that held the phone to her ear. She turned toward her window and the picturesque view of her parents' pool, barn and pasture dotted with horses, but she didn't seem to be seeing the view.

"But I wanted to do it with you," she half-whispered, then was silent, her back to me.

"Well at least come over later," she said, this time louder. "Mojo is here now, and we're going to talk about the flowers for the wedding."

She paused for a long second, shooting me an uncertain smile over her shoulder before stepping toward the bathroom.

"Of course not," I heard her say. "Ty, it'll be fine. We won't even talk about it. I promise." Then she gently shut the door.

I sat on the edge of the bed to wait for them to finish discussing me in private. A pile of flowers cascaded onto the floor. I bent to pick them up.

Then…nothing

I checked my journal. Nothing.

I sat back down on my bed and flopped back, realizing I was also late for work.

I turned on my side and opened my phone calendar, squinting in the bright light.

But the calendar gave me another surprise. I had an appointment, which I didn't remember making, with a Dr. Granger at 10 a.m. Then a separate appointment tomorrow morning, which simply said, "Stitches Out." The address for that appointment was another doctor's office.

I called Hank's cell, just to make sure he wasn't expecting me.

"Mojo," he said, answering on the first ring.

"Hey, just checking in," I said.

"Thought you had a doctor's appointment," he said.

"Yep," I said. "Everything good there?"

"I'm good. You good?"

"Yep."

"See ya."

At least I still had a job.

Next I called Dr. Granger's office, whose number and address were conveniently included in the appointment info.

thank you

denada

de dee na

"Dr. Granger's office," the receptionist said.

"Um, yes, could you, um...What kind of doctor is he?"

There was a confused pause, during which I hoped the receptionist didn't have caller id and couldn't connect this phone call with me if I showed up.

"She is a psychiatrist. Do you need to make an appointment?"

"Um, no. Thank you so much." I disconnected.

time

to begin

never

changing

I stood up and saw for the first time what looked to be an extra phone cord plugged into the power strip. The cord disappeared under the bed. I snagged it and tugged, dragging another phone out from under the bed. An iPhone, not unlike mine, except this one had a snazzy case with slots for cards. I pulled out one of the cards. Little prickles danced along my spine when I recognized Caci staring back at me from the driver's license.

I turned the phone over and turned it on, until a white screen appeared with a black apple. I waited, but then the screen asked for her passcode. I racked my brain for a second, but then realized if I got it wrong too many times I chanced erasing the phone. I tried her birthday, just in case, but no luck. I wondered about Micah's birthday, but couldn't remember it.

I remembered that one of her arrest charges was driving without a license. Had she witnessed the murder, even videoed it? Then let herself into Robbie's house to hide the phone?

linc it up

no

no good

he's no

good

My conversation with Brother Emmett came back to me. Evil. What if she wanted me to get rid of the phone because it incriminated her? No. But I couldn't just hand it over, not knowing if I was also condemning her to death. Also criminal on my part, but somehow more justified. I could protect her for a little bit, until I understood better what was going on. I would turn the phone in, I told myself, just not yet. Instead, I instinctively went to my own closet and felt around to see if there were any cubby holes that the phone would fit into.

Nothing. I looked around my room. It was bright and cheerful.

blinding

mi amigo

no grinning

I wondered what I had drunk last night and with whom. Had Ty shown up? Had it just been me and Robbie Lynn? Did I drive home? My spine tingled a bit at the thought that I might have driven Linc's truck while intoxicated. I slipped my house shoes on and shuffled into the living room to peek out the window. The truck was there, all in one piece. I stood there for a minute contemplating that. Was I really hungover?

who knows

yes

why

My thumbnails ached to be chewed on.

With a little more speed that came from a new resolve, I walked down the hall, opening the door to my mystery room. Nothing looked immediately out of place, as I scanned the contents, looking for a place to put the phone. There was the jewelry box with no jewels in it.

no

The trunk, full of clothes that had mysteriously appeared in my closet, taking up precious space as if they belonged there.

no

I checked that room's closet.

yes

Just like I remembered had been done in Robbie's closet, the builders had left the corner facing the back of the closet unfinished. The 2x4's forming the wall made a little shelf to the right of the door. Unless you stepped into the closet, which wasn't roomy enough to do, and then turned around to face out, which was pointless, then looked to your right, too much trouble, you wouldn't know it was there. To find it, you had to know it might be there, or be someone looking for a hiding spot, and then feel around with your hand. In Robbie's closet, it's where we hid cigarettes—*contraband*—We stole from Robbie's mama. I stuck the phone in there, wondering if the same builders had constructed Robbie Lynn's house and this house.

ooohhhh nooo

its

mr

biiiiill

I didn't have much time to ponder, as I had a doctor's appointment.

6

"There is nothing like looking, if you want to find something....
but it is not always quite the something you were after."

—Thorin Oakenshield, The Hobbit

I was a few minutes early for the doctor's appointment. The receptionist did not let on like she recognized my voice when she handed me forms to fill out, pointing me toward the waiting area. She was very good at her job, sending me excellent "it's ok" vibes. I was the only person in the waiting room.

I rushed through the forms, not bothering with things like my social security number and driver's license number (sorry Ms. Nicest Receptionist Ever, it's still not really your business, even if I am crazy and you're not)

especially

And writing "see card" in the space for my insurance information. Then I failed. I had given the shiny new card (another benefit of having a full time job) to her to make a copy. Why did she need me to write it all down when she made a copy of my card? I could see no logical reason. This did not infuriate me, I'm happy to report. And who was my emergency contact?

you know

Who knew the most about me that would come to bear in an emergency?

stop that

Who could provide for me in the event of an emergency?

idiot

I tried to imagine myself in an emergency situation with a psychiatrist. I suppose it happened. But what was an emergency for a psychiatrist? Any threatening of life or limb?

code blue

What is the protocol?

It doesn't matter.

It does matter. At what point did Ms. Nicest Receptionist Ever hop up and say "It's time to bring in the emergency contact."

What else could happen in a psychiatrist's office? Maybe a fit, a shooting, a disappearing act. Did those have colors?

pink

silver

violet

for violent

which is which

there is no one else

By the time I was done deciding which questions I should and should not answer, and how, I had bitten my only good thumbnail down to the quick. I tucked it, bleeding, into my fist and with the other hand gave the clipboard back to the receptionist, who smiled as if she hadn't just witnessed a break-down and handed me back my driver's license and insurance card. I was pretty sure no one read the information anyway. What difference did it make?

I made a beeline to a small table where several magazines were piled. I had just picked up a copy of a thick magazine, drawn by an article that promised it could help me "Find Happy" when the receptionist called my name and pointed me to a door. "Down the hall. Second door on your left." For some reason I was taken aback. I had expected to be escorted, I realized, as I went to the door and peeped through. I glanced back at the receptionist. She nodded encouragingly. I took a deep breath and went in.

The hallway was unoccupied by people or furniture. It was just a hallway, dimly lit, with two doors on the left. In the middle of them, on the right, like the good little remade ranch house the doctor's office was, another door was open. I saw the toilet as I passed. Then I noticed there was still another door on the right; this too was closed and I realized the doctor probably needed a place that never had patients in it. The doctor was likely in that room now.

barge in

riddikulus

emergency

for who

the doctor

contact

code blanco

denada

My room was carpeted in a light shade of pink, with a little roll top desk against the wall to the far right. I imagined the doctor sitting there immediately after the patient left, scribbling furiously, trying to get all the crazy down on paper.

juicy bits

An overstuffed armchair, a love seat, low to the ground, and a coffee table made a conversation area. Book shelves lined the walls. The blinds were drawn and the room was lit by lamps.

"Make yourself comfortable. Dr. Granger will be with you in a minute," the room screamed.

I closed the door and sat on one side of the love seat so I could study the books in the shelves: *I'm OK, You're Ok; Switch: How to Change Things When Change is Hard; Fighting for Joy; Stumbling on Happiness; Predictably Irrational; The Interpretation of Dreams; Man and His Symbols; Psychology, Theology and Spirituality; Joy Over Happiness.*

Ah. Here was real meat on the topic and wondered if she loaned her books.

take a picture

I was just dragging my phone out when a little knock sounded on the door. Then silence. Was she waiting on an invitation?

"Uh" I started; then the door opened and a jolly little woman walked in. In her sixties, with white hair, she was about four inches shorter than my 5'2" frame, and was quite heavy.

a baker

She was flushed, with crumbs on her shirt. I thought I smelled vanilla. She walked over and held her hand out to me.

"I'm Elona Granger, Moriah, how are you?"

I took her hand and made to get up, but she waved me back down with her other hand. She gave my hand a little squeeze and then collapsed into the armchair, her legs and feet sticking out. With a practiced motion, she hooked a small ottoman with her toe, dragged it over and put her feet on it. It was a relief for both of us. She reached for a little clipboard on a side table and held it in her lap. She was wearing glasses, which she peered through at the clipboard, and then over at me.

"Now sweetheart, what brings you to see me?"

When I didn't answer immediately, she smiled at me, waiting. I was further entranced.

"It's really ok, dear. Everything you talk about with me will be in the strictest confidence. My goal is to first see if we're a fit for each other and then help you through whatever is going on."

"I'm not sure how to start."

"Well just jump in, and we'll sort it all out as we go." She smiled encouragingly.

So I did. I told her about Caci, my job, and the blackouts. I told her about Linc and how confused I felt about him. At this she looked at me disbelievingly.

"Dear, I don't think you're confused at all about how you feel. Maybe a tad resentful or rebellious about it, maybe even a little outraged with some timidity and shame thrown in, but definitely not confused."

I just looked at her, and she placidly back, with a granny-elf smile of serenity.

"Well no, I think that right there might be the emotion. A kind of deer in headlights kind of feeling?"

I slowly nodded, and she scribbled something on her clipboard.

"Go on sweetheart. I didn't mean to interrupt." She looked up at me expectantly.

But before I could she circled back around to the blackouts and peppered me with questions, making notes on her clipboard.

"Because that's the heart of the matter isn't it?" she said, but not to me. Then she asked questions about my parents. When I told her about dad and Stephen dying, her brows crinkled a little and she nodded, asking me to talk about them. But I couldn't really remember a lot, so I shrugged and told her so. She asked more questions about my childhood, and the holes in my memory became apparent.

After a little while, she looked at her watch.

"Moriah,"

"Mojo," I said, without thinking.

She tilted her head at me, as if considering me in a new light. "Mojo, we're almost out of time for today. I'd really like for you to come back, at least once a week, more if you can swing it. I want to dig deeper into these blackouts."

"Do you have any idea what's causing them?"

"I have some inklings. Obviously you've had some things happen. You've talked about your dad and brother a bit. But the blackouts and these holes in your memory concern me. I really need more information before I can give you a diagnosis. Can you come back in a couple of days, at least next week?"

I nodded.

"Excellent. But first I need to be completely honest with you. My faith is intricately tied to my work. You need to know that before we go any further, because I will involve spiritual matters in my treatment. Is that something you're okay with?"

I shrugged. It seemed logical to me that psychology was tied to spirituality. I looked back at her bookshelf, remembering there had been a book titled that. I wasn't sure how I felt about it or how it fit into everything that was happening to me, but I knew I needed help. Granger seemed like a good place to start. I remembered Brother Emmett's sermon suddenly and my prayer.

"Yes, that's fine," I heard myself say.

"Good, good. In the meantime, I want you to keep a journal. Every time you black out, I want you to record what you were doing when it happened and what you were feeling and also document what happened when you came to. What's different in your location, how much time has passed, your emotions, just everything. Do you think you can do that?"

"Yes ma'am." I was already doing it as a matter of necessity.

"The second thing I want you to do as soon as possible is to record your earliest memory. Spend some time trying to go back as far as you can, and then tell me what you believe is your very first memory.

And thirdly, I need to know where you stand spiritually. What do you believe?"

I took a breath to answer her, but she held up her hand to stop me. "Not now, dear. I want you to really think about it and write it down.

"You can do all this on a computer via email or you can do voice recordings or some mixture of the two. Margo, my receptionist, will walk you through setting up an account on our server and giving you access to some journaling tools if you want to use voice. Otherwise, email is fine. I'll be the only other person with access, so don't worry about that. You can do it all on your phone."

"Yes ma'am."

"Do you have any questions?"

"Do you think you can help me?"

"I'm going to do my very best, Mojo."

Once back in the truck, I took a second to probe around. I wasn't sure how I felt. Exposed, for sure. I'd never told anybody some of those things. Relieved? Maybe a little. Still a little stunned at how she'd cut through all the fluff to identify how I felt about Linc. Deer in headlights was right. I felt like I was about to be bulldozed. My next appointment was in two days, and I was looking forward to it. In the meantime I had homework to do.

On my way to the office I thought I saw the black truck following me, but then it seemed to disappear into the traffic behind me. I had almost decided to tell Linc more about the black truck, but I didn't have anything solid. Just feelings and flashes. And there was still the phone. I felt guilty for not telling him about that, so how could I tell him about the black truck? I either trusted him or I didn't. But who really cared if I trusted him?

me

myself

and I

I turned down Courthouse Street on my way to the office. The courthouse is on the left and the sheriff's office is on the right. There is a little courtyard with a fountain in front of the courthouse and there stood Linc and Ty, heads bent together, talking intently. Linc didn't see me as I coasted past. But Ty looked up and his eyes met mine. His face tightened. He didn't look away. An odd image of his face close to mine, and maybe a little threatening, flitted through my brain. I didn't know if it was a memory or a figment of my imagination, but like the man in the black truck, it gave me a bad feeling.

The newspaper office is half a block further down the street from the courthouse. I parked and got out, but stood at the hood of the truck and watched as Ty slapped Linc on the back, and they shook hands like the best of buddies, Ty grasping Linc's right hand with both of his own.

glad

hand

Linc turned and went inside the sheriff's office. Ty walked toward me, and I remembered that his office is next door to mine.

I moved to go inside, but he waved, as if he wanted to speak to me.

no

I waved back politely, pretending not to understand, and put my head down and went inside. I didn't trust Ty. At all, I realized. I felt like I was being a terrible friend to Robbie Lynn by not voicing my distrust of him. But I had, hadn't I? Hadn't Caci and I both made it plain? I didn't know what telling her, again, would accomplish. She knew how I felt about Ty. It was none of my business. But I couldn't be around him, which meant I couldn't be around her. And now it looked like Ty and Linc were also chummy.

The rest of the day zoomed by, but I couldn't shake the bad feeling about seeing Linc and Ty together. I left the office at five, grateful there were no late meetings to attend. It was silent and almost dark when I drove into my driveway. Hebert was not in his usual stance of paws on fence, peering over to welcome me. I looked over from my side and saw he wasn't in the yard at all. I bolted for the front door, visions of him getting shot or ran over jostling in my mind. The door was unlocked. When it swung open, I lost my breath.

My house had been torn apart. The couch cushions were ripped and strewn about. All my books were on the floor. The TV stand was askew, drawers open and the contents on the floor. I ran through the mess to the kitchen and found similar chaos there. I opened the back door and was relieved to see Hebert lying on the stoop, but then panicked again when I realized he wasn't moving. When I got to him, he was warm and breathing, but completely unconscious.

My heart was hammering. Somebody knows about the phone, I thought, so I ran to the Room of Requirement to check. The room, messy before, was now a total disaster. I couldn't even get to the closet without tripping and crawling over the mess: the jewellery box lying on its side, drawers open, the trunk lid open and its contents scattered. What little furniture was in here had also been shoved over and into the middle of the room.

Then I stopped when I got to the closet. What if someone was watching me now? I peered up into the shelf over the clothes rack and then riffled through the clothes just in case. Then I turned and made my way out and into the bathroom and the other rooms as if I was assessing the damage.

I didn't know whether to call the vet or the police first. I dithered for a minute and then dialed 911. I checked on Hebert again while I was waiting for the police and found that he was coming around. His tail thumped lazily when I called his name but he didn't lift his head. I called the vet, gave her the rundown, and I was relieved when she said she would be right over.

Then I decided to pack a bag because I was not staying there alone tonight. I'd go to Mama's. I made a big deal of packing, in case someone was watching. It was chaos, really, trying to find what I needed in the mess. When I heard a vehicle approaching, the police, I confirmed with a glance out the window, I went back to the Room of Requirement and crawled over everything back to the closet. Standing, I reached into where the clothes were with my left hand, while feeling for the phone and the cubby hole with my right hand. Relief flooded me when my hand brushed the phone. I swiped at it so it dropped to the floor, then

I bent and stuffed it into a shoe which I then stuffed into my bag.

Then I went to let Linc in.

He was in a sheriff's SUV. He hadn't pulled into my driveway, but instead had blocked access to the drive with the SUV. It was now full-on dark, so the flashing lights seemed very bright and intrusive. He was standing outside his vehicle, peering at the ground. He looked up, saw me in the doorway. "You okay?" He had to holler because he was so far away. Then, curiously, he walked along the edge of the grass, avoiding walking on the dirt driveway. Even though he seemed to be taking the long way around, his legs ate up the space between us and in just a few seconds he had hopped up on the porch and was staring down at me.

"What was that all about?"

"Evidence," he said. "You Ok?" he asked again, and I realized how shaken up I was.

"I'm fine." I resisted the urge to throw myself at him like a big baby and have a good cry. As if from afar I marveled that less than a few hours ago I had resolved that he was not trustworthy. Right now he looked like everything I ever needed.

"What happened?" His voice was gentle, as if he knew I was about to shatter. I turned and indicated the open doorway and the mess inside. "It was like this when I got home," I said. He peered into the living room and whistled at the severity of the mess.

"M a n, Somebody's upset with you Mojo. Where's Hebert?" he asked.

"He's on the back stoop," I said, my voice cracking at his observation and the confirmation that it held. He looked at me quickly, wary, thinking I was upset about Hebert. "He's fine. I think whoever did this drugged him. The vet is on her way." As he turned to go check, an odd thought struck me. How did Linc know my dog's name? That I even had a dog?

I followed him, pondering this, as he made his way through the mess and out to the stoop where he squatted at Hebert's head and scratched the dog's ears. "Hey buddy," he crooned. Hebert thumped the floor with his tail once but didn't lift his head.

"You drunk Hebert?"

Thump.

"Well, it's gonna be ok."

Thump, thump.

Then he stood up. "You still got that beer?" I pointed toward the fridge. He opened it and looked inside, then ducked down and came up with one of the mysterious beers which he opened. I decided he must have brought the beer the night of my car accident, and met Hebert then as well.

He put the beer on the table, gently grabbed my shoulders and guided me to sit. "You stay here. Relax. Have a beer. Hair of the dog. Don't get into any more trouble. Let me look around," he said. Then he was gone.

Hair of the dog

trouble

he knows

Ty

After a quick walk through the house he was back, sitting at the table across from me.

"Anything you want to tell me?" he asked quietly.

I didn't know what to say, so I shrugged.

"Mojo, Ty told me that you got pretty wasted last night at Robbie Lynn's. Is there something going on?"

"What do you mean?" I tried not to let my voice squeak.

"I mean, that it's a terrible idea to drink like that, with your history."

"My history?"

"Yes," he said, sounding exasperated. "I mean with your head injury, and other stuff."

"You mean my memory problems."

"Yes." Now he sounded relieved. "Are you still having trouble with that?"

"No," I lied.

"Why were you at Robbie Lynn's?"

"She invited me!" I said. "Why are you giving me the third degree?"

"It seems pretty conspicuous that you show up at Robbie Lynn's after visiting Caci and talking about Robbie Lynn's closet. We thought

Caci was just chatting, but Ty said he caught you in Robbie Lynn's closet."

I swallowed. "What else did Ty say? Did he say that he got into my face and threatened me?" The image that had swam before me earlier that day came back into focus. Ty, angry, threatening, reaching for me. But then Robbie Lynn was there, and he'd backed off.

"If you're hiding evidence in a murder investigation, Mojo, I can understand why he might be upset and even threatening. It's for your own good. You really don't want to go down that road. Unless you're hiding something else that's even worse. I'm not sure you understand what you're dealing with here." He indicated the mess. "Obviously someone else wants something from you now, too. And I can guarantee that person won't have your best interests at heart."

I shivered, suddenly, thinking of the man in the black truck.

"Do you have anything to tell me?" Linc asked. "Mojo, did you find something?"

I almost told him. I took the breath to tell him, but I couldn't force the words out because in the end I didn't know if I could trust him. No matter what he said, I didn't trust that Ty had my best interest at heart.

"I don't remember," I said, keeping my eyes trained on my fingers, which were peeling the label from the beer. And for the first time in my life I was glad I couldn't.

7

THURSDAY, FEBRUARY 9, 2017

*"For what you see and what you hear depends a good deal on
where you are standing. It also depends on what sort of person
you are."*

— C.S. Lewis "The Magician's Nephew"

I am sitting at my desk at work, going through regional newspapers and press releases that have piled up, looking for story tips. It is a quiet way to ease into the reporting day, and I can let my mind wander a little, as I sip my coffee. I am still shook up about the break in. My house is a crime scene right now, with people sifting through my belongings looking for clues about who would break in and why. Coming so closely on the heels of my being run off the road, it's suspicious to say the least. Linc and Ty's suspicions that I had found something and was now hiding evidence, which I was, even if I didn't remember finding it, also had me upset and worried. So I came in to work early, after stopping by the clinic to get my stitches out. I told Mama this morning that I just needed things to get back to normal as quickly as possible. And it was true, but I was having a hard time identifying normal. I know for a fact that the black truck was following me this morning. It was as if the driver wanted me to know.

When I got to work, neither Theresa nor Hank had arrived. I got a big envelope, went to my desk, wrapped the phone in lots of bubble paper, stuffed it in an overnight mail envelope and called my friend Ella from graduate school. Also from Louisiana, she had moved home to Monroe shortly after getting her degree. Her father was a district attorney. I asked her for his office address and for her to give him a heads up that I was sending him a phone that I thought contained evidence of a crime, possibly involving local law enforcement. Would he please have someone look at it and then let me know what I needed to do. She agreed and gave me the address to his office. I was almost certain now that Caci had recorded something on her phone. And whoever she recorded suspected she had done so. And now the police and DA suspected as well. I had had so many blackouts, there was no telling what I had revealed and to whom. I was anxious to get the phone out of my possession as quickly as possible, even if doing so got me in further trouble later with local law enforcement.

Once I got off the phone with Ella, I addressed the envelope and got it back out to Theresa's outgoing mail box just as she was arriving. I offered to make the coffee and watch the front desk while she did the morning mail run.

"What's this?" she asked, picking up the package. It was a flat rate box.

"Oh–that's for a friend of mine. Do you mind too terribly taking it with you? Here's the money for postage."

She shrugged, took the money and left.

she thinks you're making her do your errands

I'll buy her lunch later

When Hank arrived, I filled him in on the break-in.

"You made somebody nervous," he said, but he left it at that, and I went back to the front desk, trying to avoid thinking about Linc, without much success. He had been professional, efficient, kind, even when he was telling me he thought I was lying. He'd taken care of my house, gotten investigators going, and escorted me to my mama to spend the night. He had even carried Hebert to the vet's truck so that she could take him in for overnight observation. All of that warred with my worry that I couldn't trust him. What was I really saying, that Ty was crooked? I wouldn't put it past him. That Linc was a crooked cop? I couldn't go that far, but I also couldn't erase the fear that he might be. I wondered if he had a dog. He was obviously a dog lover. If I remembered correctly, he had also rodeoed a little in high school. His parents owned a small cattle ranch, so animals had very much been a part of his life.

Part of me wanted to go into the unknown of Linc Matthews, even if he was crooked. The idea was exciting, dangerous. Certainly, if he was a dirty cop. But having him might be worth it. What if he was the area crime boss, hiding behind his job of chief detective? That would be convenient. God it sounded like I was in a crime show. Another saner part of me absolutely did not want anything to do with him because what if he simply rejected me? Let's not forget about Lana. I couldn't think of a better person to fill the role of the crime boss' woman.

Then there was the other stuff going on inside me. Stuff that I couldn't even tell my best friend...since she was a little preoccupied these days and apparently all her conversations were recorded and shared about town with every person who thought he was minutely important. And then there was the little detail of withholding evidence in a murder investigation. No, I shouldn't forget the felonies that were keeping me from jumping the chief detective. But, if he ended up being the local crime boss, we'd have a lot in common wouldn't we?

And just how did I come by the phone? It all circled back to what was going on inside me. Why did I black out? The visit with Dr. Granger had me going back through my memories and questioning the timing of my blackouts. And of course wondering what went on during them. Why did the blackouts start occurring again when I came home? I was anxious for some answers, and it seemed that seeking answers for myself, and for Caci, precluded any involvement with Linc. But still, my mind probed the possibilities.

relentless

Last night, after settling in at Mama's, I supposed it was well after midnight before I was alone, I had started my journaling for Dr. Granger. After making sure Mama was asleep, I'd used the voice recorder, starting with the evening's events, then moving to the other questions she wanted me to answer for her.

"My first memory is sitting at the supper table. I'm sitting across from Stephen. Mama and Daddy are at either end of the table. They are mad at each other. I can tell because they are using short words and they are not looking at each other.

"Mama has just asked what we did all day. But I can tell she is not very interested. She is just doing mommy things. She is not looking at me. She had left me with Stephen because she had a job interview. I think I was three or four years old. And Stephen is looking at me. For some reason, he has s scared and scary look on his face. And I'm scared too that something bad is about to happen. And that maybe Stephen is mad at me. I don't like it when he's mad at me. But then he smiled at me and told Mama that we watched TV all day. I was still scared, but I didn't know why I was scared. But Stephen was smiling at me and so I said, "We watched TV Mama."'

"And I guess we did. I don't really remember anything before that.

"As for my beliefs about God. We didn't really go to church when I was little, or none that I remember. After Daddy and Stephen died we went a few times but neither Mama nor I liked it very much because there were a lot of snooty people. I don't really know what I believe about God. I guess I'm kind of scared of someone who has that kind of power. And maybe a little angry about all the stuff I'm supposed to do to make him happy. I mean, why should I? What has he ever done for me? My life is a wreck. I don't have the time or the inclination to do all those Christian things I'm supposed to be doing.

"But something happened at church the other day that made me think maybe I needed something. I don't know. I saw a couple of people who were just so, so happy, like it was coming off them in waves. I thought it would be really kind of nice to be that happy. I've never been that happy. I wouldn't know how to act."

8

"It is a mistake to fancy that horror is associated inextricably with darkness, silence, and solitude."

—H.P. Lovecraft

Even when I wasn't thinking about Linc, he was still on my mind. So it was no surprise that when he called me at work, it felt as if I'd conjured him up. I actually jumped when my phone chirped on the desk beside me, then froze when his name appeared on the screen. I stared at it, hand stopped midair in the act of turning a newspaper page, and let the phone ring three times as my mind slowly kicked back into gear and then raced ahead, trying to determine why he was calling. Did he find out who had broken into my house? Did he know about the phone? I snatched the phone up, worried it would go to voice mail and he'd hang up, and then I'd never know why he called. I cringed at the breathless sound of my voice.

"Hello?"

"Hey Mojo."

"Linc."

"You gotta minute?"

"Um. Sure. What's up?"

"How's your head?"

I panicked for just a second, thinking he was referring to my visit with the psychiatrist. "My head?" Then I reached up to finger the place where the stitches had been. Had it really been almost a week since I'd been in the wreck?

"It's fine!" I said. "Got the stitches out this morning, and so far no ill effects."

"That's great. I was a little worried."

I just let those words hang there for a minute, mostly because I didn't know how to respond. Obviously he was referring to my past head injury, for which he heroically took responsibility. But did I acknowledge that or just let it go? Thank him? Berate him? Did he think he was still on the hook or something? I didn't know what he wanted from me, so I just said the first thing that popped into my head.

"Hey, no worries."

"I'm really glad," and he huffed out a sigh.

"Any word on my house?"

"No, not yet. Almost done collecting evidence. You should be able to go back home tonight."

I let that thought sit there for a minute, too. I didn't know how I felt about it.

"I wouldn't, though," he said. "Get the locks changed first. Work on some better security. I can give you a couple of phone numbers of people who can help you with that."

"Yes. I think so," I said. "Better security for sure. Thank you."

"Good girl," he said. "You stay put at your mom's then. How is Hebert?"

"Oh actually I haven't had a chance to call yet. I was just about to."

"Oh well, I bet he's fine."

"Yes, me too." There was an awkward pause, so I took a breath to end the call when he spoke again.

"But I called for another reason, too," he hurried on.

"Okay?" I waited.

"I'm gonna need my truck back," he said.

"Oh! Of course!" Heat flamed in my face. "Um, I actually haven't gone by to pick something out. I'm really sorry."

"It's no problem. You've been a little busy. I just have to haul some things tomorrow," he said. "Why don't I swing by your office at lunch? You can follow me back to my place so I can drop my bike off. We can grab a bite to eat and then go pick something out for you to drive. That way you'll have your new wheels and I can just drive my truck home."

"Oh, yeah, that's a great idea." Had he just asked me out to lunch?

"It's also supposed to rain this afternoon," he said, as if he'd heard my inner question and was dissuading me from jumping to any conclusions. "I'll be by about noon. See you then." And he hung up.

Despite all the reasons not to be, I was a little giddy at the thought of having lunch with him. I had a hard time focusing the rest of the morning.

At noon, I could swear I heard the Harley crank up at the sheriff's office. I definitely heard it roaring up the street toward the office, which made me feel pretty pathetic that I was listening for it. So I went to the bathroom and took my time fluffing my hair around the head injury which was now just a greenish bruise surrounding a thin puffy red line. The injury made me look like a freak, but I blotted my nose, applied a little lip gloss, swiped the mascara gunk out of the corner of my eye and then tried to see how my rear end looked in the mirror. But the mirror was just a little 8 x 10 framed thing above the sink, and the toilet wasn't lined up right for me to stand on. I considered hauling a chair into the bathroom so I could stand on it and get a better view, but Hank was sitting at his desk and it would start a conversation I didn't want to have.

just need to see my butt Hank

The news of the break-in had worried him. I didn't need to create more suspicion, or he'd regret hiring me, if he didn't already. Instead, I went back out to my desk and picked up my cell phone. I called the president of the Kiwanis club and confirmed their meeting details for later on tonight. Then I called the president of the Lion's Club, and he, bless his heart, was inviting me to their weekly lunch next week when Linc appeared at my desk.

"I'd love to come to lunch," I cooed. "Yes, thank you. That sounds great. I'll see you then," I said, all the time avoiding Linc's gaze, and wrote down the details. I clicked my phone off and glanced up at him. "Oh hey. I'll just be a second."

He smiled, making his eyes crinkle and drawing attention to his ridiculous eyelashes.

riddikulus

He gave me one of those male upward nods of acknowledgement. He was holding his black helmet between his arm and hip and looking down at me.

indulgent

as if he knew what I was up to and thought it was cute.

Hot lingered like a brand on my brain. I remained calm, wondered vaguely if I might be ovulating, and tapped the details of the Lion's lunch into my phone, then stood, sliding my phone into my back pocket and grabbing the keys.

"Ready?"

"Yep." He glanced into Hank's office as we left and spoke to him. "You doing all right?"

"Can't complain," Hank said, with a wave.

It was a bright, beautiful day outside. The temperature had risen to the 60's, a welcome change from the dreariness of the previous week. He had parked his Harley right next to his truck. I stood at the back of the truck as he swung a leg over, hefted the bike up and kicked the stand back. Then he stopped and glanced back at me. My insides felt squirrelly.

"So I don't live far from you," he said. "About two miles, actually. I bought the Miller place."

My squirreliness morphed into a shudder. The Miller place was an old homestead that had been abandoned since as far back as I could remember. It was about 40 acres of overgrown pasture, with a little two-room cabin smack in the middle, and set way off from the dirt road on which my own house was located. A winding path that in my high school days had become little more than a pig trail, led to the cabin. Because of its proximity to my parents' house and I guess our penchant for exploring, Stephen had taken me there several times. The cabin had been falling in back then. The combination of overgrown weeds, hulking oak trees and the falling-in cabin had always given me a sense of foreboding about the place. Though it was only twenty minutes from town, it seemed remote, surrounded as it was by dense thickets.

"Really? That's pretty awesome," I lied. "Did you build something?"

"I renovated and added onto the cabin," he said. "If we've got time, I'll show you."

I decided right then that we did not have time, but did not tell him that. Instead I shrugged as if I had not a care in the world. "Okay," and then went around to get behind the wheel of his truck. I felt a mild case of panic bubbling just under the surface. He pulled out ahead of me, and I followed him, aware of the opportunity to study his form on the bike. My hands were a little shaky. As we neared my house, I realized that he had to pass my place to get to his, but I didn't recall hearing his Harley roar past over the last few days. I wondered where Lana lived.

When we turned onto his driveway, I saw that he'd spent some time working on widening the pig trail. It was truly a driveway, spread with bright (glaring really) white rocks, making a winding path with a swathe of green grass up the middle and just wide enough for one vehicle, two if they were creeping toward one another. As we progressed slowly down the drive, bushes and trees crowded in, and tree limbs reached eerily up and over, seeking light, I know, but seeming to want to swallow us up. The path darkened as the trees closed like a tunnel about us. I looked in the rear view mirror to make sure the way out was still clear.

Then we burst into a clearing, and there sat the cabin. A terrifying reminder of something

what?

The cabin was still tiny, but no longer derelict, and he'd added a porch. The roof was new and metal. The siding was either different, or scrubbed; I couldn't tell. And it looked like there was another room or two, added onto the back. The cyclone fence surrounding the cabin, once sagging, rusty and dilapidated, was now a tight, shiny new fence, enclosing a clipped yard of St. Augustine grass. Tall cedar trees offered shade inside the yard while hulking oaks in the back seemed to be trying to overtake the house. A large Catahoula cur with haunting glass eyes charged out from under the porch and bounced menacingly around at the gate, barking. Linc drove his motorcycle around the side, stopped, and motioned for me to roll my window down.

When I did, he yelled over his engine, "Just stay there, I'm gonna park the bike around here. You can get out, but don't go in the fence yet."

It was obvious his dog would tear me to pieces. I nodded, put the truck in park and shut the engine off. I approached the fence warily. The dog let out a low warning growl, and I stopped in my tracks. If he wanted to, he could bound over that fence in a heartbeat. I stood still. The Harley engine suddenly went quiet, and the silence assaulted me. Then the dog growled again. The sun was blinding, so I shaded my eyes to see the dog more clearly. He was watching me, on high alert. A minute or two later, the cabin's front door rattled and opened, and Linc appeared on the porch. The dog continued to stare me down.

"Back up, Lear," Linc said. The dog obediently backed away from the gate as Linc approached, but still watching me. He snapped a lead onto the dog's collar, then snapped the other end to a stake in the yard. "Okay, you can come in now," he said.

"Nice dog," I said. "He's beautiful." And intimidating, I thought. He had a light, bluish coat, speckled with darker spots. His blue eyes completed the striking contrast of colors.

"Thanks. He's still in training. He's supposed to be a guard dog, but he's still working on discernment. And I can't trust him not to bolt just yet."

"Can I make friends?" I hated being afraid of dogs.

"Sure. Lear, sit."

The dog sat, and I approached. "Hey there, King Lear. How you doin'? You're just a big baby aren't you? Just a big ole baby!" Lear licked his chops and his tail thumped on the ground. I reached for his ear, giving him time to sniff my hand, then gave him a scratch, which clearly made him want to jump for joy.

"Be still," Linc warned him in a low voice.

Lear whined a little, but obeyed, as I scratched his ears and crooned to him. He sniffed me and wagged his tail energetically.

"You smell Hebert?" I asked. And with that he couldn't help himself and lunged to his feet, a sloppy, tongue-lolling smile on his face. I laughed. Linc became stern and stepped between us. Lear, a little deflated, sat back down and whined some more, avoiding Linc's gaze.

I went up to the porch to end the dog's torture. "He's pretty energetic," I said.

"Yes, he is. He's exhausting. I'm not sure he's ever gonna calm down," Linc said, hopping up to the porch with me. Too late I realized I'd made it easier for us to go into the cabin.

"How old is he?"

"About 18 months."

"Well, you're almost there," I said. "The puppy stage will be over before you know it."

"Thank God," he said, opening the door for me. "Have you ever been in here?"

Panic seized my throat, but I heard myself answer, "Actually, yes, Stephen used to bring me here," just before I blacked out.

9

"But it is immortals whom we joke with, work with, marry, snub, and exploit—immortal horrors or everlasting splendors."

—C.S. Lewis

I awoke in my bed in my old bedroom at my mother's house. I checked my phone. A doctor's appointment this morning at 9. It was 7 a.m. I had scheduled the appointment for this morning because I was supposed to have attended late meetings last night and could, therefore, go into work later. Hank wasn't expecting me, at any rate. I would have to check my notebook to see if I had any notes.

I got out of bed and padded to the living room to look out the window. A little gray sedan sat in the driveway. I looked at the key rack by the door, where a new key dangled. Good. At least I had gotten something to drive.

I got ready for my appointment, trying not to wake Mama.

"And did you?" Dr. Granger asked. She was referring to my note taking on the meetings last night. I had filled her in on what had happened, spilling it all out in a rush as soon as I sat down.

"I haven't checked yet. I'm kind of afraid to check."

"I see." She looked at me calmly. "You said the last thing you remember saying was that Stephen used to take you to that cabin when you were a kid."

I blinked. And then was surprised that Dr. Granger had suddenly changed positions. She was leaning forward, her notebook was lying askew on the floor, and her face had gone pasty white.

"What is it?" I asked.

"Are you all right?"

"Yes, I'm fine. I was about to tell you about visiting the cabin with Stephen."

She stared at me.

"Except that I don't really remember a lot about it. I remember going there; I just don't remember being inside. I couldn't tell you what the inside of the cabin looks like. Or looked like. I'm sure Linc has probably changed it around. I guess that's another hole in my memory. The inside of the cabin. I'm sure we must have gone inside, though. Linc and I. Well, and Stephen and I. Because I remember standing at the door, like I was about to go inside but that I really didn't want to. It's so frustrating. Dr. Granger."

"Indeed," she said, and seemed to shake herself. She took a deep breath and reached down for her notebook, held it in her lap, smoothing the pages. She had leaned back in her chair, and now she looked at her watch and then at me.

"Mojo, we're almost out of time." She seemed to study me.

I glanced at my watch. The time had flown by. She had seemed startled. Taken off guard. I peeked back up at her. "Did something happen just now?" I asked cautiously.

"Do you think something happened?" she asked.

"I'm not sure." Oh God. I put my face in my hands. It was one thing to black out and know it happened. Another thing entirely to not know for sure. That changed everything. I couldn't even trust myself.

She nodded. "Let's don't get into that now. What I'd like to do is get your permission to video our next session. And in the meantime, don't do anything but stay home tonight. And I want to see you first thing tomorrow morning for two sessions in a row. I'll just have to move things around."

"Well that sounds ominous," I said.

"Yes this is serious," she said.

"Oh, I see." But I didn't really.

"The important thing now is the video. Do I have your permission?"

"Sure, I guess. If you think it will help."

"I do," she said. "Very much. And keep writing in the journal. Now, about this trip to Monroe," she said.

"How did you know about that?" I had only been toying with the idea of going.

She looked at me blankly for a moment. "Dear, you told me."

I furrowed my brow. I didn't remember. "Oh."

"I would like you to defer or cancel that trip if at all possible."

I shrugged. As far as I knew I had no solid plans anyway. "I do think it's important to follow up," I said. "For Caci's sake."

"Yes, I agree with you, that it's important for law enforcement to look at that phone. But that's where you're involvement should end. How about if we talk more about it in the morning?"

I nodded.

"I'm giving you my personal cell phone number. If anything happens and you need help, please don't hesitate to contact me. I'm very worried about you being alone and these blackouts," she said. "This person in the black truck also scares me. However, I realize you're in a bit of a situation." Here she paused, furrowed her own brow and stared at a spot on the carpet as if she were thinking. "Maybe you should talk to Linc. Yes. I think it might be best," she mused. "Maybe you tell him everything and he could offer you protection ...."

She stopped when she looked up at me. I must have had an outraged look on my face. "Well. I can't make you, can I? All I can do is encourage you. And of course I couldn't possibly say anything myself because of doctor-patient privilege. Now look," she said sternly. "Just come back tomorrow and we'll talk more. I think having video of your session will change your perspective some."

By this time we'd both stood and were at the door to the room. She put her hand on my shoulder. "Mojo there is so much going on in that mind of yours."

"Yes ma'am." I wasn't entirely sure what she was talking about but by then I knew she knew something about me that I didn't know. And that kind of freaked me out a little. Not to mention the man in the black truck.

As soon as I got to work and got settled, I dug in my bag for my notebook and opened it to the last page I had written on. It was notes for the last story I had written, on Thursday morning before I left with Linc. No notes for any meetings I should have attended last night.

I let the full import of that sink in for a minute. Up until now, somehow, I had been continuing to take care of my responsibilities, despite the blackouts. If the blackouts prevented me from actually doing my job, how could I trust myself to keep a job? And if I couldn't keep a job, well then, I couldn't even begin to think of the implications. Right now, I could make a few phone calls and figure out a way around last night's meetings. But what if it happened again? What if I couldn't fix it next time?

I couldn't live like that. No one could. It was too much, waking up day after day never sure if I'd done something irreparable and spending all my awake time trying to figure out and fix things that did or did not occur during a blackout. Even this morning, there had been a point in my session with Dr. Granger when I was certain I must have blacked out. But it had been so subtle, I could have easily missed it. No. My condition had escalated well beyond my abilities to cope with it.

But I couldn't just quit my job or even confide in anyone. How would I even explain it?

Hey Hank, so um I think I'll quit. Oh wait, I forgot. I did that yesterday.

It was ludicrous. I had sounded like a freak when I'd told Dr. Granger about it. Indeed I was a freak or I wouldn't even be talking to Granger about it. And what about Caci? I couldn't abandon things the way they were. The phone was still out there and needed to be dealt with.

Well. I knew what I could do about that. I could stay away from the phone, for one thing. Dr. Granger was right. I didn't need to go see Ella. No, I would take that chance. If the evidence wasn't on the phone or not easily retrieved, well then the phone was in safe keeping until I could resolve some of these other issues and get back to it, if need be.

Over the next hour, I set about trying to repair the damage from my blackout by making calls concerning the two meetings I'd apparently missed. The first was a Kiwanis meeting, which was supposed to have happened at four yesterday afternoon. I called the president, who was also a real estate agent in town.

"Hey Elizabeth, it's Mojo," I said.

"Hey Mojo." Her voice sounded a bit tight. Nothing else seemed to be forthcoming, so I took it a step further.

"About the meeting last night," I hoped she could hear the apology in my voice. I waited another second, hoping she'd chime in with something, anything, but she held her tongue, so I plunged ahead.

"I do apologize," I said.

"Well we waited for like twenty minutes for you to show up, and we finally had to just go on and give Mr. Hilton his award without you."

"I'm so, so sorry, Elizabeth. I'm not always in control of my schedule or when things crop up that I have to take care of immediately," I said, which was the absolute bitter truth about my life, but not necessarily my job. Then I took a leaf from Linc's book. "And, unfortunately, I can't always pick up the phone to call immediately."

"I understand that you probably have lots of other more important things to cover, Mojo, like murder trials and stuff. It's just that Mr. Hilton has been in Kiwanis for 30 years. He's done sooo many awesome things."

I jumped at the chance to do a story without fangs.

"I totally get it, girl. Tell you what. Why don't you give me Mr. Hilton's phone number and let me do a full feature on him. That would be so much better than just a photo and a cutline."

"Oh Mojo, really? That would be fantastic!" I finished getting the details, including her agreeing to send me the photos she took and clicked off, heaving another sigh of relief. Two hurdles down, one to go. I was feeling like I was nearing the summit of a huge mountain.

The second meeting had been a town meeting at 6 p.m., for which I already had the agenda. There was only one item on the agenda that might have caused some discussion: the town was applying for state aid to make sewer repairs. According to Hank (I hadn't been on the job long enough to make it to a meeting), sometimes the guy over the sewer system got snide with the town council, which caused words to go back and forth. As entertaining as that might be, it wasn't something we generally put in a story, as it made the town look bad for no good reason and would jeopardize the paper's relationships with just about everybody concerned.

Everything else on the agenda was pretty straightforward. But Hank would still be expecting a story, written from someone who had been there. Eventually the meeting minutes would be sent to the paper for publication. But I couldn't wait that long. I could go and get a copy of the audio recording, but that might prove to be complicated. I doubted anyone had ever asked for that before. And the clerk would be using the original recording to finish up her minutes. If she didn't know how to get me a copy, she would ask the mayor or someone else for help and then it could get back to Hank. It was better to come clean. I got up, knocked on Hank's door, and poked my head in. He looked up from his computer.

"Hey, so I just wanted to give you a heads up. I've got a nice feature coming up from the Kiwanis meeting, and probably some great art to go with it, but the town meeting was a bust. I couldn't get to it. And besides that the agenda was very low key. I could try and get a copy of the audio recording, if you want and go from there?"

"Oh yeah? What's the feature," he asked.

"Thirty-year service award for a Mr. Hilton. But I thought I'd go interview the guy and maybe some others who remember him? Maybe scan some old photos if I can find some?"

"I like that. Hilton's a good guy. Give it some serious attention."

"And what about the town meeting?"

"Call the mayor and ask him what happened. Write it like an interview. Don't worry about art on it."

Bam.

I shut his door and went back to my desk, jittery with adrenaline and anxiety.

Once I calmed down with a cup of coffee, I spent the rest of the day working peacefully and blissfully on the feature article about Mr. Hilton, who was a very sweet man. I went to visit with him, spending an hour chatting on his front porch, and, glory hallelujah, another hour going through old photo albums which had enough pictures for a center spread about his years of service to the community. His was truly a life well lived, I reflected wistfully on the drive back to the office.

I would give anything to be able to have such an uncomplicated life full of doing what I loved and helping others.

Once in the office, I got straight to work on the article, which was a cinch to write. No writhing over appropriate legal jargon, no struggling with how trustworthy my sources were. Just straightforward feature writing about an interesting fellow. I was just putting the finishing touches on the article when my cell rang.

I looked at the caller id and my heart sank. It was Linc. I had been avoiding thinking about him. Very successfully, too. It was good to know that the threat of pending unemployment could take my mind off him. But, crisis with employment averted, here he was back on the radar.

The thing was, I had been with Linc a huge portion of the day yesterday, at least some part of it at his house alone with him, and I had no idea what had transpired between us. If I couldn't trust myself to do my job, I dang sure couldn't trust myself to be alone with Linc. I toyed with the idea of sending the call to voicemail. At least then I could gauge his state of mind by the message he left. But I couldn't picture him leaving a message. He'd figure he was in my phone and that I'd see he called and expect me to call him back.

I answered it like a good girl.

"Hello?"

"Hey. I'm just getting off work here. I've sent Jimbo out to your place. I'm gonna run home, pick up Hebert and bring him to you."

"Oh! Ok." He had Hebert? My face flamed. I had gone the whole day not knowing he had my dog. And why did he? "Thanks," I added. "I really appreciate that. What do I owe you?" Maybe I had offered to pay him?

"Shut up," he said. "He's a great dog and distracted Lear from being bad. I should be paying you."

"Okay, good, I could use a hundred bucks," I said.

He laughed.

"I was totally kidding," I said, just in case he thought I was a moron.

"Well, I may have to rent him in the future for winding Lear down. What are the rates?"

"Free for you, since you're such a nice guy," I said, smiling now.

"Ohhh," he said. "Well that's good to know."

Is this flirting?

What about the divine Lana?

"Okay, well I'll be by with your pooch in a bit," he said.

"Okay. Oh, wait!" I said before he hung up.

"Yeah?"

"Who is Jimbo?"

"The security guy," he said and disconnected.

10

I clocked out and drove home. When I got there, a blue van with Locks Unlimited painted on the side was already in the driveway.

"Hello?" I called, after I parked, got out and approached the van. The back door of the van was open and I could see a man in coveralls squatted down and digging around inside.

"Oh, hey! You must be Mojo. I'm Jimbo. Friend of Linc's," he said, standing as much as he could inside the van and offering me his hand, which I shook quickly. He was so tall and lanky, it was obvious that he was uncomfortable in the position he had to take to look at me. As soon as I let go of his hand he sank back down into a squat and smiled. "Can't stand up in here too long," he said. "Gives me a crick in my neck."

"I can see that," I said, smiling. "Nice to meet you. Thanks for coming out. What do you need from me?" He looked distracted and I suspected I'd interrupted him from looking for something. The back of the van was a jumble of tools and mysterious equipment.

"Oh nothing much. I'm just gonna take a look around at your doors and windows and then come up with a plan for you."

"OK that sounds pretty good," I said. "Just let me know if you need anything." He nodded absently, already absorbed in looking through his stuff.

I went inside and changed into jeans and a T-shirt, trying to ignore my own mess left over from the break-in.

It was going to take me days to get it sorted out. Though I picked up a few things here and there and put them away, I resisted the urge to dive into it right away and went to the kitchen instead to stick my head in the fridge, wondering if Linc would want to eat. I was starving, but I had absolutely nothing interesting to eat. I was considering picking up the phone to call out for pizza, when I heard Linc drive up, so I went out to get Hebert settled.

I heard him barking before I got to the door. I was glad to see him, but he was concerned with the unfamiliar van in the driveway. He was snapped into the back of Linc's truck with a lead and pulling at it, his eyes on the van. Once he parked, Linc hopped into the back of his truck with Hebert, unsnapped the lead and handed it to me over the side. Hebert took a flying leap to the ground and began pulling me toward the van.

"Whoa, boy," I said as sternly as I could. "Sit." He whined, but couldn't break his attention from the van.

I stood in front of him and adopted my fiercest attitude. "Sit."

I am always relieved and a tad bit surprised when this works. Hebert, who is a large dog and could easily jerk me around, sat like a champ, and finally turned his attention toward me. His tongue lolled in a sloppy grin as he finally relaxed and waited for me to tell him what to do next.

"Impressive," I heard Linc say. I resisted the urge to show off and earn even more praise from that mouth. Instead, I rewarded Hebert with lavish ear scratches which made him melt to the ground and expose his belly to be scratched.

"Hebert, you're so easy," I told him in the high voice I used when he was being a good dog. "You're just so easy. Anything for a good belly scratch huh? But he's a good dog. Yes he is. Just the best dog ever. In the whole world. I mean it." Hebert lolled ecstatically on the ground.

"Dude," I heard Linc say and looked up to see he had hopped down and was standing beside me. "You can't just roll over like that," he said looking at Hebert. "Have some self-respect."

"He knows the source of all good things," I said.

"I have no doubts," Linc said, a smile playing around his mouth. "I see Jimbo made it. I guess y'all have met already?" I nodded.

"Bit absentminded," I said, but not unkindly.

"Yeah, but he's a good guy and he's good at what he does. And he's self-aware," Linc added. "He doesn't charge by the hour. He charges by the job. He knows he takes longer than other people."

"Oh, well," I said, shrugging. "In that case," I trailed off.

Hebert had hopped up and began sniffing the ground and pointing again toward the van.

"Let me go speak," Linc said, and also headed toward the van.

I led Hebert over to check it out just as Jimbo whooped from the back of the van. "Found it!" And then he hopped to the ground right in front of Hebert, who barked and jumped up on him, forepaws on his chest. Not missing a beat, Jimbo, grabbed Hebert's ears and gave them a massive rub down, teaching him, I was sure, to jump on every person that ever came into the yard.

"Nice dog," he said.

"Thanks," I said. "Hebert, down!" I gave the leash a hearty pull.

"Oh it's all right," Jimbo said.

"If he jumps on my mother like that, he'll break her hip!"

That got Jimbo's attention, and he stepped back, forcing Hebert to drop down.

"Sorry," I said, realizing I'd been a little too aggressive.

I dragged Hebert over to the yard and put him inside the gate, finally distracting him with one of his chew toys. I hung his leash on a hook by the door and sneaked a look back at Linc. I was relieved to see that Jimbo had caught his attention. They had extended their hands to one another as soon as I'd backed away with Hebert, gripped each other's hands strongly and clapped each other on the back, smiling; then they stood and spoke, their arms crossed comfortably over their chests, legs planted.

man talk

I was always slightly bewildered by the way some men greeted each other and spoke to each other. Their conversation took on an abbreviated tone full of understated nods and grunts and non sequiturs. I remembered lots of similar conversations between my brother Stephen and our father. We'd be riding along in Daddy's truck, me sitting in the middle as they talked. I could barely follow along, and I never knew if it was because they weren't speaking in a way I could understand or because my mind drifted away.

What sounded to me like some unimportant detail uttered with little fanfare by one which barely elicited a response from the other, often ended up being the topic of conversation for hours. Inevitably the importance of the detail and the ensuing conversation was lost on me because I simply didn't accurately translate their facial expressions, tones and grunts. I would often just let my mind drift because I wasn't usually interested in what they were talking about even if I could translate.

Briefly I wondered if men felt similar bewilderment or tuned things out when confronted with a group of women talking. Did the hand flying and extreme facial expressions punctuated with gasps and ever-changing tones of voice puzzle and overwhelm them?

And then there was the way men and women communicated with each other. There was a fine line between flirting and exchanging information. Sometimes I caught myself with a flirtatious tone in my voice when I didn't mean it at all. And other times I found myself praying for the ability to flirt. I wondered about married couples. My own parents had rarely flirted. Well, my mother and stepfather. My biological father had been a soldier, stationed at the nearby military base for a short period of time, just long enough to get my mother pregnant. She'd never heard from him once he left. She'd always told me that it had been a lighthearted fling between the two of them. She had just graduated high school and he was here on a training mission. By the time she found out she was pregnant with me, he'd already left. I always thought that maybe she'd been too prideful to tell him. I could totally see her thumbing her nose at him for not caring enough to check on her after he left. Anyway, a few years after I was born, she saw that he'd been killed in the Gulf War. In the meantime she'd waited tables, put herself through school for an associate's degree in business management and gotten a job with an insurance agency.

Not long after she'd found out my real father had died, she'd married my stepfather, Frank, but I had always called him Daddy. Frank's son, Stephen, was four years older than I. When our parents got married he was seven and I was still a baby. Both Stephen and Daddy died the year I turned twelve. I don't remember many happy times between Mama and Daddy. In fact the best I could remember, they had struggled to speak civilly to one another. I didn't know if that was the whole truth, though, since I could never rely on my own memories. And Mama never wanted to talk about Frank and Stephen. My stomach growled and I went inside, intending to make some iced tea and order a pizza, leaving the men to their chat.

I was just stirring the tea when someone banged on the door. I came around the corner to holler "come in," as I was sure it was either Linc or Jimbo. The door opened and Linc poked his head around.

"You don't have to knock," I said. "Come on in. You want some iced tea?"

He came in, stepping carefully around stuff that was still strewn about, and then looked at me so seriously I stopped.

"What?"

"Well, it depends," he said. "Have you yankified it?"

I laughed. "My tea? Absolutely not! It's so sweet the spoon stands up."

"Good," he said, obviously relieved. "I'm pretty thirsty."

"Well sit yourself down, boy," I drawled, going back into the kitchen and pointing to the table. "I'll fix you a glass." Oddly, the kitchen was the one room in the house that had escaped complete annihilation. Drawers had been opened and riffled through, cabinet doors were open, but nothing was destroyed or thrown on the floor.

"It shouldn't take Jimbo more than an hour to get you set up. I'm not sure how much you want to spend, since this is a rental. But your landlord should cover a portion of it. Jimbo actually did my house," Linc said.

"Oh yeah? New locks and all. That makes sense."

Linc gave me an odd look, and I looked away quickly as I poured the tea, aware that I must have said something weird. Probably more blackout fallout.

"I plan on giving my landlord a copy of the estimate and then going from there," I said, to distract him.

Linc nodded as he accepted a glass from me. He drank half of it in one go and then rattled the ice cubes together. "Thank you," he said. "I was dying."

I turned to get the pitcher and refilled his glass. "Don't go dying here, buddy. I got too much else going on," I said, trying to be light.

But he didn't smile.

"Yeah," he said, resting his eyes on me. "About that."

I made to turn back to the kitchen, but he put his hand lightly on my wrist. "Sit down Mojo."

"Dang Linc, I was just kidding." He looked very serious. "Don't go all chief detective on me."

But he didn't lift his hand and his eyes didn't flicker.

"Ok, fine," I said, sitting and putting the pitcher of tea between us. What is it?"

"About yesterday," he said.

Crap.

"What about it?" I said and stood back up, not making eye contact and wishing desperately for more information. He reached for me again, but I pulled away. "I'm just getting my tea glass." I stepped over to the kitchen counter and grabbed my glass. I sat back down and busied myself with pouring my own tea, hoping he would move on to something else.

When my eyes landed back on him he was still looking at me.

"Fine," he said, looking down at his tea glass. My eyes followed his to his right hand, which was holding the glass lightly, his long fingers curved around the glass. His hand was rough, as if he spent time working with tools, which made me wonder what he did when he wasn't at work.

"I'm just trying to clear the air after yesterday," he said. "I'm sorry I kissed you. It was very unprofessional of me."

My tea gushed out of my nose like a little tea fountain. I turned to the side, to spare him the sight and to also cough. The front of my shirt was soaked with tea. It was dripping on the floor. If I hadn't felt like I was suffocating, I would have been mortified.

He stopped talking immediately and got up to grab a paper towel. I was still in a really bad way, trying to catch my breath. A headline flashed through my mind: *Forgetful* Times *Reporter Drowns In Sweet Tea Tete a Tete.*

He handed me the paper towel, which I held over my mouth while I coughed.

"Are you ok?"

"Yes, I'm fine," I said, finally catching my breath. "I'm sorry. You just caught me off guard." I started mopping up the tea off my shirt, the table, the floor, but I still saw how he looked at me and knew I had again said something that sounded odd to him.

"Off guard?"

I squirmed a little. So he had kissed me, and now he regretted it. Did that mean I should regret it too? Probably, especially if I wanted to spare my own feelings. Dang it. How unfair to have to regret something you didn't remember. I cleared my throat and looked at what remained of my sweet tea and then thought better of trying to take another sip.

"Well, I was just hoping we could forget about it," I said, trying to be airy.

He raised an eyebrow at me, and for the third time, I got the distinct feeling I'd said something wrong.

"Tell me about your head injury," he said, shifting topics so quickly I blinked. "What did the doctor tell you? Do you still see a doctor from the accident in high school?"

"Whoa!" I said. "Dude, are you interrogating me?"

He looked taken aback. Then he seemed to relax. "Sorry," he said. "I just have a lot of questions."

"Okaaay," I said, not sure where he was going.

"Mojo, I didn't kiss you yesterday," he said. When the words sank in, I felt a familiar sinking sense of hopelessness, very similar to earlier in the day when I'd realized that my condition could cost me my job. That there were times when I didn't know for sure if I'd blacked out. And now I was realizing that if people knew about my issue they could use my condition against me.

It was suddenly abundantly clear to me that Linc was trying to manipulate me. He had somehow deduced that I didn't remember parts of yesterday. And now he knew that he knew something about me that I didn't know. And he had some kind of plan to use it against me. Oh God. What was wrong with me? It felt like my life was falling apart or that I was the star in a play where everyone but me had the right script. All eyes were on me but not only did I not know my lines, I didn't know if I was in a comedy or a tragedy.

"You need to leave," I said, plucking his tea glass out of his hand and taking it to the sink. Without making eye contact, I glided to the door and held it open for him.

"Now."

"Mojo, hear me out," he said, standing and holding his hands out to me defensively. "Why are you so mad? I was just trying to figure out what's going on."

Ha, I thought. *Aren't we all?*

I pressed my advantage. "Why am I mad? Why am I mad? Oh my God you've got to be kidding me. You think it's ok to come into my house like you're my friend and then interrogate me and lay traps for me like I'm a suspect or something? Like you're investigating me?" I slammed the door, because it seemed like the only appropriate way to punctuate my words.

His sheepish look made me feel triumphant.

"I'm sorry," he said. "I didn't mean to come off like that. I should have just asked you, you're right. But I was sure you'd find a way around talking about it. Mojo you always find a way around talking about it."

"Talking about what? Your deep-seated and incredibly conceited fear that you gave me brain damage in high school?"

He went a little pale, but before he could say anything there was a knock on the door. I slung it open.

"What?" It was Jimbo and he was blushing deeply.

"Just wanted to let you know I'm done. I'll be on my way. I'll drop the estimate off tomorrow evening." If he'd had a cap on his head he'd have swiped it off and wrung it mercilessly in his hands, he was so nervous.

"I'm sorry, Jimbo. Of course. Thank you so much!" I tried to smile, but it was more like a snarl. He ducked his head and turned toward his van. I shut the door gently behind him and turned with my back to it, facing Linc, but not looking at him.

"As a matter of fact, no," he said, as if Jimbo had never interrupted us. I looked up at him then. He was frowning and staring at me with an intense look. Not defensive now exactly, but not offensive either. Just standing his ground. "Your mom cleared that misconception up a long time ago. It's your issues with remembering things that I'm so concerned about. Particularly since somebody might have identified you as a target."

"Oh," I said. But I wasn't entirely convinced. He had been interrogating me. And he had laid a trap for me.

He took a step toward me, and then another, until he was standing much closer. I still had my back to the door.

"Mojo you obviously still have memory problems. You handle it very well, but it makes you vulnerable. It worries me that maybe you know something about Roberto's murder that you don't realize you know. Caci has been mixed up in all kinds of crap. And you two go way back. I think when you went to see her it made someone very uncomfortable."

Again, I found myself feeling off kilter. "You don't think she killed him?"

"Just because we arrested her doesn't mean we're done investigating. And believe me, more points away from Caci than to her."

I nodded, glad they hadn't stopped looking.

His words had echoed exactly the way I'd been feeling all day: vulnerable. But I wasn't done being angry.

"You lied to me. And you were manipulating me. That really ticks me off."

He shrugged, which made me even angrier. I turned and opened the door for him, not looking at him.

He didn't move. "Being your friend comes second to doing my job," he said. "It's unfortunate that hurts your feelings or ticks you off or whatever. But ultimately me doing my job protects you, and it might just get your friend off a murder rap."

His phone rang and he answered it. I didn't look at him, but I could feel him staring at me.

"Yeah," he said and then listened as the person on the other end talked. "Send me the address," he said. He holstered his phone, stepped into the doorway and turned to look at me.

"I have to go," he said. "There's been a shooting in town." I still didn't look at him. "Look, I'd really appreciate it if you'd go to your mom's tonight. You're still not safe here until you get better security."

I finally looked at him as coldly as I could, but didn't say anything. I had been planning to go to Mama's anyway. I didn't want him to have the satisfaction of having the last word or thinking I'd agreed to something he said. He had stepped out onto the porch.

"You can do your job without being a jerk," I told him, and let the door swing shut with a satisfying click. But it was an empty sense of satisfaction because he'd told me what I had suspected all along: he was over me. And now I knew how he must have felt in high school when I'd told him I didn't remember him.

11

When I was sure he was gone from the driveway, I packed a small suitcase and took it to the car. Then I put an old blanket on the backseat of the car, tucking it in, and told Hebert to hop in, which he did happily, lying on the back seat as if he were a king about to be chauffeured. I left him there with the windows partway down and went back in for a last sweep of the house and to lock up. Then we drove to Mama's. I fed Hebert in her fenced backyard, hauled my suitcase to my old bedroom and then joined her in the kitchen where she was pulling a small pot roast from the oven.

"Well, I'm glad you're here," she said. "I don't eat roast very often because there's never one small enough at the grocery store. This one will feed us tonight and then we can have roast beef sandwiches for lunch tomorrow," she said. "I was worried about the leftovers, to tell you the truth."

"It smells great," I said, glad now that I hadn't ordered pizza. "I'm starving."

"There's salad makings in the fridge," Mom said. "Let me whip these potatoes." Her hand mixer whirred to life as I dug lettuce, tomato and cucumber out of the fridge. "Awesome!" I said to myself when I saw she had sugar snap peas. She glanced at me while the mixer whirred, and I held up the bag to her. She smiled and nodded. She had obviously shopped recently with me in mind.

When everything was done, we sat at the table.

"I like to say a prayer these days," Mama said, surprising me. I had already picked up my fork, so I put it down again.

"Sure," I said, putting my hands in my lap and bowing my head.

"Lord, thank you for this time together and for this food," she said. "We pray for our safety, too," she added awkwardly. "In Jesus' name, amen."

"Amen," I said, feeling a little uncomfortable. Mama had never been very religious, so this was new.

But being completely honest, I'd have to say that Mama had changed quite a bit. Part of it was because I was an adult, of course, but most of it was because of her stroke, I supposed. Only occasionally did I get glimpses of Mama as I remembered her from my childhood. For one thing, I wasn't the only one suffering from memory problems. She sometimes had days when her memory was as unreliable as mine. Then other days she was fine. Unlike mine, her memory issues had to do with tasks. Sometimes she drew a blank when presented with a phone or a remote control. She would turn them over in her hands, studying the objects as if they were artifacts from a different civilization. Other times, she struggled with remembering how to do something, like tie her shoes, or make a meal. And still other times she struggled with words and getting them out. Today's meal was a testament that she'd not struggled in the cooking realm today.

"What did you do today?" I asked her. "Oh I read a little bit. Do you know that Tom Cruise is beginning to regret he got involved in all that Scientology mess?" she said.

I stared at her blankly. This was another issue, deceptive in its subtlety.

"I've been worried about him," she said, shaking her head. I could almost see the intimate conversation that had led her to her worry. Except I knew it had probably been a talk show or some other video or an article. "I just don't know what he's been thinking all these years." She chewed her roast beef thoughtfully. I didn't know what to say. I didn't even know what to call this, a grandiose delusion that she knew the inner thoughts of movie stars? Almost, but not quite. Leave it to Mama to have a delusion that couldn't be pigeonholed.

As is often the case when I come face to face with one of her issues, I can't find anything to say. I don't want to encourage the delusion by engaging in a conversation about Tom Cruise's feelings. Neither do I want to contradict her because that will only upset her. I wouldn't change her mind and she'd likely forget we'd ever had the conversation, but still feel the effects of having gotten all worked up. On top of that, her behavior was so bizarre to me, I couldn't think beyond it. So I usually let her prattle on, becoming more and more uncomfortable.

Now she was talking about someone else. "I really believe that if Charlie hadn't had it in for him, Steve would have gone to hell," she said. "I don't know if you know it but Steve McQueen was a very famous movie star."

"Well who was Charlie?" I asked, not able to resist.

"Manson," she said. "You know that helter skelter guy. If he hadn't had Steve on his hit list I don't think Steve would've gotten saved before he died. You know it's just amazing how the Lord works."

"Yes. It is," I said. Befuddled, I pushed back from the table. "Mom, this was delicious. I love your pot roast."

She beamed at me. "I'm so glad you liked it. I bet you'd rather have dinner with Tom, though. All the girls would, you know. He has a terrible time with it."

I had no response.

She brought her dishes to the sink, and we both washed up.

"I think I'm gonna have a bath and watch some tv," she said.

"Okay. I've got some work to do, then I'm gonna walk Hebert."

As she moved toward her bedroom, I decided to walk Hebert first. It would be good to take a familiar walk. When I was a kid, I had walked often, usually with a dog or two following me. Mama's house was far enough out that the nearest neighbors were several miles away. I had never worried about leashing the dogs because we were so far from other people. Hebert would love a leash-free walk before dark, I thought.

As soon as I started off down the road, Hebert immediately took off for the woods. I didn't bother calling him back, knowing he was on the scent of some critter. Then I realized I had forgotten my phone. I paused, looking at the sky. It was almost dark. If I went back for my phone, it would cut the walk short, and I really needed to unwind. I walked on, but within minutes I regretted it.

As I came to the end of the driveway, which is about a quarter mile long, the man in the black truck was just turning in. We both stopped.

His truck was idling in a low growl. My stomach clenched. I stepped to the shoulder of the road just as the driver door opened. I heard a shot as I slipped into the undergrowth. My heart slammed into my throat as I took several strides and found myself caught by briars. I didn't stop, but ripped through, vaguely grateful for the jacket and jeans I was wearing. It was nearing the end of winter, and the trees were mostly bare except the low-growing holly and invasive privet. The area around Mama's house had been logged a few years ago. The regrowth had created a tangled thicket of tightly growing trees, bushes and briars, both excellent camouflage and a possible death trap at the moment.

I had to stop again to untangle myself. I strained to hear the truck, but all I could hear was my pounding heart and the blood rushing in my head. Branches, briars and limbs snatched at my clothes and hair, whipping my face and arms as I shoved my way through. In the direction I was going, and a short distance away, I knew a logging road ran parallel to the driveway. Both roads originated from the same dirt road from which the man in the black truck had come. I was willing to bet he didn't know about the logging road. He'd turned into the driveway from the opposite direction. If I could get to that road and on down it before he figured it out, I would be way ahead of him. He wouldn't be able to get all the way down the logging road in his fancy truck, no matter how big his tires were. And I would eventually come out behind Linc's cabin.

When I broke through the brush, it was in time to see the truck's brake lights flare as he passed the logging road. Then, thrown into reverse, the truck sped back and turned toward me.

I could either melt back into the underbrush or make a run for it in plain sight for the woods on the other side of the road. I decided to run for it. I didn't want to be trapped in the brush, and I didn't want him to go back to my mother's house. If I could make it to the other side of the creek, I would gain access to acres and acres of woods with no road access. And I could get to Linc's house. The truck was bearing down on my position so I took a deep breath and sprinted toward what looked like a game trail in the older growth pines on the other side of the road.

I heard the truck's engine rev as I crossed in its path, but it was still far enough away that it was no threat. I didn't stop running until I reached the creek, about a quarter of a mile away. I had heard a truck door slam when I'd made it to the other side of the road and knew the man in the truck had gotten out and possibly even followed me into the woods. But I knew where I was going.

Ever since I'd stepped into the woods, the box stand my stepfather had built had pulsed in my mind like a beacon. Now, the image of it reared sharply in my mind. It had been a small shelter he and Stephen had built, especially for me. At 12, I had been a good shot, but was afraid of heights. Daddy had been afraid to put me on a tree stand alone, but I had begged to hunt alone. Stephen, 16, had suggested it to me. "Just think if you get a deer all by yourself. You'd be such a badass." I had very much wanted to be that.

But the memories are shadowy and strange for me. I remembered hunting, but not the fear of heights, and to this day I don't have trouble with high places. I don't know where the idea came from. I haven't actually hunted since the year they died. The same year they built the stand.

They'd used plywood to build a 4x4 room in the woods. Then we painted it with black, green and rust-colored spray paint to blend in with the surroundings. We'd strung netting over it which that fall caught the leaves and pine straw as they fell to make a perfectly camouflaged blind. You had to be looking for it to see it. But that had been more than 15 years ago. It was most likely rotted by now. But still the image of it hung in my mind like a full moon on a clear night. Unavoidable.

I trekked through the woods, now with much less underbrush to contend with, breathing hard, but slowing because I sensed my hunter had given up. I thought I had heard an engine roar down the road far to my right, but I couldn't be sure, so I continued on. After a few more minutes, I stopped to catch my breath and realized that it would be dark very soon. The woods were vaguely familiar in that I had a good knowledge of the area and a decent sense of direction, but in the dark was a different matter. And it would be getting colder. The trees became eerie, familiar shadows. I'd reached the creek bottom, which snaked lazily around the roots and fallen companions of monolithic trees with the hairpin curves of a body always taking the path of least resistance. Mosquitoes hummed around me. The creek bottom held heat and water enough for hordes of mosquitoes, surviving on the blood of larger mammals coming to drink, to hatch and survive in an endless cycle, even in winter sometimes.

I remembered finding a log bridge here once with Stephen as we'd tromped through the woods. The log bridge had been a perfect place to play, but I don't remember ever going back there to play after we found it. We had climbed on top of it and looked down into the creek where a natural, deep hole had formed, perfect for swimming. We could see clear to the sandy bottom. Little minnows darted in the sunlight which dappled and sparked the water. Water bugs zoomed in and out of crevices near the banks on either side.

"Let's go swimming," Stephen had said.

"We'll get in trouble!" Mama did not like for us to swim unsupervised.

"Nobody has to know. We don't even have to get our clothes wet," he said. Then he stood up, whipped his shirt over his head, kicked his shoes and socks off and shucked his pants and underwear. He jumped into the water and hollered. Then he ducked his head under and I could see his whole body, two-toned from going shirtless in the summer sun, skimming under the surface, before he emerged further down the creek in much shallower water. He stood up, slicking his dark, wet hair back from his face. He was glistening, standing in water just below his hips. I turned away.

"Aw don't be a baby," he said. "Come swimming!"

He walked closer to me and hopped up onto the bridge so that he was sitting beside me. Water slid off his skin and beaded. He was muscular and tall.

"Why you gotta carry that stupid purse everywhere? You're such a girl," he said. The derision in his voice hurt my feelings. I didn't like carrying the little pink purse which I'd hung crosswise over my body. But I had to. Ever since that day at the end of my seventh grade year, I had been carrying it and making frequent trips to the bathroom to check for blood.

I'd been in gym class, and I saw Lana Dowd, the prettiest girl in eighth grade, whisper behind her hand to one of the other girls and then look at me and laugh. I didn't know what was going on until class was over and we were changing clothes.

"Want a bloody mary?" she asked, walking past me. This caused all the other girls to howl with laughter. I was still not aware of what they were talking about until Janie, someone I'd always considered friendly, threw a tampon at me, hitting me in the chest. It bounced off and landed at my feet. When I realized what it was, I ran to the bathroom and hid out in a stall, humiliated and bewildered.

Caci, who had P.E. a different hour, came and checked on me when I didn't show up for the next hour. And of course she'd heard about it from the other girls. She brought me some of her own clean clothes and my gym bag into which I stuffed the mess I had been wearing, and then she went to the nurse's office to tell them I was puking in the bathroom so they'd call my mom.

I'd been carrying the purse, stuffed with pads, ever since, terrified it would happen again. I had even told Stephen that I didn't want to go in the woods, worried I would bleed all over, but in the end he had talked me into it, telling me about the log bridge he'd found and how pretty the creek was.

"What's in it anyway?" he asked, laying back on the bridge.

"Just girl stuff," I said.

He had lain down on the bridge, but came up on his elbows. "What kind of girl stuff?" He asked suspiciously, one eye squinted shut in the bright sunlight.

His nakedness bothered me, but it never bothered him. He walked around the house in a towel a lot, usually getting in trouble for it if Mama was home. And when she wasn't, he didn't bother at all with a towel. Without waiting for me to answer, he sat up and grabbed my hand. The bridge must have rotted and been washed away, like my memory of the rest of that day. I had wanted to remember the spot, so that I could go back to it without Stephen, so that I could enjoy the pristine water, the perfect bridge over it, but I had never gotten the chance.

The box stand was near where the bridge had been. Daddy and Stephen had built it later that summer.

It was really dark now. I was grateful for the light of the moon, which gave everything a silvery, haunted glow. And then suddenly there it was in front of me, barely discernible in the gloom. I had noticed it only because the leaf litter on its roof seemed to hang bodiless, three feet thick with no support, and to pour itself to the ground where a corner sagged. Trees grew up around it, masking it even more. In summer it would not be discernible at all. Eventually branches and roots would crash through it, obliterate it and then bury it. When I reached where the door should have been, I saw that it had long since rotted away. The floor looked brittle and was strewn with pine straw and leaves. In the corner sat the old propane heater, rusted and useless now. Low, wide windows all the way around gave the hunter an excellent field of vision. A folding chair lay rusted and bent in the corner, like someone had crumpled it in a rage. A couple of screws in the wall served as a place to hang things, and something hanging on one caught my attention. It was my little pink purse, mouldy, dry rotted, brittle. I reached for it.

Daddy had taken me and Stephen hunting. He had put me in this new stand while he and Stephen hunted in tree stands nearby. Stephen had again made fun of me for bringing my purse. "Hunters don't carry purses," he'd said. He had become difficult to be around ever since he'd killed his first deer a few weeks before that. He'd gotten even more insistent about me being a sissy. I had begun to think that he was different, somehow. He didn't quite seem like the other boys at school. Sometimes I thought some of the boys in my class, and especially the class ahead of me, were more mature than Stephen.

I had to carry the purse, I told him again. Just in case. Even though it was supposed to happen once a month, Mama said, it hadn't happened to me again. When I told her about it, she had said not to worry. Sometimes it took awhile for your body to get in rhythm. I'd felt like my body was having a really hard time getting in rhythm. She'd said keep my purse with me, just in case. And I had and I had been glad Daddy had told Stephen to hush when he'd made fun of me. It hurt my heart and made me mad all at the same time. And he'd kept calling me a sissy girl.

In my mind, I saw them leave me in the stand, saw myself hang the purse on the screw, lean my gun carefully in the corner and warm my hands at the heater that Daddy had lit for me before leaving with Stephen to go to their stands. I sat in the chair and waited. I waited to hear something, some rustling in the leaves, something approaching.

I had expected it. When I heard it, I looked out the window and thought I could see the shadow of something in the brush off to my right. I picked up my gun like Daddy had shown me, checked the safety was on, raised the muzzle, looked through the eyepiece toward the spot in the woods, my finger hovering over the safety. The shape became more distinct before things went dark.

I tossed the little purse against the wall, frustrated that, again, the memories just weren't there or seemed inaccurate. A noise outside the stand caused my heart to leap into my throat. I looked through the slit but couldn't see anything except the dark shapes of trees and bushes. The noise got louder and louder until I couldn't distinguish between it and my own heart beating.

Oh God

I crouched in a corner of the stand, knowing I was trapped. The man was running now, crashing through the woods toward me. I turned toward the door just as a huge shape entered and hulked above me as I tried to shrink into the floor. And then I felt him licking my hand. My eyes had been shut tight and I opened them to see Hebert standing above me, licking my hand. I wilted in relief and Hebert wagged his tail, his tongue lolling like he was delighted to see me. I wrapped my arms around his neck and buried my face in his fur.

I'm told, but I don't really remember, that Daddy accidentally shot Stephen in a hunting accident that same year. Later, out of grief, guilt too, I guess, Daddy shot himself. It happened sometime that fall, the year Stephen turned 19 and shot his first and only deer, the year I turned 12, the first and only year that I had hunted myself.

12

"It is the very underground palace of the Serpent, the spirit of changing shape and color, that is the enemy of man."

—G.K. Chesterton

There is a huge gap in my memory from that year until the morning I woke up and discovered I was in a relationship with Linc. I was 16 and in my junior year of high school. I've never told anyone about the breadth of that particular gap in my memory. It just seemed too much to admit, too extreme. It was unbelievable enough that I didn't remember Linc.

I remember waking up that morning very clearly. I opened my eyes and knew that something was wrong. When I looked in the mirror, I saw me, but a me who had lost all the baby fat and developed cheek bones and breasts and hips. I stood staring at my reflection for a long time until I heard Mama calling me to hurry up, I'd be late to school.

I opened the closet door to choose something to wear. It was a sparse collection of mostly black clothes. I chose jeans and shoes, black of course, then spied a pink sweater hanging on a chair and threw that on. In the bathroom, I brushed my teeth with the only available toothbrush and washed my face, noticing that makeup was strewn on the counter. Black eyeliner, black mascara, black eye shadow. There was even a bottle of black nail polish.

I left it all there and went back into the bedroom, looking for a purse or a notebook or something. A backpack on the floor caught my attention, so I sat down on the bed to rummage through it, pulling out a sleek, heavy rectangular object made of metal and glass. It had a small screen which flipped open, like a Star Trek communicator. A little screen showed the time, the date plus a picture of a cute guy.

It was April 12, 2005. I had lost four years.

I heard my mother calling from just outside the door a few seconds before the doorknob turned, and she stuck her head in.

"I've been calling and calling. Are you up?"

I zipped the bag and stood, slinging it over my shoulder. "Yes." I studied her face. She did look older. And her hair was a lot shorter. There was more gray. She was a little chubbier.

"Oh no ma'am," she said, point at my outfit and then crossing her arms in a "you shall not pass" stance. "I'm glad you chose to wear something besides black, but you are not leaving this house without a bra," she said.

I looked down and blushed. I could see that my breasts had gotten quite large. I looked around for a bra. The last thing I remembered, I had been wearing training bras. The contraption I saw slung on the desk chair looked complicated. I grabbed it and went into the bathroom, shutting the door. I heard what sounded like "hurry up," then the bedroom door closed.

Ripping the sweater over my head, I studied the bra, leery of its size, then consulted its confusing array of straps and hooks. The last bra I remembered wearing had been much simpler. I'd only had to slip it over my head. I slipped my arms through the straps and quickly realized I'd done it the wrong way. But when I had my arms right, I couldn't reach behind me to hook it.

I searched my memory and finally landed on something helpful: watching Mama get dressed when I was little. She'd done a strange little series of moves: hooking the bra in front, twisting and turning it around, then sliding her arms through the straps. Then a bend and a dance. I tried it and it worked. I threw the sweater back on and looked in the mirror. Much better, even though my face and body were completely foreign to me.

I poked my head out the bedroom door and looked around to get my bearings. The house was still familiar, and I could hear noises coming from the kitchen. I could also smell frying bacon. My stomach rumbled, so I followed my nose to the kitchen where Mama was standing over the stove flipping bacon.

"Hurry and get something to eat. Linc'll probably be here in a few minutes." She put a few pieces of bacon on a plate that already contained a heap of scrambled eggs and handed it to me.

I took it and sat at the kitchen table, snapping a piece of bacon between my fingers and biting into it. I took a few bites of eggs. I was very, very hungry, as if I hadn't eaten in days. Truthfully, I couldn't remember the last time I had eaten. I stared at my plate as I chewed. I couldn't remember anything. I was trying to cast back to what I did remember, but the only thing that surfaced was the hunting trip with Daddy and Stephen. But that was impossible. By the date I'd seen on what I was assuming was my cell phone, that was more than four years ago. I forked more food into my mouth and chewed.

"Girl," I heard Mama say, which caused me to look up. She was looking at me with her eyebrows raised, tongs in hand as she waited for the last of the bacon to get done. "That's quite an appetite you have this morning."

I felt myself flush and put my fork down, wiping my mouth. I pushed my plate away, uncomfortable that she was noticing how much I was eating.

"Baby I didn't mean it like that. It's good to see you eating." I didn't look at her but heard her sigh deeply.

Suddenly I wondered where Stephen and Daddy were. She'd cooked enough bacon for two more people. Herself and Stephen? I glanced around when she wasn't looking but didn't see any sign of him. No men's shoes by the back door. Only women's.

But Mama had always had breakfast cooked well before she woke me for school. Would she be taking me to school? I was 16, did that mean I drove? I rummaged through my backpack, looking for keys or a wallet or license, but also because it kept me busy, as if I knew what I was doing.

Four years? My mind kept repeating it. How could I figure things out after four years? I was desperate for more information.

Doing the math in my head, I realized Stephen must be about 20. Maybe he had a job or had gone on to college? Daddy had always left before I got up for school.

Mama fixed herself a plate and sat down across from me.

"Linc must be running late," she said.

Link? She'd said something similar earlier. Was that a person?

A horn honked in the driveway.

"There he is," she said. "Better hurry or you'll be late."

I went with it, gathering up my backpack and taking my plate to the sink.

"Don't forget his," Mama said as I headed for the door.

I stopped. *His what?*

When I just stood there, Mama pointed. "His bacon Mojo! He'll starve to death, poor boy."

I grabbed up the bacon in a paper towel before heading out the door.

"Bye! Have a good day! Love you!" Mama called after me.

"Love you too," I said instinctively.

Link the bacon eater was the same person whose picture was on the phone. He was waiting for me in a very shiny dark gray truck in the driveway. It was cold outside, but a blast of warm air hit me when I opened the passenger side door, climbed in and shut the door. Linc was a handsome fella, and he was fiddling with his own Star Trek Communicator when I got in.

beam me up

He glanced at me and smiled and then looked back up. He looked surprised.

"Nice," he said, seeming to take in the sweater and my face just as Jim Morrison crooned my name in stereo.

"You like it?" he asked.

"The stereo, girl!" when I gave him a puzzled look. "What else? I can control it from my phone," he said, looking over at me and turning up the volume as Morrison sang my name again.

I nodded. "Pretty cool. Sounds good," which was not a lie.

boyfriend

He put the truck in reverse and backed out of the driveway, his arm along the back of the bench seat as he peered out the back glass. It was one of those older Ford trucks. My Papaw had driven one, blue and white striped, like his engineer's cap. I had loved to ride in the back down dirt roads as Papaw drove. Once, when Caci had come with me and before we met Robbie Lynn, we had stood in the back as Papaw drove on a winding dirt road through the woods, what seemed to us like a bat out of hell. We looked out over the cab, alternately holding on for dear life in the hairpin turns and holding our arms out like super girl in the straightaways. The wind was in our faces as we sang, pretending to be the precious baby girls of some god-like alien as we rocketed through a place we didn't belong.

Link's truck was tricked out. It had a shiny paint job, big tires and now, apparently, a new stereo system. The inside of the truck was spotless.

"So," he said as he accelerated down the street, toward school, I assumed. "Got my bacon?"

The bacon was clenched in my right hand, but I didn't tell him this. Instead, without thinking, I said. "You'll have to work for it." I added a sly sideways look, hoping he'd think I was flirting.

He responded with a grin. "Oh yeah? What did you have in mind?"

"You just have to answer a few questions."

"Hit me," he said, with all the confidence in the world.

Before I lost my nerve I blurted out, "Are you my boyfriend?"

His ears turned pink, and his grin widened.

"If you want me to be?"

I snapped a piece of bacon and handed him half.

"I guess that was half right," he said, chewing his bacon. "But I'll take it."

"How long have we been seeing each other?"

He wrinkled up his brows. "Is this like a test? To see if I've been paying attention?" he asked. I didn't answer but gave him another sideways look.

"You've had the hots for me ever since the accident," he said, grinning.

I saw the grin, but didn't know what it meant. Instead, I plowed ahead.

"When was the accident?" I asked, only halfway trying to be lighthearted, as if I were still testing him, not trying desperately to figure out what was going on. But he knew something was up. He stopped smiling.

"November," he said quietly, glancing into his rearview mirror.

I tried to give him a piece of bacon, but he wasn't playing anymore.

"What's going on?" he asked. He didn't look at me, but his face was tight, as if he were bracing himself for bad news.

But I still needed information. "I didn't see Dad and Stephen this morning," I said.

He shot me a look I couldn't interpret. "Stop messing around, Mojo," he said. "Really, what's going on?"

"I'm not messing around," I said. "Nothing's going on. I'm just wondering where Dad and Stephen are."

"That's not funny," he said. And now I could tell he was angry. "Don't joke about stuff like that."

"I'm not joking," I said, as seriously as I could. His mouth tightened, and he pulled over on the side of the road. We were on a two-lane highway with wide shoulders. He put his hazard lights on and put the truck in park before he turned to search my face. "Tell me where Dad and Stephen are," I said.

"Mojo…" he looked confused. "Why are you doing this?"

"I just want to know where they are," I said. "I didn't see their shoes by the door this morning. Their shoes are always by the back door. We always take our shoes off at the back door," I said. I was beginning to fear the worst. Something had happened, or he wouldn't be having such a hard time telling me. "Please, just tell me what happened."

I saw something in his face, then, as if something were dropping into place, some sort of understanding. "It's the accident, isn't it? You don't remember because of the accident." The last was a statement, not a question.

"I don't know," I said. "I just know I don't know where they are."

"Mojo," he said. His face had lost all its color. "You're not messing with me? You really don't remember? I swear, Mojo, if you're messing with me, I won't ever forgive you."

"I'm not messing with you," I said.

After a minute of searching my face, he finally took a breath and let it out. "They died," he said.

His words rolled over me like an icy wave, numbing me. I think he continued to talk, but I couldn't hear him. They were dead? How could they be dead?

I was choking, trying to keep a sob from ripping out of me. I felt him gathering me up.

"Oh God Mojo, I'm sorry."

I became aware of his words, his arms around me.

"I'm sorry. Geez I thought you were playing around. I shouldn't have said it like that. I should have taken you back home."

I didn't say anything. The idea that I'd never see them again was more than I could bear, so I cast about for something else. He had stopped talking and was simply stroking my hair and back. My head was buried in his chest. He smelled really good, a little spicy. I pulled away, keeping my eyes averted from him, and started to rummage in my bag for a tissue, except I still had the bacon in my hand. I shoved it at him and felt him take it, but I still wasn't looking at him.

I couldn't find a tissue. "What are you looking for?"

"A tissue or a napkin or something," I mumbled, still not looking at him. By now I was a drippy mess. Then a napkin appeared in front of my face and I took it from him, using it to blow my nose.

"I'm sorry," I said. "I didn't mean to do that." He handed me another napkin, which I used to wipe my eyes. I flipped his visor down, looking for a mirror.

He looked at me strangely and tipped the rear view toward me. Under better control now, I tried to smile and used the mirror as I mopped my face. I looked spooky.

"No worries," he said. "Do you want me to take you back home? I think I should."

I shook my head. "No, I'd rather just go on to school. I don't want to think about this."

As if it were against his better judgment, he pulled back out on the road, looking to make sure I meant it, and we went to school.

He kept glancing at me as he drove, so I tried to keep my face composed, but it was a struggle. My mind kept drumming on the word dead, the shock rattling through me. Blessedly, the drive to school was short. When he parked, I made to hop out but he reached out for my hand.

"I'm sorry," I said, pulling away. "I have to go."

I heard him say my name, but I didn't respond and got out. Too late, I realized I didn't know where to go.

I looked around. We were parked across the street from the school, and there were no people outside. We were late. Everyone was in class. I had no idea what to do. I glanced over at Link, who was taking his sweet time getting out of the truck. His head was down. I guessed I'd hurt his feelings. I was just about to go back and try to smooth things over and hope that maybe he'd give me some clues, when I heard someone call my name.

13

*"You've got to jump off cliffs all the time and build your wings
on the way down."*

—Annie Dillard

I looked around and saw a girl with long, curly blonde hair
approaching. It wasn't until she was up close that I recognized her. I
smiled in relief. Caci glanced at Link, who was still in the truck. We
could hear he had something with deep bass playing because the truck
seemed to be thumping.

"What's up with him?" Caci asked.

"I hurt his feelings," I said.

She rolled her eyes. "What else is new? Looks like he hurt yours
too." She kept walking past me, so I fell into step with her, but didn't
respond. What would I say? He ripped half my world to shreds? "That
is quite possibly the ugliest sweater I've ever seen, Mojo," she said. "I
mean, pink? Did your mama dress you, like Ty-Baby?" I looked down
and shrugged, grateful for the distraction, but not really caring. I was
just relieved to see her. We crossed the parking lot, then the street, and
went into the building where a door was marked "Office."

Inside a woman sat at a desk behind a counter and frowned at us.
I glanced at the big clock on the wall behind her. It said 8:05. Caci
picked up a pen and signed her name on a sheet that was attached to a
clipboard on the counter. Then she handed the pen to me. I signed my
name too. I saw that the sheet had a spot for the time next to my name.
Caci had written 8:05 in her slot, so I did the same.

"One more tardy, Caci, and you'll have to talk to the principal," the
woman said, handing her a slip of paper. Caci rolled her eyes and took
the slip. Then the woman handed me my own slip of paper. But it was
useless to me because it didn't say where I should go next. I followed

Caci out of the office and left down an elevated catwalk toward a set of stairs. We went up the stairs and entered another part of the building. It was lined with lockers. Caci stopped at a locker and opened it.

"I hate math," she said. "I especially hate math early in the morning."

"So skip it," I said. "I really need to talk to you, anyway."

As we walked, I had remembered that Caci knew about my memory problems, to an extent. I had told her about them when we were little, and she'd experienced the after effects with me before. I knew I could trust her, and I didn't think I could bluff my way through this, not if Stephen and Daddy were... I couldn't even think it without tears choking me. I felt like an alien.

She stopped what she was doing and looked at me intently. "Is it about Lincoln?"

"What? Lincoln? Like Abe Lincoln?" I wrinkled my forehead.

"Linc, idiot. Lincoln Matthews. Your jock boyfriend," she said. "I guess NOT," she said. "Obviously your mind is not on him." I stared at her blankly for a few seconds, fixated on his name. Linc, not Link.

Caci waved her fingers in front of my face. "Hellooo!"

I focused on her with some effort and then said, "Let's go somewhere." I really did need to figure things out.

She shut her locker, leaving everything but her purse inside. "Heck yeah," she said. "What you got on your mind?"

I shrugged. "You tell me, Caci. I don't remember anything."

"Oooh is this one of your waking dreams? Like you don't remember anything as in, what happened yesterday?" When we'd gotten older, after the scene I'd made in the restaurant when we were little, she'd taken to dramatizing things, as if the blackouts were a grand adventure.

"Longer than that," I said.

Her eyes widened and she grabbed my arm. "Let's go to my car," she said, leading me further down the hall, where another set of stairs took us down to a more secluded catwalk, tucked between buildings. We emerged in time to see Linc walking across the street to the office, his head down.

"Oh the poor honey," Caci said. "His wittle feewings are hurt." I wondered why she disliked him. When he'd gone inside, Caci looked around to make sure no teachers were lurking about, and we made a run for it to her car, hopped in and drove out of the parking lot.

"Where to?" She asked, not looking at me.

"No idea," I said.

"Let's go to the lake," she said.

"Okay."

"But I can't wait that long for you to tell me what's going on. You talk while I drive," she said. Then she dug in her bag with one hand, eyes fixed on the road, and came up with a pack of cigarettes. She shook one up and drew it out of the pack with her lips. Then she handed the pack to me and pushed her car's cigarette lighter in. I took a cigarette too, but held mine between my fingers and remembered that we'd both started smoking, along with Robbie Lynn, in seventh grade. Suddenly the need for a cigarette was overwhelming.

She handed me the lighter, and I held the cigarette to my lips, the lighter to its end, and puffed, inhaling experimentally.

"Talk," Caci said. And I did. But I didn't tell her how big the gap was. I think she concluded on her own that it went as far back as the accident, which had happened, as Linc had said, the previous November.

"Tell me about the accident," I said.

"Well, your mom was pretty upset with you and made you promise to get involved in activities at school. I really think she believes I'm a terrible influence on you. You know, all the black, and stuff. I think she suspected we were smoking for sure. And maybe other stuff. She kept giving me the stink eye when I came over.

"Anyway, I'm not sure where you came up with this Mojo, but it drove her crazy...." She looked over at me. "Do you remember this at all, your mom telling you to join a club?"

I made a noncommittal sound, hoping she would go on. She did. It helped that she was driving and couldn't keep her eyes on my face.

"Ok so you were kind of being mean to your mom, but I went along with it because she was being mean to me.

"I'm not gonna lie, though. I was thrown for a loop because you aren't usually mean, you know? You can explode and all, but ongoing mean

131

from you was something different. I just figured you'd had enough. And I get that you were mad at your mom because of your dad and Stephen." she said.

"They're dead," I said.

"And I guess you were mad at your mom because she sort of moved on, you know? So we started wearing black, like all the time, like even our makeup. Then you started playing this song, that James Taylor song, Fire something. I'm not gonna lie; it wasn't my favorite. I was getting kind of sick of it. Like every time your mom was around you had it going. And then the meanest thing was that book you got." She paused, as if thinking. "The *Harold and Maude* movie was also kind of..."

I just let her talk.

"Your mom called it the death theme. You said she was afraid of death, ever since, well, you know, your dad and brother and stuff. I think you're mom thought you were thinking about suicide," Caci said. "God, we were really mean. That *Harold and Maude* movie was pretty bad but that book was downright sinister. Do you remember it?"

I did not.

"It was like old-timey death photographs. You left it open on the kitchen table at this super heinous picture of a man and a woman crammed into a coffin with their dead baby. Your mom saw it and threw the book across the room. And then she got all gentle and kind with you.

"I didn't know you could be so mean. But hey it got you a phone. But it was the song—*Fire and Rain*—that's it—that finally made her mad. I guess she knew more about that song than we thought. She came barging into your room and stood there with her hand on her hip with her mouth all pressed together. She told you to turn that crap off. She was pretty scary looking. When you turned it off she got up in your face and told you to stop all your nonsense, stop moping and join some clubs and meet some people. And then she looked at me and said if I wanted to keep coming around I'd better do the same thing.

"'Your father and Stephen are gone,' she said 'but we are not. You still have a life to lead. I'm not going to let you throw it away pining.'"

Caci did an excellent job of imitating my mother. Then it dawned on me that Dad and Stephen had been gone for years. Mama had moved on.

I had not.

"Oh and let me tell you that made you mad! You started screaming at her that they were dead and she didn't even miss them and you were stuck with her. And then wham, she slapped you right across the face.

"'Don't you dare assume how I feel. You have no idea, little girl. No idea.'" This time Caci's impression was through clenched teeth. She was enjoying telling the story, changing her expression, her voice with each character. I could easily imagine my mother making this speech and thought Caci should probably try to be an actress or something.

"She was like totally about to cry, she was so upset, and I guess you finally felt sorry for her.

"You were like 'why won't you talk to me about it?'

"And she's all 'I have to keep going for you. If I talk about it right now, I won't ever be able to climb out of that hole. I can't afford to talk about it. You can't afford for me to talk about it. Let's just keep going forward for now.'

"Then I was about to cry because y'all have been through so much and finally ya'll were about to make up. It was pretty intense Mojo. We probably would have done anything she wanted us to right then.

"She made us promise to give up the death theme and told us if we didn't she'd take your phone and never let us see each other again.

"And then we joined the yearbook staff."

By this time we had made it to the lake. A place to discuss life and death, it was the largest man-made body of water in the South, according to Bobby Hudson, the kid who did the social studies project on it. Bobby, too, had made it to state that year. I had stood and talked to him as we'd waited our turn with the judges, letting him practice his speech on me.

"Did you know that the land for the lake was taken by inanimate domain?" he'd asked me, stuttering over the last words, which I had never heard before. I guessed by the way he stopped, as if thinking, his eyes wandering above mine, that he didn't know either.

"What the heck is that?" I interrupted him.

"It's where they let somebody take something from you for your own good," he explained, impressing me with what he seemed to know. I had more questions, like who "they" were, but the judges were nearing my project.

"Cool," I said, "I gotta go."

Bobby nodded, "Good luck."

Neither project progressed beyond the state level.

Caci pulled into a paved parking lot that looked out over the glassy water, put her car in park and turned off the ignition. It was too cold to get in the water and too windy to get on the beach area. But the sun was shining brightly. Caci had put on dark shades when we got in the car. I found myself wishing that I had some. The sun was too bright in my still-weepy eyes and Caci too intent on my face. Despite the wind, I got out of the car and said "let's walk some."

Hiking paths wound around the lake. We took one, twisting through pines, the way often single file. The whole time Caci talked. When she fell silent, I asked questions.

14

According to Caci, Linc and another basketball player fell on me one night at a game. "One side of your head hit the floor, your camera hit the other side of your head and his jaw," Caci said. "He actually got a fracture. Well you both did. Your head and his jaw. And I guess your brain got bounced around. And a couple of your ribs got cracked."

The other boy was uninjured.

I lost consciousness for three days. Traumatic brain injury, Caci said. My mother had been beside herself with worry.

"Once you came out of the coma, or whatever, Linc was like by your side. He visited you every day, and when you were ready for school work, he brought it to you and hung out with you. And when you came back to school, he was like your self-appointed driver. I mean, I'm like you're best friend and all, and I came two or three times a week, but it's like he staked you out, or something. 'Linc's property.'"

I could tell that Caci felt hurt, as if maybe I had let our friendship fall by the wayside and realized that's probably why she wasn't fond of Linc.

"I'm sorry," I said, stopping to look at her. She stopped too and shrugged.

"No biggie," she said. "You had a lot going on. And I know he felt really bad. Still does."

"So, are we like together?" I asked.

She shrugged again. "I don't think it's official or anything. But most everybody assumes you are. Even Linc. And your mom adores him because he's so freaking perfect." She rolled her eyes.

"I picked up on that," I said, continuing to walk. "What do you think of him?"

"Meh," she said. "You don't want my opinion. I'm just jealous."

Later that night, at home, I knew Mama knew something was up. I was an emotional wreck after all the things Caci told me, and I couldn't hide it. I told her the same thing I had told Caci. That I didn't remember Linc or the accident, or Daddy and Stephen dying. By then I knew she would attribute it to the accident with Linc. And I knew she would help me. "I just can't believe they're gone," I said, overcome once again by that one, stark, unyielding fact. Mom had looked at me so oddly and reached out her hand to touch my face.

"You astound me, honey," she'd said. "It's like you live on a different plane of existence sometimes."

"What does that mean?" I'd sniffled.

"Nothing," she'd said. "Nothing."

And just like I knew she would, she took care of Linc. I only ever saw him one more time after that, except in passing, before he left for college. Mama filled me in that Dad and Stephen died the same year they built the hunting stand for me. Stephen was accidentally shot by Dad. A few days later, Dad committed suicide over it.

The temperature was dropping with nightfall. I wasn't so scared I thought I needed to stay the night in the woods, freezing my butt off. I'd walk out, I just didn't know where to go. I didn't want to go back out to the road because I was afraid the man in the black truck was still waiting for me. Mama's house was closest through the woods, but I didn't want to give her another stroke with me tromping up and stumbling around in the dark after she'd gone to bed. Linc's house was too far away, more of a long shot. While I was thinking it out, Hebert had curled up beside me and was resting. I didn't have a leash, but I really didn't want him to take off without me, so I stood up, took off my belt and hooked it to his collar to use as a leash.

"You have to stay with me, Hebert."

He sat up and thumped his tail on the ground. He seemed ready to go.

We had been walking less than 10 minutes, picking our way through the woods trying to avoid briars and stumps and other pitfalls in the dark, and hopefully back the way I had come, when we both heard something and froze. Hebert pricked his ears up and looked off into the woods toward the sound. Then to my dismay he barked.

"Shhh, Hebert! Be quiet!" I whispered fiercely. I heard someone shout, and Hebert barked again and started pulling me in the direction of the sound, which was clearly someone coming through the woods toward us.

When Lear broke through the woods and made a mad dash toward Hebert, I at first thought it was a crazed animal. When he got closer and I made out his markings, I almost collapsed in relief. Lear was upon us and barking a full minute before Linc emerged from the woods. I saw his headlight glancing off the trees well before I saw him.

"What the hell are you doing Mojo?" he hollered at me. I didn't answer. Instead, I gave Lear the most excellent rub down I could. I was glad to see him and Linc.

"Well?" he said when he got closer.

"It's nice to see you too, Linc," I said, straightening. I was truly glad to see him, but also still miffed. Plus he was yelling at me and blinding me with his headlight which was perched on his head as if he were a miner.

"The shooting was a set up," he said, grabbing my hand and pulling me back the way he'd come. The dogs jumped and played at our feet. I had released Hebert, knowing he would stay with us now that Linc and Lear were also here. Linc whistled at Lear and they both fell in beside us.

"There wasn't a shooting?" I asked.

"Oh yeah," he said. "There was a shooting. But it was somebody in a big black truck, tinted windows. He took off after spraying some bullets into an empty car in a parking lot. When I heard it was a big black truck, I thought it might be a set up. So I called your cell. No answer." He looked back at me and frowned when he said it but continued to walk briskly, almost dragging me behind him. "I called your mom's house. She said you went for a walk." His voice was clipped and tight.

"Would you stop!" I dug my heels in and jerked my hand away from him. "Quit dragging me around like some rag doll, for Pete's sake!"

"Well stop acting like an idiot, Mojo!" He turned on me. He was really mad.

"Somebody is obviously out to get you and you're off traipsing around in the woods after dark! Without a cell phone."

I let the cell phone remark go. I didn't need him to lecture me.

"Linc, I know! That's why I was in the woods. He was chasing me!" This made his Spidey senses tingle. He came to a full stop and turned to look at me.

"Did you see him? Can you describe him?"

"No. He shot at me. I was trying to get away from him so I took off running into the woods. And it's a good thing I went for a walk," the truth suddenly hitting me in the face. "He was turning into Mama's driveway. He was coming to my mama's house. Oh my God. Have you talked to Mama? Is she ok?"

"She's fine," he said. "I have a deputy there now." I almost fainted with relief, but Linc didn't give me time to. He grabbed my hand again, dissatisfied with my bad-guy detecting abilities, and started pulling me along. "Quit dragging me Linc!"

"Well keep up," he said. But he let go of my hand. "My truck is just up here." We emerged on the logging road, but by then I was so disoriented, I didn't know exactly where. I was relieved when we reached his truck. He opened the door for me, handed me the keys and said "Go ahead and start it. Turn the heat on. Should still be warm."

I climbed in and did just that, cranking the heat all the way up, while Linc put the dogs in the back of the truck and came around to the driver's side.

I held my hands near the vent and let the warm air blow on them.

"Oh my God I am so cold."

"How long were you out there?" he asked, handing me another jacket that was on his back seat and then putting the truck in gear. He drove us toward my mom's house.

"Since before dark," I said, snuggling into the jacket. It smelled just like him. I was beginning to thaw out.

15

"Grace does not merely blot out the evil past but in the most literal sense 'makes it good.'"

—Dorothy L. Sayers

The next morning at Mama's I felt dizzy and groggy, with a headache vaguely pulsing behind my eyes. I was acutely aware of Linc on one level, desperately not wanting him to know that I had an appointment with a psychiatrist. But some other part of me didn't care and delighted in being irritable over breakfast. Breakfast, in fact, was a kaleidoscope of emotion, words and voices that I had difficulty sorting through.

"So, I probably need to have someone stick close to you today," Linc said. We were sitting at Mama's dining room table. His chair was pulled out away from the table, and he was leaning forward, elbows on his knees as he cradled a cup of coffee in his hands. His hair and shirt were rumpled from his night on the couch, and he needed a shave. He hadn't yet put on his shoes, and his socked feet on my mother's linoleum seemed too intimate.

Mama was standing a few feet away in the kitchen frying bacon, the tongs held in her hand like a wand and an odd smile plastered on her face as she gazed at us sitting at the table.

"That's not necessary," I heard a voice say, and realized, from the look on Linc's face that it had come from my mouth. But it was necessary, I knew, and I wanted to take it back. I was scared to death the man in the black truck would find me and kill me. "No, that's not what I mean," I said, interrupting Linc before he had a chance to argue.

Then, "I can take care of myself," the now petulant voice said. I was still puzzling over this when both Linc and Mama spoke at the same time.

"Moriah!" Mama's voice was shrill as if she were scolding me.

"Unless you have a license to carry a concealed weapon and you also have a weapon, I'm not inclined to believe you," Linc said, looking at me skeptically. He seemed to dismiss me as he drained his cup and stood. Then he held up his hand, as if he were stopping me from saying anything else. "I don't care how you feel about it. You aren't leaving here until I have a deputy to escort you." And then he left the table, his phone already to his ear as he tried to slip past Mama with his coffee cup. She intercepted him and took it from him with a smile, and then motioned to the bacon.

"It's almost ready!" She said in a stage whisper, and as if they were on the same team.

He nodded at her and then turned away toward the living room as he began speaking.

"Yeah, Jake, I need you at my location as soon as possible." His voice faded, and I looked at Mama. She avoided my eyes and busied herself with removing bacon from the pan and putting it on a plate lined with a paper towel.

My head throbbed, and the dizziness had not abated. I felt like I was looking at the world through a thick glass. Sounds were muted, and objects seemed almost blurry. But I stood up quietly and went down the hall. I watched my hands gather my purse, phone and keys, watched my feet go into sneakers, caught a glimpse of myself in the mirror as my arms went into a jacket. I felt odd. I looked odd. I knew I was sneaking away before anyone could say or do anything about it. They were all expecting me to

toe the line

I went back up the hall and when Mama had her back turned, went out the back door without a sound. Linc, I assumed, was still in the living room. Their inattention after bossing me around—*their own fault* and the car's quiet little motor both meant, somehow, the universe was on my side. And Hebert, too, seemed to be on my side. He had stared at me and thumped his tail as I walked past him, but didn't bark. I felt a distant gratitude and justification. I was pulling into Dr. Granger's parking lot when my cell rang. It was Linc, so I turned the phone off.

16

"The path to paradise begins in hell."

— Dante Alighieri

The parking lot was in the back of Dr. Granger's office. Most of the houses on the street were doctor or dentist offices, with parking for each office in what used to be backyards, paved over, but still hemmed in by their privacy fences. I locked my car, got out and walked around to the front entrance and went inside. The receptionist greeted me and directed me back to the room I had been in last time. In less than five minutes, Dr. Granger joined me. Almost immediately she detected that something had happened and began peppering with me questions.

I told her everything.

"And where is he now?"

"The man?" I asked foggily. By now, the headache was fierce. I wished I had brought my sunglasses inside because the light was hurting my eyes. I guessed I was still tired from the previous night's ordeal. I'd had to rehash it with Mama when Linc took me to her house. Then she'd fussed all around Linc, delighted to see him again, bringing him pillows and blankets so that he could sleep on the couch. He had insisted, and Mama had agreed. I didn't have any fight left in me, but I'm not sure I would have fought it.

"No, dear, Linc," Dr. Granger said.

"Oh. I kind of gave him the slip this morning. He wanted to give me an escort, and I really didn't want anyone else knowing I'm seeing you. No offense."

"None taken. Are you ok? You seem to be a little worse for wear this morning. I know it must have been a terrible ordeal last night."

"My head is hurting," I told her. "I guess I didn't get enough sleep. I feel foggy."

"That's understandable," she said. "And I'm afraid you aren't out of danger as long as that phone is still out there. Have you told Linc about it?"

I dropped my head. "No ma'am." I knew I should have. I wasn't sure why I hadn't yet, beyond the vague uneasiness I had felt when I'd seen Ty slapping him on the back in true, good, ole boy fashion that day as I had driven past. And now, with the weird stuff between us, my blacking out, him and his false kissing, I didn't want to tell him anything.

"Maybe after our session you can bring him up to speed on this?"

I nodded, but it was more as an acknowledgement of her words than agreeing to them.

"Now, I've got the video camera all set up," she said, indicating the camera in the corner on a tripod. "You're not having any misgivings are you?" It was a tiny thing, and inconspicuous, the camera. I truthfully hadn't had time to consider being videotaped. But it felt like a brick was on my stomach, heavy, dense and unmoving. I was struggling to keep my eyes on Dr. Granger. I just wanted to close my eyes and drift into the chaos of thoughts running through my mind.

Dr. Granger seemed to go on. "Ok, then, let's get started," she said. "I'd like to try something with you," she said. "Have you ever heard of hypnotherapy?"

I nodded.

"Good, good. So what we'll do," she said, reaching up like an angel and dimming the lights with a switch on the wall behind her, "is, I'll guide you into a state of deep relaxation and ask you questions. The point is that this state of relaxation will help you to remember things you might not otherwise be able to remember. How does that sound?"

I nodded again; I didn't seem capable of speech. I wanted to remember, I knew there were things missing, but suddenly I realized there must be a very good reason I couldn't remember.

Why would you want to mess up a good thing? The words echoed around in my brain.

But there are so few memories.

We need her help.

Whose help?

Dr. Granger's?

No you idiot. We need your help.

Did I say that out loud?

"Yes," Dr. Granger said. She seemed so far away. In fact, I could barely hear her. The noise in my head was growing. It was difficult to surface.

"Now, I'd like you to get comfortable."

"Do you want me to lie down?" I heard myself say and found myself looking over at the couch, which was big enough, but it looked too uncomfortable for anything but sitting.

"No, no, not unless you want to. I'd just like you to put your head back. You know that chair reclines," she said.

"Really?" It was an overstuffed club chair, with a comfy headrest. I felt around for the lever to make the chair recline and couldn't find it.

"Just push back on the arms, dear," Dr. Granger said. I did, and the chair unfolded neatly, putting me into a reclined position.

"Comfy," I said.

"Good," she said. And I almost cried with relief at her next words. "Now, close your eyes and take some deep breaths. In a moment I'm going to start counting backward from 10. But I want you to concentrate on breathing deeply and relaxing. Are you ready?" I nodded, already drifting back to the fascinating bends and turns in my mind, the need to process was overwhelming and I succumbed to it, only dimly aware as Dr. Granger continued to talk.

Her voice drifted over me. "Now here we are at 10. I'd like you to take a deep breath and let it out slowly and as you do, think about relaxing your feet.

It was too much effort to think about my feet. Instead, I tried to empty my mind, focusing on a white spot that seemed imprinted on my brain. Dr. Granger's voice seemed to come from far away.

"Yes, just let them fall apart. There's no need to worry. Just relax. Nine." The white spot seemed to take on a growing brightness, so that the area around it became darker and darker.

"Take another deep breath and let it out, relaxing your calf muscles. You're doing wonderfully. Now breathe in. Eight, and out, relaxing your thighs."

But the darkness was not so dark that I couldn't see anything else. Forms seemed to flit around the edges of the white spot, but they moved too fast, just beyond the periphery, so that I couldn't focus on them. I settled again on the bright white spot.

"Breathe in seven, let it out slow, relaxing your hips."

Then I became aware of voices on the periphery as well. They were whispers, and not loud enough for me to discern, though I strained my ears, becoming aware again of the flits of movement just outside the spot. The voices were coming from there too.

"Now we're at six, and you're breathing in and then out and your stomach is letting go of all the tension. It's just flowing right out of you. Deep breath in."

I tried to block the voices out, but they seemed to grow louder, so I tried to concentrate on them, which made them recede, as if they knew I was eavesdropping and didn't want me to hear.

"Five, and let it out and all the stress in your chest. No more tightness there. Just relax. Breathe in four, and let go of any clenching in your fingers or arms."

As she spoke, the feeling of distance I'd been experiencing all morning increased until I could barely discern her words and so wasn't at all certain of what I heard next. Her voice was far away, and I was floating above the white spot. And suddenly I could see that there were people standing around the spot, but none were actually in it.

"Breathe in three and let your mouth relax, even your lips, your jaw." I seemed to float further away from the spot, which was growing smaller. "Breathe in two, and out with any tightness around your eyes and forehead. Breathe in one, and out and now you are completely and totally relaxed. You are safe. Nothing can harm you."

"Can you tell me your name?" I could barely hear her; the spot was so far away now, I thought I must be imagining the girl that stepped into the light.

"People call me Mojo, but my name is really Molly."

"Well it's very nice to meet you Molly. How old are you?"

"I'm twenty-eight, the same age as Mojo," the voice said. I was trying to protest, but I was too far away now. And it really didn't seem worth it. Molly, whoever she was, could handle it.

"And why do people call you Mojo?" I heard her ask. I could barely see the shape of the girl who answered as the darkness closed around me.

17

Psychiatrist: *That's very interesting, Harold, and I think, very illuminating. There seems to be a definite pattern emerging. And, of course, this pattern, once isolated, can be coped with. Recognize the problem, and you are halfway on the road to its, uh, its solution. Uh, tell me, Harold, what do you do for fun? What activity gives you a different sense of enjoyment from the others? Uh, what do you find fulfilling? What gives you that... special satisfaction?*

Harold: *...I go to funerals.*

—Harold and Maude 1971

"And now you're feeling alert in your legs as we're coming around," Dr. Granger said. "Go ahead and wiggle those toes and fingers. And now, ten," she said. "You are fully awake and alert, feeling refreshed and renewed."

I opened my eyes. "That's it?"

"Yes, that's it," she said. "How do you feel?" I thought about it for a moment. My headache was gone. I didn't feel blurry or foggy anymore. The distance between me and the world had faded.

"Much better than I did."

"Good," she said, pointing the remote at her camera. "Now, for the second half of the session, I'd like to show you the video of the first half of the session," she said. I looked at my watch and was surprised to see that an entire hour had gone by.

"Did I fall asleep?"

"No," she said. Then she shrugged. "Are you ready? I'm afraid this might be a bit of a shock for you," she said.

146

I couldn't imagine anything being more shocking than what I'd already been through, so I shrugged.

She nodded and, using a remote, turned on the monitor to our right.

I was wrong, though. At first, it was quite mundane: my body, reclined in the chair, filled the screen. I could hear Dr. Granger's voice encouraging me to relax. When she asked my name, it all suddenly became surreal. I was transfixed as I saw my mouth say "People call me Mojo, but my name is really Molly."

I remembered seeing the white spot, like a spotlight on a stage, in my mind's eye, the girl stepping into the light as I floated into the darkness above her, hearing those very same words.

The person on the screen was me, but not me. I had never been comfortable with my reflection. The picture of myself in my mind has never matched what I saw in the mirror. I mean there was a resemblance of course, but I am often shocked by some aspect of my appearance like my size or the way my eyes crinkles when I smile.

Is that really me?

That can't be me.

This time, watching myself on the video, the feeling was more pronounced than ever.

"I remember hearing that," I said aloud, continuing to watch myself on the video. I was reclined, eyes shut.

"Do you?" Dr. Granger asked, pausing the video. "Do you know you said it?"

The chaos had quieted in my mind, like a crescendo of silence, as if my mind was waiting with bated breath for answers. "Do you think I'm possessed?" The thought had never occurred to me before now, but suddenly there it was, and it was terrifying.

"No, dear, I don't think so." She pointed the remote again and peered at me over her glasses. "Would you like to continue?" I nodded, afraid of what I was about to see because I couldn't remember much beyond this point in the video, but I was also suddenly intensely curious to find out.

The girl in the video was me, but not me. I was awkward and ugly. The girl in the video claimed to be Molly. She sat up, her eyes open and bright, and tucked her feet underneath her. Her arms moved, suddenly graceful, and she looked at Dr. Granger with such confidence, I couldn't see myself in her at all.

"It's just easier that way," the girl was saying. "It's very difficult for people to understand us. You know," she shrugged, "more than one person in one body."

"I beg your pardon?" Dr. Granger said.

"We've been trying to tell you. But not her. Not until today, anyway. The video was a pretty good idea, though. We've all agreed that she needs to know. And the video is just the thing to help her. Way to go, Dr. Granger. Mya is very pleased that she found you."

"Oh my dear," Dr. Granger said. She sounded surprised.

"I'm sorry," the girl said. "I'm too blunt. I don't really see the point in beating around the bush, but it throws people for a loop, sometimes. I really thought you had caught on."

"I suppose I did, in a sense," Dr. Granger said. "However, I wasn't expecting things to move this quickly."

The girl shrugged and held her hands out. "I guess we're sick of hiding," she said. "I know I am. And it's hard being home. Being home makes it all boil to the surface, and everyone is all stirred up."

"I see," said Dr. Granger. But her voice was faint.

"You know how certain places can give you the creeps and certain people push all the wrong buttons?"

"Yes."

"Well, that's how it is with us. Some of us surface to deal with certain places or certain people. I guess you can say those things bring us out."

"Well what brings you out?"

The girl shrugged again. "Right now? Curiosity, mostly. I'm the intrepid one. Everyone else was too scared or too wrapped up in their own angst. I'm ready to get things resolved; plus I like to see how people tick. I've never met a psychiatrist before. I wanted to see your reaction."

"So you like shocking people?"

Another shrug. "I guess."

"And you say you're twenty-eight?"

A nod.

"You keep saying 'we.' What do you mean?"

"Just what it sounds like. First person plural. Me and Mojo and a few others."

"How many others?"

"There's Mya, and of course Moriah, but no one has seen her in a really long time. And MJ." The girl rolled her eyes.

"Why do you say it like that?"

"MJ is a total pain. She's always messing things up."

"Oh, how so?"

"Well she's always wanting to do things she ought not."

"And how does she accomplish this?"

"Well, we don't let her, but sometimes she gets out and we can't do anything about it. Mya and I try to keep it from happening, But we can't always stop it."

"And who is Mya?"

"She's the one who takes care of us. She makes sure we all get our stuff done, you know, sort of like a mother. She's just in charge of stuff. And I let her. She's actually kind of good at it. I don't want to be bothered with keeping up with appointments and job stuff. I prefer to handle the people, you know? Except Mojo has gotten pretty good at that. Usually I don't come all the way forward, just part way, and I can help her like that."

"How do you help her?"

"Well, when you deal with people, it's all about being in control of the information."

"How do you mean?"

"Okay take the other day for instance. MJ kind of took us by surprise the other day. And when she comes forward none of us can really edge in at all. It's like none of us know what is going on. She can block us all out. That's why we don't let her, you know? That's a really good way to get in trouble. And we have a job and a mother to take care of. Anyway, at Linc's house, MJ suddenly comes rushing in and we're all left in the dark, for like the rest of the afternoon, and until the next morning. It caused us to miss a work appointment."

"Yes, she told me about it. She was quite upset. She didn't remember a thing."

"None of us did."

"But Mojo seemed to handle it okay. She seemed to figure a way to make up for the missed appointment."

"Yes, that's exactly what I'm talking about. I helped her."

"You helped her? How, exactly?"

"Well, I was kind of part in and part out, you know?"

"No, I'm afraid, I don't know."

"Well, even though Mojo was in control, I could push her some."

"Push her?"

"You know, I guess influence her with my thoughts."

"Really? Can you explain how?"

"I just sort of think about what I want her to do and she does it. That way I don't have to take the spot from her. I can just guide her from inside."

"The spot?"

"Yes, forward. You know, up front and talking and walking and stuff."

"As opposed to…?"

"Not up front," she said, shrugging, as if that explained it.

"Molly, would you say you're separate from Mojo?"

"Definitely. We are so different."

"But yet you are in the same body."

"Yes, but still, we aren't the same."

"I see. Can you explain how you came to be?"

18

"They say you die twice. One time when you stop breathing and a second time, a bit later on, when somebody says your name for the last time."

—Banksy

Molly

The only reason I was even there was because the Mother refused to let us grieve. I could barely wrap my mind around it, but Stephen and Daddy were gone. But the Mother wouldn't let us talk about it, so I had found other ways to bring it up.

"Find something else to interest you or else," she'd said. "I'm sick of this morbid fascination you have with death. And that goes for Caci too. Both of you join a club or something or Caci can just stay home." I could think of nothing worse than being separated from Caci too. We could not survive any more separation. It was what she called the death theme that had the Mother so upset. I had dyed my brown hair black and taken to wearing deep black eyeliner and black clothes. Caci had also taken up the theme, wearing all black all the time. But she left her hair alone.

I knew Mother was afraid of death. I didn't actually remember this happening, but somehow I just knew, the same way I knew, when Mya pushed me out—she had been sobbing on that hospital bed—that something had happened. I knew that Daddy had accidentally shot Stephen while they were hunting. The Mother had told us that. And then a few days later Daddy shot himself, committing suicide out of his terrible grief and guilt. I was only twelve when they died, but like I said, I don't really remember it. But I do remember the shock, which seemed to reverberate through me each time the thought of it appeared in my brain. It was easy for me to forget, and sometimes MJ and Mya would too, and then suddenly they would remember and it would be awful inside. No one could believe it and everyone was upset. MJ was so distraught I had to completely shut her out. So I just took over and blocked them both out. Only Mya remained. She was also grieving, but she wouldn't talk to me about it. She thought I didn't know it, but she was always crying and always trying to hide it. With any of them out, truthfully, I think Mother feared we were also headed toward suicide. So I just took over. But I was furious with the Mother because she wouldn't let me talk about it and find out what happened. So, like I said, I found other ways to bring it up.

After a while, I'll admit, I started working it to my advantage. And sometimes I pushed things a little far. Like the *Harold and Maude* movie. I would leave it playing at the morbid parts when I knew she was about to come in. and then the post mortem photography really freaked her out, especially when she found my copy of *Beyond the Dark Veil* opened to a photo of the Kellers. Mary, the wife, had murdered both her husband, Emil, and their nine month old daughter Anna with a revolver before turning the gun on herself. In the photo, the three were crammed into the same coffin, Mary with her head on Emil's shoulder (to cover their wounds) and the chubby baby snuggled between them. Thanks to the Kellers I got the newest phone. I wasn't anxious to relieve the Mother of her fears. Instead I wanted to strike a balance of just enough morbidity on my part to keep her worried, but not so much that she felt the need to act and do something I'd regret.

My feelings toward her had grown increasingly cold over the years since Daddy had killed himself. If only she'd been a more watchful wife and mother, I told myself, maybe we wouldn't have lost everyone who ever mattered. And besides, it didn't seem to matter to her. Life just kept ticking along for her. She never seemed to have paused enough to grieve. Maybe she never felt the need.

Caci was in on it with me of course; she would giggle when I would suggest a new twist in Mother's torture. Oddly enough my persistent playing of James Taylor's "Fire and Rain" is what sent Mother over the edge. I had thought that it was subtle enough, but apparently she knew more about the song than I had thought. I had been playing it every time she came home from work for two weeks, when on that last day she came into my room unannounced. I could tell she had reached a limit of some sort because she usually knocked a little timidly. Not this time. She swung the door open and stood there with her hand on her hip. Her mouth was pressed together.

"Turn that crap off," she said.

I didn't argue with her. In fact I'd never seen her looking so stern, and I was quite interested to hear what she would say, so I turned it off. Caci, who had been lying on the bed, jumped up and put herself in the corner, her eyes wide. Mother and I were only vaguely aware of her.

"You will stop this nonsense," she said. "You will stop moping, you will join some clubs and get out of this house and meet people. Things happen in life, Moriah Elizabeth, and you must learn to deal with it. Your father and Stephen are gone, but we are not. You still have a life to lead. I'm not going to let you throw it away pining."

"Pining?" I said. "Gone? Things happen?" I couldn't believe she was putting such soft words on what had happened. I knew that the others were completely bereft, still, after several years, but clearly she was over it. When did she get over it? How did someone simply get over people they love dying?

"They are dead, Mother. They are never coming back." The stark words were familiar. I uttered them often in my mind to quell the incessant grief. "And I'm stuck here with you, and it's like you don't even miss them." I screamed it at her. I was so angry at having to deal with the mess I couldn't stand the sight of her. I thought that would make her slink away, but instead it only made her angrier. She came further into the room and slapped me hard across the face.

"Don't you dare assume how I feel. You have no idea, little girl. No idea." This she said through clenched teeth. I put my hand up to my face, which was burning. Her eyes were bright with tears. But her eyes were also hard, like she was trying to keep me from seeing everything she felt.

"Then why won't you talk to me about it?" I asked. I hated myself because it felt like I was blubbering and desperate for her to tell me it would all be okay, that I would be okay, despite it all, that what was going on in my head was normal, somehow. I bit my lip until I thought it might bleed, trying to keep from crying.

"Moriah, I have to keep going for you," she said. "If I talk about it right now, I won't ever be able to climb out of that hole. I can't afford to talk about it. You can't afford for me to talk about it.

"Let's just keep going forward for now," she said. She reached up and cupped my cheek where she had slapped me. "I'm sorry." Then her eyes hardened again and she straightened. "Now, all this preoccupation with death, it's got to stop." She swiveled her eyes around to look at Caci and include her in the ultimatum. And then she laid out the consequences in a hard tone that I knew we couldn't combat. At least not on the surface.

So Caci and I joined the yearbook staff. When I showed promise with photography, the advisor put a camera in my hands and sent me to the school's sporting events.

I was at a basketball game, standing at one end of the court, under the goal, snapping photos. I had been charged with getting action shots, especially of the seniors. The boys were playing, but I was having trouble with the camera's settings. I should have stepped away from under the goal to fiddle with the camera, but I was absorbed with trying to figure out what I was doing wrong.

And then I looked up and a handsome face with soft brown eyes was suddenly in front of me. I saw a bead of sweat rolling down his cheek like a runaway tear. I remember thinking how odd that I was so close to see that wet path on his face. His eyes widened, his mouth grimaced, and I thought he said "Oh my God I'm so sorry" before his arms wrapped around me.

And then I felt crushed as everything went black.

My memory of regaining consciousness and the following days is sketchy at best. Mother told me that Linc, the boy who had barreled me over, had visited me every day since the accident.

Even though I tried every way I could think of to get rid of him, he stuck with me.

He told me exactly what had happened. He had been going in for a layup. As he jumped, a player from the opposing team suddenly appeared to block the layup. His momentum had carried him out of bounds, under the goal, and into me. As he was coming down, his arms tangled around me.

"I didn't want to fall on you," he said, "so I twisted, but the other guy was right behind me, and he fell too. I wasn't able to twist enough to keep you from hitting your head on the floor. We were like a sandwich, me, the camera, you, between the floor and Allen. I guess your brain got bounced around. The camera was totally smashed. Allen got a T."

"Unnecessary roughness," I said.

"That's football," he said. I shrugged to show I didn't really care. "Anyway, we won by two points. My two foul shots." He made it sound significant. His falling on me had won the game, perhaps.

"But you didn't get to finish the game."

"Yeah, I finished. Just two minutes left. We didn't realize my jaw was fractured til after I got to the hospital to see you. My dad said by the time we got there it looked like a purple Easter egg on my jaw. Since we were at the hospital we went ahead and had an x-ray."

The game had been paused for some minutes as officials rushed to the aid of the tragic Goth girl, lying unconscious half beneath the star basketball player.

"You were limp as a rag doll," he said. "When I was finally able to get off you, the ref bent over you and was about to pick you up, when some guy stopped him. I guess he was a paramedic or something there watching the game. He said not to move you until your neck and head could be stabilized. You kind of laid there while they worked on you for a few minutes. I couldn't really see what was going on.

"By the time they got the neck brace on you, the ambulance was there and they picked you up."

"I won't ever forget it," he said.

"What?"

"My first full body embrace," he said, "was in front of a packed gym." He waggled his eyebrows at me, but I looked away because I was on the verge of laughing myself, and I knew I was blushing.

It was difficult not to like someone who obviously liked me, but I was giving it my best go. I was not into the jock scene. Or the happily ever after scene, for that matter. So I just looked down at my hands. My fingernails had tiny remnants of black polish on them from before. My life was beginning to fall into two categories: before Linc and after Linc. My black nails seemed trite and desperate.

"Tough crowd," he said.

I shrugged again. "You could just leave," I said, having recovered my disagreeable attitude. I couldn't ever allow myself to feel bad for being rude to him or I was done for. I think that was one of the reasons he liked me so much. In the beginning, not so much later.

We were in my living room. I was tucked into the couch. It was around 5:30 on a late January afternoon, several months after the accident. And truthfully I was glad to see him, having spent a long boring day doing homework by myself, watching tv and reading. It had been the same for weeks it seemed.

Headaches and bouts of dizziness still plagued me and also kept me home, but I was catching up with my school work. And the others had gone completely silent. I had never felt so alone.

Linc was helping by bringing me my assignments everyday after ball practice. Basketball had ended with a loss during the playoffs the week before, he'd told me, and baseball was now going strong. Mother would be on her way home from work.

"Why are you so mean to me?" He seemed serious, and I couldn't answer that question truthfully.

"Um, you gave me a traumatic brain injury," I said.

"There is the issue of your brain damage," he said. "And let's not forget the broken ribs. I have a lot to make up for."

I laughed despite myself, and he smiled at me. He was sitting at the other end of the couch, his long legs stretched out, sock feet crossed on the coffee table. He was a solid six foot two. He looked like he could use a good meal. Despite his thinness, I could see the hard, muscular curve of his thighs under his jeans. I resisted the urge to tuck my toes under his leg and tried to remind myself that I resented how cozy he had gotten with me.

"You actually kind of get on my nerves," I said, instead. "You're like a puppy starved for affection."

He turned his big brown eyes on me and blinked. "I am starved," he said. "Do you have anything to eat?"

"Stop," I said. "You're pitiful."

"I know. It's because you're so cruel to me. But I know you can't help it. I think it's a symptom of your brain damage. I take full responsibility for your not treating me the way I deserve."

"Oh my God you're impossible," I said, throwing a pillow at him.

He caught the pillow and tucked it under his head. "Thank you," he said. "But I was serious."

"About what?"

"Do you have anything to eat?"

I rolled my eyes again.

"Girl they gonna get stuck like that," he said.

I pointed to the kitchen. "Leftovers," I said. He didn't need any more invitation than that. I read while he shuffled around in the kitchen. A moment after the microwave dinged, he plopped back down on the couch, a full plate of leftover pizza in his lap, and picked up the remote. "Now be quiet. I need to catch up on the game." He flipped through the channels until he found the game he was looking for, put down the remote and patted me on the top of my bare foot. He curled his fingers around my arch as he turned his attention to the t.v. and his pizza, which he ate with his other hand. I felt a sinking sensation in my stomach. His fingers were both hot and cold on my foot. I didn't know what he thought he was doing, but him touching my foot was just more than I could bear, so I kicked his hand away. He glanced at me and winked, then turned back to the game and became immediately engrossed again, this time the offending hand holding his plate of pizza. I turned my attention to the book I had been reading, but I couldn't concentrate. My foot mourned his hand.

He always stuck around until Mother got home. She would give him the welcome he deserved, gushing over his thoughtfulness, his continued care of her invalid, and clearly ungrateful, daughter. She would fuss over him and fix him a snack and make sure he knew he was welcome any time, and oh how he made things so much easier for her by checking on the Ungrateful One while she, the overworked mother, was at work.

"Why do you keep coming over?" I put a sneer into my voice.

He glanced at me and a slow smile spread across his face, revealing white, straight teeth. Brown eyes with a ring of hazel around the pupil. His square jaw had a little black stubble on it. He was very handsome, with curling dark hair and olive toned, clear skin. He was not the typical tall and skinny basketball player. Tall and skinny, yes, but it was clear he was going to be a big man. Extremely athletic, he seemed to be good at everything. He even rodeoed for crying out loud, roping or something like that. I couldn't remember exactly what he'd called it. He made good grades and was able to answer my questions about my assignments with no difficulty and often offered advice. His abilities and talents were actually a bit sickening.

"You need me," he said. And that was the worst part of him. He was his own hero and was convinced he could be mine as well. It nauseated me and excited me at the same time. He gave me a feeling in the pit of my stomach, as if at any minute something might happen which would cause me to lose control. Sometimes I wondered if my lingering symptoms weren't caused more by him than the accident. I knew that if he were to stop coming I would be hurt, but not as much, I thought, if he didn't stop coming. And more than anything I wanted to avoid that hurt. I had seen how the others had been affected by people disappearing. I needed to end it before they got too attached.

His father was a rancher. He had an older sister in college. He was the youngest. I could never work out then why he was obsessed with me. He would tell me all the time that I needed him. Who else would bring me my assignments? Who else would sit with me while I waited for my mother to get home? I would remind him that I was alone all day while he was at school and Mother was at work. But he just used that as further evidence of my need.

"It's a good thing I show up in the afternoons, huh?"

Caci, who, after the first couple of weeks I was home, began making herself scarce, now hardly ever answered her phone or called me back. I often wondered what had happened to our friendship. Robbie Lynn also seemed scarce. While a part of me missed them terribly, another part of me thrived on the attention from Linc. I needed it like I needed air.

19

"It does not matter how small the sins are provided that their cumulative effect is to edge the man away from the Light and out into the Nothing. Murder is no better than cards if cards can do the trick. Indeed the safest road to Hell is the gradual one--the gentle slope, soft underfoot, without sudden turnings, without milestones, without signposts."

—C.S. Lewis, The Screwtape Letters

Her words—my words?—hung in the air, heavy as unpicked fruit.

"And so what happened next?" Dr. Granger asked. I glanced over at her, curious as to why she was asking me, but then realized it was the Dr. Granger on the video asking her.

Molly.

"After a little while, when I saw I couldn't get him to leave," the girl said, "I pushed Mojo out. I knew he wouldn't be able to handle being forgotten." She paused, studying her fingernails. "And I was right." She looked up at Dr. Granger, and there were tears in her eyes. "He freaked out a little, you know. I was watching while Mojo handled it. She was actually quite good at it. That's her job, to handle things when we don't know what the hell is going on. She's very good at discerning the circumstances and not giving us away. I think that's why she was created. You know, to handle that part. And I help her when I can. I can tell how to handle people, too. I just sometimes don't care as much as I should about them. But handling Linc was really hard for me. The Mother helped us, too."

And then she grew silent and pensive, studying her nails.

"You know what's really irritating about this whole thing?" she asked, looking up with a bewildered expression. "We can't seem to grow our nails out. Someone is always chewing them off. I'd really like to have pretty nails one day."

Dr. Granger didn't reply, and I couldn't see her in the video. I glanced over at her, and she was looking at the screen, her mouth slightly open. She glanced over at me, and nodded toward the screen, as if to say "it's almost over."

Molly said "I'm really tired. I think I'm going to go back in now." And I watched as she unfolded her legs from beneath her, reclined the chair again and lay back, her eyes closed. "You can start counting now. Isn't that the way it works?" Already her voice was beginning to fade.

And Dr. Granger, the one on the video, began counting forward to ten, her voice disembodied and floating around the room. When she reached 10, she said, "You are fully awake and alert, feeling refreshed and renewed."

I saw my eyes open. "That's it?" my voice asked.

"Yes, that's it," she said. "How do you feel?"

"Much better than I did." And then the screen went blank.

I looked down at my hands. She was right, the nails were chewed. I didn't remember doing it, and felt a shot of irritation. I was sitting upright now. I searched my mind, but everything was silent. There was no noise, no sound, as if it had all fled in the face of this, this...I didn't even know what to call it.

"Mojo?" Dr. Granger asked. And I didn't blame her for the question in her voice. "Yes," I said. "I am Mojo. But who was that?"

"That's an excellent question," Dr. Granger said.

"You're the doctor," I said, angry at her for not just coming out and telling me what was wrong. "What the hell is wrong with me? People don't just suddenly become somebody else. Are you telling me that every time I black out this other person, this Molly comes out? I thought you said I wasn't possessed? This looks like possession to me. Maybe I need a preacher or something."

"Mojo, just take some deep breaths and let's work through this."

"Work through it? How do you work through something like this? I'm crazy. I don't even remember saying all that stuff. I don't remember all that stuff about Linc when we were kids. God, no wonder he looks at me like I have horns. No wonder he.... How can I not remember? How does that even work? It's crazy."

The more I thought about it, the more it terrified me to realize that I wasn't in control of my life, that someone else was calling the shots, and even manipulating me without me knowing it. How could a person manipulate herself? Oh my God that was crazy talk.

The rest of the session was spent with Dr. Granger trying to comfort me and get me to deal with this new information and me trying very hard to block her out so I could absorb this new, surreal information. At any minute I felt like I would just dissolve in a heap on the floor. How could this be happening?

Crazy—the word reverberated in my mind like Patsy Cline's voice at the Grand Ole Opry. The space around had gone black, looked empty, as if chaos had been hushed or blown away. But who knew what was beginning to wake there?

I stood up and said, "You know what, this is not something I can deal with right now." And I walked out. Got my purse and left like a big girl. That's what big girls do, after all, they gather their things and leave if they can't keep on keeping on.

It's her job to handle weird circumstances. Isn't that what the girl, Molly, had said? Mojo handles it when we don't know what's going on.

And we certainly didn't know what the heck was going on. When I got outside, I took a deep breath. This went far beyond coming to in a strange situation. This was coming to and seeing how I had gotten in the strange situation. And the answer to all my questions was ridiculous, terrifying on multiple levels.

I fumbled with my keys and opened the driver's side door. I would go home. Back to my little house, shut the door and lock it with my new locks and get in my chair with my blanket and Hebert at my feet. I was inserting the key in the ignition when I heard something behind me and then felt something cold and hard at my throat, and a warm arm snaking around me, a hand covering my mouth.

A man said, "If you bite me, I'll slit your throat."

I went absolutely still. The man's arm tightened, pulling me back against the seat, his fingers solid against my mouth. The cold blade at my throat pinched into my skin. It was the man in the black truck.

Memo.

I didn't have time to wrap my head around that before he was speaking again.

"Little Mojo, the rabid little bunny." The sound of his voice, his thick Hispanic accent, so familiar, caused my bladder to release. At the same time, my mind began to swirl into darkness. The warmth of the urine soaked into my sweatpants. The smell wafted up to me, and I heard the man give a little laugh. I fought to stay conscious, while another presence tried to push me aside.

"It's like old times, little one. I'm flattered," he said as if from inside a tunnel. His breath was stale and rancid, as his words floated over me. I focused on that smell, that awful, terrible smell that seemed so familiar.

It's me, I heard someone say inside my head, as if to confirm and clarify: the man knew a different me.

It's me he wants. Let me.

I shook my head.

No. Get back. I'm staying. I'm so sick of this. I'm staying.

I'm ready, it said.

"Now listen," his arm tightened, pulling my head back next to his face. I heard a whimper and realized it was me making the sound and almost relented, almost sank into the darkness.

"Shh," he said. "It's okay little one. I got you," he crooned.

His voice hardened. "You know you've always been my favorite," he whispered. "But I can't have you messing in my business. I need to know where that phone is," he said. "Do you understand me?"

Somehow I was able to nod. The presence that had been pushing me aside had relented and my mind was clearing, though someone was still there, in the shadow of my mind, watching, waiting.

I'm ready, it said.

"I'm gonna let you go, but if you scream, I have a knife at your throat. Your blood would be so warm, little one. I wouldn't mind seeing it, you know. But you're warm other places, too. You remember? I remember like it was yesterday. I've always wanted to know where you learned your little tricks.

162

"Now, you tell me, just nod, you got the phone?"

I shook my head, no.

"No? What did you do with it? Did you give it to the police?"

I shook my head no again.

"I think you're lying, little one. I have a knife at your throat." He pressed it harder into my skin, as if to remind me. "I'm gonna take my hand off your mouth. If you scream, I'll slice you. You understand?"

I nodded. He loosened his grip on my mouth. "Where is it?"

"I didn't have the passcode, and I was afraid I would erase it accidentally," I said. "I sent it to someone out of town. Someone who could break into it."

"Who?"

"Her name is Evie," I lied. "Evie Stanton."

Good girl, the presence said.

"Where?"

"She lives in Shreveport."

"Where in Shreveport?"

"1275 Line Avenue," I said, giving him an address I'd typed into my phone countless times since I'd been home: Mama's doctor.

He was silent for a moment, as if trying to decide what to do. Then I felt his breath on my neck.

"The only reason you're alive right now is because I'm choosing to let you live. You understand? I'm gonna be watching you. If I think you're stepping out of line, telling our secrets, I'm gonna be back. We'll have a real reunion then. If you're lying to me, I'll drag the truth out of you, you hear me? And you won't like what I do near as much as you did last time. You understand?"

I didn't, but I nodded anyway, praying he would leave.

I heard him laugh. "I might drop by just for fun, too. You never know."

I felt the pressure at my throat release, and then with a whoosh, the presence, as if it had been biding its time, knocked me out of the way and everything went black.

I came to sitting in the deepening dark amidst the wreck of my house, my life. It had been close to noon when I had stepped out of Dr. Granger's office. With consciousness, terror, guilt, confusion, anger, and every other emotion washed over me. I wasn't able to control the tears at all, and simply sat there and sobbed until I became aware that someone was beating on my door.

At first, the sound caused me to cower into my blanket. Was it him? Had he already discovered I'd lied? Was he back to hurt me? How could I get away? But somehow, Linc's voice penetrated.

"Mojo?! Open the door! Mojo!"

I got up stiffly, vaguely aware of a soreness in my body that comes after a heavy workout, and went to the door, sliding the dead bolt back. I didn't open the door, just went back to the chair and huddled back in my blanket, an unfamiliar ache flared in my hands as I grasped the blanket. The skin on the backs of my hands seemed to catch on the fibers of the blanket, but I ignored it. It was too much effort to find lotion. The door opened and Linc came and stood before me. Then he knelt in front of my chair.

"What the heck, Mojo? Where have you been? Geez, what the hell happened?" He leaned back from me and blinked hard.

My own smell assaulted me, then. Mortified, I huddled deeper into the blanket, bringing it in tight about me, my hands snagging on the fabric, praying he couldn't smell me, wishing he would go away and regretting having opened the door to him.

"I'm fine," I said. "Just go away. I need to be alone."

"Mojo," he said. And he reached for me. But I raged at him.

"Leave me alone! Get out! Get out! Go away!"

He pulled his hand back, as if avoiding an animal. I saw it and knew that he probably knew that I was psycho. How could he not know? It occurred to me then that he probably knew more about me than I knew about myself because he knew that other girl, Molly. But still, I couldn't let him see just how deeply it went. I couldn't bear it if he looked at me and pitied me. Holding the blanket tight in my aching hands, I pulled it around me tighter still to hold in the awful smell. "Look, Linc, thank you for checking on me. Really. But I absolutely need to be alone. Please. Call me later or something." And I looked him in the eye, and I knew he knew that I was hiding the smell, but he was a gentleman and backed off.

"I'm gonna leave here and come back in an hour, Mojo," he said, his voice gentle.

I stared stonily at the wall behind him. "When I come back, we're gonna talk. If you don't answer my questions then, I will haul you to the sheriff's office for questioning. And I can guarantee you won't like that." He paused. "Are we clear?"

"Yes," I said. I didn't look at him though. And I was relieved when I heard the door shut behind him.

20

As soon as he left, I went to the bathroom and stripped down, preparing to step into the shower. Something fell out of my pocket and hit the floor. I bent to pick it up. It was a slim, wicked looking knife, closed. A tiny button on the side made the blade pop out, which spooked me and caused me to drop it again.

Was it his knife? What was I doing with it? I turned it over, trying to figure out how to close it. When it wasn't immediately apparent, I set it on the counter and stepped in the shower, deciding to worry about it later.

By the time Linc got back, I had not only showered but had put the stinking clothes and the blanket in the wash, hoping to eradicate all evidence of what had happened. In the process, I'd examined my hands, which were raw and swollen, as if I'd punched a concrete wall. My body ached all over, reminding me of a hard workout, but also of how I'd felt after the wreck. I'd mentioned it to Hank, and he'd said he'd heard that an adrenaline rush can be the cause of sore muscles later. I rubbed lotion into my hands, wondering what had happened after I blacked out. How had I gotten the knife?

I stopped short of wrapping my hands, though the scrapes were very raw looking. Instead, I let my sweatshirt sleeves hang down to cover them.

I had also stopped short of going out to the car to clean it. I was still afraid, but the thought of Linc coming back made it possible to get up and move, to think beyond the fact that the man in the black truck could come back, had promised to come back, to kill me. Would most assuredly do that when he found out Evie Stanton in Shreveport didn't exist. Might even do it anyway, just for fun, he'd said. How could I keep a secret I didn't know I knew? How would I know if I was telling one of his secrets when I didn't even know my own secrets? How could I possibly protect myself from him?

I was trying to build a fire in my wood stove with my sore hands when Linc knocked on the door again. I made sure it was him before I opened the door, then turned back to work on the fire without looking at him before I realized my predicament. I couldn't build a fire without exposing my hands. He would ask me questions I couldn't answer. So I shut the door on the wood stove and turned my back to it to face him, my sleeves hanging over my hands. I was surprised to see Hebert coming in with him.

I knelt and he came bounding across the room. I wrapped my arms around his shaggy neck. He seemed to sense that I needed comfort and he sat down, panting a little as I crooned to him and rubbed his ears, being careful to keep my hands inside my sweatshirt.

"Hey! I'm so glad you're here! I'm such a terrible mommy, leaving you and not coming back for you. But you still love me? Even though I'm so mean to you and forget about you?" Hebert smiled and panted. Then, apparently done with my pity party, he went to his spot on the other side of the stove and curled up.

Linc had come in and shut the door, moving surely toward the wood stove. He had it open and a match lit before I realized what he was doing. I had stacked a small pile of pine kindling in the bottom of the stove. He held the match to it until the flame leapt and caught the kindling. After a minute, I heard the sizzle of pitch. I moved to the couch and watched as he added a small piece of wood on top and then gathered more to feed the fire as it grew.

"Are you feeling a little better?" The fire was going now, and he turned to look at me.

I nodded, not trusting my voice.

"Mojo, I need to know where you were. Where did you run off to this morning?"

"Why? Why do you need to know? Has something happened?"

"Yes!" he exploded. "Yes, something happened! The DA is getting ready to file charges against you for obstruction of justice at the very least and possibly conspiracy to commit murder!"

My eyes swung around to him, and I could see that he was serious. His face was a bit ashen, his eyes wild. Probably not as wild as mine, I thought. Despite my feeling earlier that nothing else could annihilate me further, I knew I had been wrong.

"What are you talking about?" I managed to ask in what sounded to me like a very calm voice.

Linc sat down on the couch, leaning forward, his elbows on his knees. He still had his jacket on. The fire popped and hissed, burning brightly.

"The DA got a phone call today from a colleague in Monroe. It seems that he came into possession of a phone with video proof that Caci did not murder Roberto. Instead, she caught the murder on video. Roberto's nephew, Memo, shot and killed Roberto.

"Mojo, we know you went to college with Ella, the daughter of the DA in Monroe. And that means you're involved. You either have withheld evidence or you're involved some other way. Or both. Both DA's are now inclined to think you're involved. The fact that you snuck off this morning to go do God knows what isn't looking good for you."

I looked at Linc disbelievingly. He looked terrible. I felt something (someone?) pushing me out of the way, similar to earlier when Memo had held a knife to my throat. I was amazed at how easy it was to relinquish control. This time, though, in my mind, I simply stepped aside, but I didn't allow the blackness to overtake me. Out of the corner of my eye, before Molly had taken completely over, I saw Hebert pick his head up and look at me.

Curious, I said, but I don't know who I said it to.

"I had a doctor's appointment," I heard Molly say. And I knew she was here to handle Linc.

"I'll need to corroborate it," he said.

I felt my body shrug. "Fine. Her name is Dr. Granger. I'll give you her number. I'll have to call her too to give her permission to release the info. And you may as well know, it's a head doctor."

He nodded and stared past me at the fire. Molly pressed her advantage. "I didn't want you to know because you feel guilty enough."

"Is everything ok?" He asked.

"No. Everything is not ok," she said. "I'm pretty messed up."

"I'm sorry," he said. And she let him take the blame because it was the only way she knew to keep him at a distance. We both agreed that no one could know about the crazy.

"Does that mean Caci will be released?" she asked, and I could feel her retreating, but not all the way.

"Yes, it does," he said.

"Well that's good," I said, amazed that I could come and go like that. If it weren't so strange I'd call it a super power, I thought.

It is a super power, she said, and I almost laughed out loud at the absurdity.

Linc leaned back on the couch beside me, seeming to relax and wrenching my mind back to him. I felt Molly rush past me to the front. She pulled her legs up, using them as a shield between us and Linc. I could tell he was aware that she was trying to keep our distance.

Hebert thumped his tail.

"I can probably keep the DA off your back if we can verify your whereabouts today," he said. "Are you going to tell me about the phone?"

"What do you want to know?"

"How did it come to be in the possession of the Monroe DA?"

"I mailed it to him after I found it."

"Where did you find it?"

"Robbie Lynn's closet." I didn't know that for a fact, but I had deduced it. "Ty's fiancé?" he asked. "Yeah, Ty thought you'd found something."

Molly nodded, then retreated again and I guessed she must have been the one to retrieve the phone.

"How did it get there?" he asked. "And how did you know it was there?"

I shrugged. "It was just a hunch from some things Caci said when I visited her. I guess she put it there. We both know how to get into Robbie Lynn's house. Robbie Lynn invited me over..." I trailed off, shrugging, letting him fill in the blanks. "But the phone was locked. So I sent it to Ella's dad. I knew he would do the right thing."

I felt dizzy as Molly rushed forward again, hissing *Idiot*, as she zoomed past.

"Mojo why didn't you give it to me?" he asked quietly.

Hebert stood up and barked. Molly stretched out our legs. She shrugged again and changed the subject. "What about Memo?"

Linc let it go. "We've got an APB out on him, but I'm afraid he's gone. We checked his address. The truck is gone. His house is wrecked, like somebody left in a hurry. He has ties to Mexico, of course, so he probably headed south. He is a bad dude. We know he's the middle man for the local meth dealers. There's no telling what else he's involved in. We've heard rumors of human trafficking, prostitution. But we haven't been able to pin anything on him."

"Why did he kill Roberto?"

It was Linc's turn to shrug. I didn't know if it was because he didn't know or didn't want to tell. "Who knows?" he said. "Roberto could have gotten mixed up in something."

My phone rang, vibrating from its place on the table beside the couch. I grabbed it and saw it was Dr. Granger calling. I saw Linc's eyes go to my hand and cringed. But I didn't try to hide it. Too late for that.

"Hello?"

"Hello Mojo, it's Dr. Granger. I was just calling to check on you. I know our session was quite difficult for you today."

"Yes ma'am," I said.

"Are you okay?"

"Yes ma'am," I said. "It was pretty hard."

"Well, we probably don't need to ignore this, but I also don't want to push you too hard. When do you think you'd like to come back? Maybe we can work through it some."

"Yes ma'am," I said.

She was silent for a moment and then, "Have I caught you at a bad time, dear?"

"Yes ma'am," I said.

"Oh, I see. Well why don't we do this? Why don't you give me a call first thing Monday and we'll make another appointment. In the meantime, try to write in your journal some about what happened today."

"Yes ma'am I will."

"Okay then," she said. "And don't forget to tell Linc about that phone. I'm worried about that."

"Yes, ma'am, I've just done that. In fact, he's sitting here with me," I said.

"Oh?"

"He'll probably be calling you to verify that I had an appointment with you today. I'm giving you my permission to confirm that."

"I see," she said.

When I didn't add anything else, she said, "Very good. I'll see you next week then."

I clicked off and returned the phone to the table. "She'll confirm that she saw me today," I said.

Linc nodded and looked at me, his head cocked a bit. "You know that won't necessarily keep the DA from pressing charges against you."

"Well, won't Caci telling what she knows help?"

"Possibly. Let's hope so."

I nodded, knowing I could rely on Caci. I still wasn't sure at all that if I had turned the phone in to Linc or Ty that it wouldn't have been lost.

He's completely trustworthy, I heard Molly say. *It's sickening how trustworthy he is.*

Linc was saying something so I couldn't respond to her.

"First thing in the morning would be best," he said, looking at me sternly.

"Let me see," I said, instinctively grabbing my phone and opening my calendar.

"It's not an invitation, Mojo," Linc said. "You have to come down and give a formal statement."

"All right!" I said, "but I still have a job! I can't just not show up and expect it to be ok." The realization suddenly hit me that I probably wouldn't have a job after this. How was I going to break all this to Hank?

"No later than 8:30," he said, "or I'll have you arrested."

"Fine," I said. There wasn't anything on the calendar anyway.

He got up and went to stand with his back to the fire, hands behind him. He stared at the floor for a minute before he looked up at me. "Are you hungry? Do you want me to cook you some eggs or a grilled cheese? Do you have any tomato soup? My mom used to always cook me grilled cheese and tomato soup or mac and cheese out of the box when I had a bad day."

He was serious and intent. The idea that he still cared enough about me to try and make me feel better made my throat tight. I blinked back tears and looked away from him.

"Yes," I choked out, barely above a whisper. He was already moving into the kitchen before I could get out a strangled "Thank you." As he left the room, Hebert, always keen to check out the kitchen, hopped up and followed him. I felt like I would dissolve in tears at any moment.

"Get ahold of yourself," Molly hissed at me. I took a deep breath.

"How do you know so much about him?" I asked her, still at odds with the idea that there was someone else in my head.

"You'll have to get used to it," she said. "There's more than just me," she said. "I was the one he was into during high school, but since we're so messed up, I had to keep him back. It wasn't easy. He's persistent. I think he's still into me." I could hear her as if she were standing right next to me, but I still couldn't see her. I had so many questions.

"You mean me," I said.

"You what?" Linc said, coming back into the room with a bowl of soup and a grilled cheese.

"What?" I said, realizing that I'd spoken to Molly aloud.

"You said 'you mean me,'" he said, looking at me with his head cocked.

"Oh, I was just thinking out loud," I said, unfolding my legs and reaching for the plate, which had the bowl on it and two wedges of grilled cheese balanced on its edges. He put the plate in my hands, and I almost dropped it.

"Whoa," he said, catching it and sliding it onto the table. Before I knew it he had captured my hands and pushed my sleeves back, one after the other, exposing the raw skin and swollen knuckles.

"Dang it looks like you've been in a fight," he said lightly. "What'd you do Mojo?"

"I fell," I said, saying the first thing that came to mind, but knowing it sounded fishy. I reached for the plate of food, and cradled it up against me, pulling my legs in to help make a shelf.

"You got it?" he asked.

I nodded. "Are you gonna eat?" I was relieved that he seemed to be letting the condition of my hands go. I let the steam from the soup hit me in the face.

"Yeah," he said, looking around dubiously. "But not like you." He indicated my folded position, and I realized he wanted something to put his plate on so he'd know to do the same. He joined me and we ate as Hebert snored by the wood stove.

"There's a TV tray in my other room," I remembered, putting my plate down on the couch cushion and hopping up.

"I'll get it," he said. "Just tell me where."

"No," I said, already down the hall and opening the room of requirement. "It's all the way across the room," Molly said. "He's gonna come in here and see all this crazy stuff. You should have just let him use the coffee table."

She was right, so I turned immediately around, but he was standing right there, so close I bumped into him. His arms came around me to keep me from falling, but he wasn't looking at me. He was looking around the room.

"You know it might be easier to just use the coffee table," I said.

"Are you a hoarder too?" His voice rasped, as if the thought of one more strange thing about me was more than he could bear.

"No," I said, pushing against him to get him out of the room. My touch seemed to draw his eyes back to me. "Out," I said.

He gave me a little half smile, and I felt his hands tighten at my waist, which caused my heart to jump around. I looked away, then reached over and turned the light off in the room. "Nothing to see here, mister," I said.

And I thought I saw a sheepish look flit across his face before he let me go and turned back to the living room and then into the kitchen. I went back to the couch and pulled the coffee table closer, putting my plate on it so he'd know to do the same. He joined me and we ate in silence, Hebert snoring by the wood stove.

"I still have a lot of questions," he said, dunking a corner of his grilled cheese in his soup and taking a bite. He studied his soup. I knew he was not looking at me on purpose. I swallowed. I didn't know what to say. I didn't want to answer any more questions, but I knew he wouldn't leave it alone. Plus there was tomorrow to think about. Might as well get my story straight now. I waited for Molly to say something, but she was silent, so I was too.

"What happened after you left the doctor's office?"

Yes. That was the one I didn't want to answer. How could I possibly answer it without lying and without putting myself in danger.

"Idiot. You're already in danger," Molly said. "You think Memo was telling you the truth? That if you keep your mouth shut he won't ever bother you again? You are such a moron. Tell Linc what happened. He can help you."

So I did, without looking at Linc. By this time, my soup was cold, but I kept stirring it in order to have something to keep my eyes on. I couldn't possibly look at Linc.

"He literally scared the pee out of me," I said, trying to make light of it. But instead of a laugh, a sob escaped and I couldn't hold it in. I dropped the spoon in the soup and curled up on the end of the couch, digging the heels of my sore hands into my eye sockets to keep the tears and shame from leaking out.

Then his arms were around me, scooping me up. He sat back down with me on his lap and he tucked my head under his chin, his arms around my body. "Shhh," he said. "It's ok."

I was so relieved that he wasn't disgusted with me that I cried all the harder.

"Now you're snotting all over him," Molly said. "Come on. Stop it."

I sat up, my face away from him, and rubbed my sleeve across my nose, disgusted with myself even more.

"I'm sorry," I said, feeling suddenly very awkward on his lap. I slid off and into the seat he'd vacated, facing him, my legs crossed in front of me like a barrier and looking down at my hands.

"What happened to your hands?" he asked.

"I don't know," I said, capitulating on that issue as well. He already knew anyway, I reasoned.

Yep, Molly agreed.

"That's why I'm going to the doctor. I forget things. I think you already knew that."

When he didn't say anything, I looked up at him. He was looking at me with such a deep sense of remorse, I almost started crying again. That look was what I had been dreading. You help someone you pity, and then you move on. You don't stick around pitiful people.

"We'll catch him," he said. "I promise we'll catch him. But it changes things a little."

"How?"

"I can't possibly leave you alone."

Alarmed at the thought of him staying here when I had so much to think through and maybe even talk through with Molly, I blurted out the first thing that popped into my head. "You can't stay!"

"Relax," he said, not a little shortly, and standing up. "I'm not the bad guy, Mojo." He picked up our plates and headed for the kitchen.

I was mortified all over again. He cooked me supper, comforted me when I cried, didn't get disgusted with me when I peed my pants for heaven's sake, and snotted all over him, and even accepted my forgetfulness, and now it looked like he was about to wash my dishes. I stuck close to his heels.

"I'll do that," I said, when he put the dishes in the sink and made to start running hot water. I bumped him out of the way. "I didn't mean it the way it sounded," I said by way of an apology when I shut the water off.

"It's no big deal," he said. Hebert had followed us into the kitchen. I hazarded a peek behind me and saw that both of them were a little hang dog. Linc was propped on my lone kitchen stool, absently rubbing Hebert's ears, my traitorous dog's head resting on Linc's thigh.

"So you're not staying," I said, trying to figure out what he had on his mind. I rinsed the last dish and put it in the drain board and dried my hands.

"No," he said. "I don't think I can take another night on someone's couch. I'll have a patrol unit come over and park in your yard all night."

"Thank you," I said, breathing a sigh of relief. I might actually get some sleep, I thought, then realized he probably wanted some sleep as well.

"He'll also follow you wherever you go. And if you aren't in your car heading for my office by 8:30, he'll have instructions to bring you in the patrol car."

"Ok, I won't sneak off. I promise," I said. "When will Caci be released?"

"Not immediately," he said. "I've got questions for her, too. I'm sure the DA will have questions; plus her lawyer will have to file a motion with Judge Stewart." He ran his hand through his hair, stood up abruptly, and looked at his watch. "It's almost 10. I'll call the unit now," he said, unclipping his phone from his belt and walking back into the living room.

I heard low tones while he talked on the phone, but couldn't make out his words. I was wiping down the stove when I heard silence and then the squeak of the wood heater door. I hung the rag to dry on the edge of the sink and went back into the living room. Linc was poking at the hot coals. They were a brilliant orange, with a black shadow to them. He spread them out, dragging them forward to the front, before he threw another small log on top of them and shut the door.

"The unit should be here in a few minutes," he said. "Bobby Hudson is one of our best deputies." He stepped away from the fire, which had caught up and was roaring nicely behind the glass door. "You'll be ok with him on watch."

"I know him," I said, delighted that I could remember something. He did a social studies project on the lake.

"Oh yeah?" Linc said. "He's a pretty smart guy. I think this is his third career change since high school."

When the lights from the patrol car fell on the back wall a few minutes later as Bobby turned into my driveway, Linc headed toward the door and Hebert gave a bark. "I'll see you tomorrow," he said. "Lock this door!" And then he was gone. And I was alone. With Molly.

21

*"Heaven wheels above you, displaying to you her eternal
glories, and still your eyes are on the ground."*

— Dante Alighieri

Surprisingly, I fell right to sleep soon after Linc left. I did try to
quiz Molly on the issue of my hands, but she was as clueless as me, and
said as much. Then she went quiet, even though I waited for her to say
more. I wasn't brave enough to speak to her out loud, to call to her, and
she simply stopped answering me in my head. Crazy. So I drifted off
to sleep.

When I awoke the next morning, it was with a sense of foreboding.
I would need to tell Hank something, and hopefully preserve my job.
I didn't think I should put it off. I should probably speak to him this
morning.

My stomach was too nervous for any breakfast, but I was bleary-
eyed, so I made coffee and took a cup to Bobby. My soreness had
dissipated some, but my hands still ached. The warmth of the coffee
cup felt good. He was standing outside his car. Hebert went out with
me and ran over to sniff him. Bobby, obviously a dog person, gracefully
deflected the snout in his crotch and scratched Hebert's ear, making a
friend for life.

"Are you a coffee drinker?"

"Yes ma'am!" he said, taking the steaming cup gratefully and giving
me a bashful smile. He noticed my hands but didn't say anything.

"I've got cream and sugar in the house. I don't know if you're allowed
to come inside, but you're welcome to."

"No ma'am. The chief would skin me. And this is fine. I like it black," he said, and took a sip.

We both leaned against the hood, watching Hebert, but then I felt him eyeing me out of the corner of his eye.

"I was thinking of you the other day," I said, "and the social studies fair. Remember that?"

"I sure do," he said, then he was quiet. It felt like a short eternity before he said anything else. Awkwardness had descended on the situation. "To be honest I'm surprised you remembered."

I glanced at him, wondering if he knew about my problems. Who would have told him? I tried to imagine Bobby gossiping about me, and I couldn't conjure it.

"What do you mean?" I finally asked.

"Oh, just that I hardly ever talked back then. I didn't figure I made your highlight reel, is all."

I just looked at him, remembering why he had been so quiet.

"Of course you made my highlight reel, Bobby. We were in the same class."

He looked over and nodded, with an appreciative smile. In a second, he pressed on.

"So what were you thinking about me?"

"Well, I was thinking about the lake, actually, which made me think of that day at the state social studies fair when we were waiting on the judges."

"Oh, yeah, I remember that!" And then he started laughing. "You probably thought I was an idiot," he said.

"What? Why?"

"Inanimate domain," he said.

"Ohhhh yeaaah," I said. "No, I didn't think you were an idiot. I thought you were brilliant. I didn't know anything about eminent or inanimate domain then."

He laughed. "Well, I think that's what caused me to lose," he said. "I saw it in the judge's eye when I said it to him. I was still feeling high and cocky from impressing Moriah Jordan." he was smiling down at me. "But it was too late." His face took on a mock dejected look. "I'd already said it. I looked like an idiot," he said again. "Inanimate domain." He shook his head and rolled his eyes, took a sip of his coffee.

"No, you didn't," I told him. "At least not when you said it to me. Not ever to me did you look like an idiot, actually," I said, and it was the truth. "I always knew you were trying. Idiots don't try."

He smiled at me behind his coffee cup, which made me jittery. I hopped off the car. "Well ok, I'll leave you to it then. I'll be heading into the newspaper office in a little bit. I'll just be a few minutes while I talk to my boss, and then we'll head over to the sheriff's office."

"Yes ma'am," he said. A solemn note had entered his voice, as if he knew I was in trouble and felt sorry for me.

When I was fully awake and after I'd rubbed more lotion into my hands, this time opting for some with a little peppermint oil in it, I texted Hank.

"Got some developments. I need to see you in person. Can we meet at the office around 8?

"Yes." Maybe he already knew something was up. If not, he was certainly suspicious now. But that was all he said. No demands to come clean immediately. Maybe Hank was more patient than I gave him credit.

After my shower, and more peppermint oil on my hands, I was able to get down a few sips of coffee and was beginning to feel a little more human by the time I got out to the car. My soreness was completely gone, and except for the skinned places which were now scabbed over, my hands were a lot better. I had opted for long sleeves again so that I could hide them easily. I stuck my head inside my car tentatively and sniffed, not knowing if I was nose blind or if the smell was really not there. I was armed with some clean towels and a spray bottle of cleaner, and after testing the seat, I sprayed the cleaner on it, wiped at it with one towel vigorously, then covered it with the other towel so I could sit without getting wet. I tossed the dirty towel on the porch, then gave Bobby a wave. He had been watching me wordlessly and maybe a little mystified the whole time. For all I cared, he could stay mystified, I thought as I hopped in, then started the car and backed out. I confirmed in my rearview that he was right behind me. He kept a respectable distance the whole way to the office and pulled in to park a few cars down from mine, but where he could see me when I left the building. Bobby was boy-next-door nice, but no fool.

Hank's car was in the parking lot. I took a deep breath and went inside. He was at his computer, even though it was Sunday, and barely glanced at me when I came to stand in his doorway. Maybe he'd already planned to be at the office. Maybe he lived here. When I lingered in the doorway, my arms crossed to hide my hands, he glanced up and said, "What's up?"

"I need to tell you some things," I said, and before he could say anything, I started with the phone, and rushed through the act of sending it to Ella. His face took on various shades of red, then pinked into purple, so I moved on quickly to keep him from bursting in on my story or having a stroke, to the man in the black truck, whom we now suspected was Memo, shooting at me in the woods, and then accosting me in the car. His face drained of color. I rushed ahead to the part about Memo being the murderer and Caci being cleared, and the possibility of charges against me for obstruction of justice (left out the conspiracy to commit murder part) and how I needed to go to the sheriff's office first thing to be questioned and give a formal statement. By this time, he'd taken on a greenish hue. I ended it all in a rush of apologies.

"I know you told me to keep you informed. I'm sorry. I guess friendship comes first for me. I understand if you need to fire me. I'd probably fire me too."

He rubbed his beefy hand over his face. "I need a drink," he said, looking around absently. I remained silent. I didn't know he was a drinker, but didn't think this was the time to mention it. When he failed in locating a drink, he stared distractedly at the top of his desk and rubbed his face again.

I took this as my exit cue, and turned to pack up my few belongings at my desk. It was a pitiful amount of stuff. A little desk calendar. A cute little pen holder. I hadn't been around long enough for things to collect. I guessed I could start freelancing again. Cost of living wasn't nearly as high in Bethel as in Charlotte. I could probably make it.

When I had my stuff, packed into a plastic grocery bag like a real redneck, I turned to go and almost ran into Hank.

"What're you doing and what happened to your hands?" Gathering your stuff is not easy with your hands stuffed in your sleeves.

"I fell and leaving," I said.

"You fell? Looks like you got in a fight," He was staring at my hands. I resisted the urge to hide them behind my back. He blinked and seemed to mentally shake himself and brought his eyes to mine. "Well, I know you got to go to the sheriff's office, but leave your stuff here. Come on back when you're done over there and we'll talk it out." He looked a little shaken.

"Really?"

"Yes," he said, and that was all. He turned around and went back into his office, shutting the door. I stood there for just a second and let the relief wash over me. Then I put my grocery bag back down on my desk and left the building.

I pulled into the parking lot at the sheriff's office and got out, waiting on Bobby to pull in behind me. I needed him to tell me where to go. Was I supposed to go to Linc's office? Or maybe I should go and be booked?

Bobby met me at the door, and I gave him a questioning look.

"This way, ma'am," he said, opening the door.

"Stop that," I said.

"What, ma'am?" he said.

"Stop 'ma'aming' me."

He opened the door to Linc's office for me and looked down at me, winking as I walked past him. "Yes ma'am," he said, letting the door shut behind us.

Gloria wasn't at her desk, probably because it was Sunday, so Bobby rapped on Linc's partially opened door and then stuck his head in. I heard murmuring, then Bobby stepped back out and with a mumbled "see ya" left when Linc appeared.

"Good," Linc said, giving me the once over from the doorway of his office before stepping out. He was wearing jeans, boots and a t-shirt. It was casual Sunday. He had shaved and trimmed his goatee. He looked grim, as if he'd been dreading my arrival. No smile of encouragement here. In one hand, he had a thin blue folder which he tapped against his thigh. For some reason that movement made my heart constrict. He was all business.

"Let's go to an interview room," he said, leading me back out and down the hall. I kept my hands in my sleeves and followed him. Bobby had disappeared. Linc tapped on a door before opening it, and then led me into a room with a table and two chairs across from one another. He directed me to a chair facing a wall where a two-way mirror dominated. He sat in the chair with his back to the mirror, the table between us. I wondered if anyone was on the other side of the mirror, and if so, who.

Linc picked up a remote control on the table and pointed it to a camera in a corner facing me. "Mojo, I need you to tell me about how you came to find a cell phone belonging to Caci Molejo and your reasons for mailing it to the DA in Monroe, Louisiana."

I took a breath to answer, but the door swung open and an older man needing a shave but dressed like Linc, in boots, jeans and a tshirt, walked in and stood beside me. He rested a briefcase on the edge of the table. "Let's not answer any questions just yet, Mojo."

"Who are you?" I said.

"I'm Benjamin Self. Hank sent me. I'm your lawyer. You can call me Benny." Then to Linc, he said, "Are you charging her with a crime?"

"We're trying to determine that," Linc said.

"Well, I need a few minutes to consult with my client," Benny said. "Privately."

Linc stood up, almost looking relieved. "Absolutely." He pointed the remote at the camera, presumably to turn it off.

"I'm sure you won't mind if we leave the premises for our consultation." It was more of a statement than a question.

"We don't mind at all," Linc said. "However, If you're not back in an hour, we will arrest her and hold her for questioning."

"Understood," Benny said. "Mojo, let's go get some air. Linc, we'll be back in under an hour." They shook hands. My head was spinning. Did they know each other? Benny reached for my elbow, and I stood. He propelled me out of the room, down the hall and out the double doors to outside. I must have looked like a troubled teen, except for the bags under my eyes, with my hands tucked into my sleeves, being escorted firmly by an older man holding my elbow. I went with him wordlessly, but when we got into the sunlight, I put the brakes on and extricated myself from his hold on me.

"Hold on a minute," I said.

"Mojo, I know you might be a little confused, but let's get in my car before we have a discussion. Hank sent me on behalf of the paper. My job is to make sure you get a fair shake here. Please. Let's get in my car." He pointed to a black BMW parked at the curb.

I did not decide easily to get in a car with a man I did not know, but stepped around to the passenger side, anyway. He unlocked the doors, and stayed on his side. I did not get in, but instead called Hank. "I think I'd like to talk to Hank," I said to Benny over the hood of the car.

This caused Benny to smile patiently and nod with approval. "Good girl," he said, reminding me of that protective presence from last night.

Hank answered on the first ring.

"Hey," I said.

"I guess Benny showed up?"

"Yep."

"I'd appreciate you going along with what he says. There are more things going on here, more players, than you realize. I'm sorry you've been caught in the middle."

"Oh," I said, and then put my hand over my mouth to prevent a hysterical giggle from erupting.

Oh Hank, honey, You just don't even know how many players!

Molly?

The giggle I was trying to hold back echoed in my brain.

"Are you good?" Hank asked.

"Yes," I said. "Thank you."

"No worries. Come back here when you're done, and I'll fill you in."

"Ok," and I clicked off.

"You good?" Bennie repeated. He tilted his head, and I knew he was trying to see my eyes. But I kept my face down, looking at my phone, and let my hair fall to shield myself for a minute.

Molly?

Yeah, I'd just go with it, she said. "Can't hurt to have a lawyer with you. Linc has a job to do. He can't protect you if his boss or the DA is crooked."

Or if he is, I thought.

He's not, Molly fired back.

I looked up at my lawyer. "I'm good." And then opened the car door and slipped in onto a comfy leather seat. The car was immaculate.

Bennie slipped behind the wheel and started the car. "We'll just sit here for a minute," he said. "Now. Let me fill you in. Hank has reason to believe that your pending arrest might have something to do with local corruption. He also thinks something else was going on with Caci than just a dope head accused of murder. He's actually been suspicious for a while about some of the local law enforcement and some elected officials. The involvement of this Memo character and all he brings to the table makes it all quite fishy.

"He called me in to help make sure you don't get railroaded and take the fall for something they're trying to cover up. I'll be representing you, paid for by the newspaper. It's important that you tell me your version of events before you say anything else to the police. You tell me what's been going on with you, and then we'll go back in and answer their questions on our terms. That's the best way to keep them from filling charges against you.

"Okay, so tell me what's going on."

"First, you tell me how Memo makes it all fishy," I said.

"Well, he's been around for years," he began. "At least 15." Memo was not old enough to be my father, but he was quite a bit older, maybe late 30's, I thought.

"At first he was just this low-life, doing a little B and E here, some shoplifting there. Then he suddenly moved into the big time, pushing meth. It's suspected that he's done some human trafficking. For sure prostitution. It's also suspected that he's the main supplier of meth around here and that he's funded by some locals."

"How do you know all this?" I asked. "And which locals, exactly?"

"Hank's been covering it for years and has pretty much watched Memo work his way up and miraculously get out of some nasty predicaments. So it's mostly hunches, right now. No proof. No names I'd care to repeat right now.

"Now you," he said. "Give me the low-down."

And I did, giving him the same details I'd given Hank. He was silent for a moment.

"You've had a rough weekend," he finally said.

I nodded, wondering if I should tell him about Dr. Granger. And Molly. On the one hand it would probably help him understand more, especially if it ever became apparent that I was missing time. On the other, I could still lose my job. And my credibility.

He's your lawyer. He's sworn to secrecy, just like Granger, Molly whispered. I considered that. But I wasn't paying his bill. Hank was.

So ask him.

"If the newspaper is paying for your services, does that mean they're privy to any details I share with you?"

"Not necessarily," he said, looking at me again. "Hank will obviously help in your defense, so some things he'll need to know. But ultimately you get to decide. If he thinks we're withholding information he feels he needs, he may stop paying the bill in an effort to compel you to share those details. But he can't legally compel me to share them. And I wouldn't unless I had explicit permission from you."

I nodded and took a deep breath.

"You don't have to worry," he said. "If it's something that will help me help you, I most definitely need to know. If you don't tell me and it could possibly help, I can't do my best for you."

"Okay," I said. "The only other person who knows is my doctor. Her name is Dr. Granger, and she's a psychiatrist." I stopped. Then gave a little laugh. "I didn't even know until Saturday morning, so I'm still trying to process it."

He nodded encouragingly.

"She called it dissociative identity. It's a disorder, but Dr. Granger doesn't like to call it that. Basically, I'm not the only person in here," I said, tapping my temple.

"Well, I wasn't expecting that," he said.

"It's complicated," I said.

"I bet it is." Then, after a minute, he said, "I'm just trying to understand and not trying to make comparisons at all. But are we talking Sybil?"

"Ha!" I said, making the connection myself for the first time. Mama was a big fan of Sally Field's and had made me watch the movie with her. I wondered now if she'd had ulterior motives.

"The most complicated thing about it so far as all this mess is concerned is that I have memory problems," I said. I can't remember everything I do or everything that happens to me." I looked up at him. His eyes were on mine, waiting. I couldn't detect any sort of scorn or skepticism, so I plunged on, letting my eyes drift to the floorboard of the car. I didn't want to see if his face swung toward incredulity.

"Yesterday, I met...I don't even really know what to call it...how do you meet yourself, you know? Anyway, this other personality. Her name is Molly. She remembers some things, but there are others, she said, so she doesn't know about everything that goes on. And now Molly and I can sort of talk to each other."

"Wow," he said. "That must be really intense." I swiveled my head back to look at his face, but he was still with me, it seemed. He was puzzled, but had not adopted a sense that he needed to escape yet.

"And with everything else that's going on, I'm thinking it's pretty important that I not forget things, you know?"

"You're absolutely correct," he said. "So why don't we do this. Why don't you tell me where you have holes in your memory, so I can be sure to help you to avoid any pitfalls with those parts if they come up in questioning."

I told him about waking up and finding the phone, and how I thought I came by it, but that I didn't really remember it. He asked why I didn't turn it over to the police and I told him about seeing Linc and Ty buddied up one day, which caused me to second guess Linc. I for sure didn't trust Ty, I said.

"Good instincts," he said. "He's someone on Hank's radar as well. I don't know about Linc, but for certain law enforcement has to be involved or Memo wouldn't have walked so often."

"I think it's funny that Ty and his father Edward didn't recuse themselves."

He shrugged.

"Small town only goes so far," I said. "Plus, considering the relationship between Edward and Roberto. I mean, they were friends. Why would you want to be the judge in your friend's murder trial?

"I mean I'm friends with Caci and I didn't want anything to do with covering the story. Because she's my friend. It just doesn't sit right with me."

Benny nodded, but didn't comment. After a moment, he said, "So are there any other holes in your memory?"

"I don't have any memories of Saturday a week ago. Brother Emmett told me he saw me at the Desperada playing pool."

"Brother Emmett?"

"The preacher at First Baptist."

He shook his head as if confused. "What was the preacher doing at a bar?"

I shrugged. "He said it's a ministry. Like, he tries to intercede for addicts, talk to them. Help them." He nodded in understanding.

"Did he say what you were doing?"

I shrugged again. "Playing pool with some bad characters."

"Hm," he said. "Anything else?"

"On Sunday afternoon, with the car accident, I was kind of in and out. And then on Thursday, I was with Linc, at his house, and blacked out then, too."

"Okay, so all of last Saturday, parts of Sunday afternoon, Tuesday evening, Thursday afternoon. Anything else?"

"No I think that about covers it. No, wait. Most of the day on Monday afternoon is a blank."

"Saturday, Sunday, Monday, Tuesday and then Thursday. But since then you've not had any blackouts?"

When he listed it like that, it sounded as if I'd not had any lucid moments at all.

"Last night," I said. "After Memo threatened me. I don't remember how I got home."

"Anything else?"

"Not that I know of." He gave me a strange look. "I'm pretty sure some of me comes out to play when the rest of me is sleeping. And, apparently, there are small moments when I think I'm aware but I'm really not."

"No offense, but that is just creepy," he said.

"None taken," I said. "And you're right. It is creepy. And terrifying."

"And how does that work exactly?"

I told him about my experience with Dr. Granger, when I thought that I'd blacked out, but it had happened so swiftly I was only aware because of Dr. Granger's reaction.

"I bet that's tricky," he said, before pausing for a minute, as if to gather his thoughts.

Then I remembered my hands, and held them up to him. "There's this too," I said.

He whistled. "Looks like you got in a fight."

I shrugged. "I don't know what happened," I said. "They were like this when I came to, after Memo put a knife to my throat and threatened me yesterday."

"You think...?"

"Memo is a big guy. And a very bad guy," I said. "He must have done something to me."

"And Molly doesn't know?"

I shook my head, remembering the knife. "I think I brought his switch blade home with me."

"You have his knife?"

"I have "a" knife that I don't recognize. It was in my pocket when I got home last night."

"Don't say anything about a knife in your possession, unless asked directly," he said. Then he seemed to think for a minute before going on. "Well," he said, pursing his lips. "I didn't notice your hands until you showed me."

"Linc knows and that I don't know what happened."

"That's a bit of a problem," he said. "But don't lie. Just say you don't remember. You don't have to give an explanation of why you don't remember."

"That's true," I said, "but it still makes me look kooky."

"Kooky is not against the law," he said. "Better to seem kooky and be free, then to seem not-kooky and go to prison," he said.

"Good point."

"Okay, when Linc asks questions about these time periods, only say what you remember. Don't make anything up. Don't fill in any holes. And it's a plus if you can do all that without letting anyone know you can't remember. But if you can't, just say you don't remember."

"Easy, peasy," I said, with a sick feeling in my stomach.

"'I'll try to deflect them as much as I can when it looks like it's getting rough, okay?"

I nodded. "Them?"

"Yes," he said. "I'm sure there's someone on the other side of that two-way mirror, probably Caci's attorney and Ty Stewart. He might want in on the action."

I digested that for a second.

"One last question that is for sure going to come up. Where were you the night of the murder?"

"At home, I guess."

"You guess?"

I told him about unpacking most of the night but leaving the room of requirement for another time.

"Room of Requirement? Wait, isn't that from..."

"Harry Potter," I said, nodding. "It seemed fitting," I shrugged. "Anyway, the next morning the room was all unpacked."

He gave me a sideways look. "I'm not gonna lie. I'd like to look in that room," he said, as if to himself. "So, your physical body, most likely, spent the night unpacking that room. But you don't really have anyone who can testify to that." Again, he seemed to speak to himself.

"All right, well, let's hope it doesn't come up. If it does, don't mention the room of requirement for crying out loud. Just that you were unpacking and went to bed. Let's get back in there before they send a posse for us." He put his hand on the door handle and then paused. "Can I ask you a question?"

"Sure."

"Do you know what causes you to disassociate? I mean, I don't know anything about it, but is it stress induced? Genetic?"

"I have no idea. I do know from experience that being home upsets things."

"So there's some kind of trigger here for you? But it's completely different from say, someone trying to kill you," he mused.

I looked at him carefully. "What do you mean?"

"Well, you don't seem to black out when someone is shooting a gun at you. That's a pretty stressful situation. More stressful than moving home for most people. And then last night, when Memo had a knife to your throat, you didn't black out until the last minute."

The question took me off guard. I had almost blacked out, but had controlled it somehow, but then, when it seemed he was about to leave me alone, I had blacked out.

"So," he continued. "I guess I'm saying it looks like only certain kinds of things cause you to black out. If you can identify what, then maybe you can discover your triggers."

"My triggers?"

"Yeah, you know, the things that make you do what you do. Everybody has them. Take for instance a smoker who is trying to quit. Certain situations cause him to want to smoke more than other situations. Triggers. Identifying and then avoiding the triggers or learning to deal with them differently, helps him overcome smoking."

I felt light blooming. I knew exactly what he was talking about. I had used smoking as a crutch to avoid certain situations in college and graduate school. It had been almost comical, in fact, once I realized what I was doing. When certain people had entered a room during graduate school, I had felt an immediate urge for a smoke break. Smoke breaks had also been a necessity when overwhelming amounts of work loomed. Maybe he was right and certain situations caused part of me to take a check from reality.

"It's just a thought," he said. "I'm not saying it's that easy, but there might be something there to work with."

For the first time in my life, I felt a glimmer of hope where the blackouts were concerned.

22

"Kilroy was here."

—James J. Kilroy

In the interview room, we took our seats, and Linc picked up the remote control again, pointing it to the camera, which blinked a tiny red eye at me in response.

"Mojo, I need you to tell me about how you came to find a cell phone belonging to Caci Molejo and your reasons for mailing it to the DA in Monroe."

I looked down at the table hoping Molly would come forward to help me out here. It felt like an eternity that I stared down at the table waiting. I could feel Linc staring at the top of my head, but I didn't dare look up.

"Well, I saw Robbie Lynn at church last Sunday," I started. "And she asked me to come to her house to talk about her upcoming wedding. She wanted me to come over on Tuesday. So I did."

"Before we talk about that, tell me what happened on the afternoon of Friday, February 3," he interrupted.

"You mean about getting run off the road?"

He nodded. "Just for the record," he said.

I told him everything I could remember about being run off the road. He questioned me minutely about the details, such as the time of day it happened, where it happened, the description of the truck.

"Did you recognize the man in the truck," he asked.

"No. The windows were tinted. I couldn't really see anything but a shape."

"And so on Tuesday, you went to Robbie Lynn's house?"

"Yes. I went up to her room. She was on the phone, and there were flowers all over the bed," I said, stalling for time.

"Where did you find the phone?"

"When we were kids, we used to hide cigarettes in a hole in Robbie Lynn's closet. We called them contraband. That's what I thought Caci was talking about when I visited her at the jail."

"So you found the phone in Robbie Lynn's closet?"

"That was our hiding spot when we were kids," I said, glancing at Benny who gave me a very slight nod.

"But the phone was dead," I said, jumping ahead to Wednesday morning.

"Did you show it to Robbie Lynn? It was in her closet, after all."

"Did she say I did?"

"No, but it seems logical that you would."

"I hate getting innocent people involved in stuff they don't know anything about."

"Why wouldn't Robbie Lynn know the phone was in her closet?"

"We know where the house key is," I said. "Caci and I both know where it is. Ever since we were little, we've known."

"Are you saying Caci snuck into the mayor's house on the night of the murder and planted the phone in Robbie Lynn's closet? How would you know something like that?"

"From our conversation at the jail."

"Mojo, that never came up in the conversation. It sounds like you're making this up."

"That's enough of that," Benny said. "My client is doing her best to help you."

"Withholding evidence is hardly my idea of helping," Linc said.

I shrugged. "You all listened to the conversation," I said. "Go back and listen again. She talked about contraband, about smoking and then just before she walked out she gave me our old sign for a smoke. It was very clear to me."

"Why did you send the phone to Ruston?" Linc asked, apparently done with that particular subject.

I shrugged again. How could I tell him that I didn't trust him? Or Ty, who was probably listening on the other side of the mirror? "It just felt like the right thing to do. I knew Ella's dad is a DA: I gave Ella the gist so when the phone arrived, she could tell her dad what to do with it."

"You mean tamper with it. He tampered with evidence at your request."

I didn't respond, but inwardly I cringed. It seemed like a minor technical detail to me. He was another DA. What difference did it make? What else should a law-abiding citizen do with evidence when the only law enforcement around was suspect?

"So in other words," Linc continued. "You didn't trust law enforcement in Bethel to do the same thing?"

"I don't really know much about law enforcement in Bethel," I said.

His eyes didn't so much as flicker, as he moved on. "Tell me what happened the night of February 10, last Friday night," he said.

I did, repeating the story about the man in the black truck shooting at me and hiding in the woods.

"And did you recognize him then?" he asked.

"Who Memo? No, but he was far away, and it was getting dark. I haven't seen Memo since I was a kid."

"According to the assistant DA this isn't the first time you've had an altercation with Memo," Linc said.

I felt my heart go still. I had forgotten to tell Benny about the restaurant. I glanced at him, and he smiled benignly at me and said, "Just listen, Mojo. Don't say anything else."

I looked back at Linc.

"According to Ty Stewart, you attacked Memo; he says you bit him and drew blood, when you were in seventh grade. At Los Palomas, Roberto Molejo's restaurant." Linc was studying me, so I looked down at my hands, tucked into my sleeve, then Benny.

"What's your question, detective?" Benny said.

"What is your relationship with Memo Molejo?" Linc asked softly.

I looked at Wilson who nodded. "You can answer that."

"I don't know," I said. "He's always terrified me," I said. And that was true, but I knew it sounded like I had been around him more than I actually had. Maybe I had, and I just didn't remember anything but the terror.

"And Saturday morning?" Linc asked. "You were under police protection, but slipped away," he said. "Where did you go?"

"I went to a doctor's appointment," I said.

"And the doctor's name?"

I told him, throwing in her address and phone number for good measure.

"What kind of doctor?"

"A psychiatrist." I didn't look at him when I said it.

"And what happened after the appointment?"

I told him about Memo getting in my car.

"And you know it was Memo? How did you know if he was behind you?" he said.

"You're right, I didn't see him. But who else would it be, but the same man who shot at me and ran me off the road? And plus he said 'Don't bite me.' Plus he was Hispanic, and I recognized his voice."

I went on and explained what Memo had said about the phone, how I'd given him a Shreveport address. I left out the part where I peed my pants, about his threat to visit me just for fun. Linc had been taking notes and had remained what I would have to call "professionally aloof" during the whole interview.

I was watching his hands, one of which held a pen he lightly tapped on the folder. He didn't say anything, and I knew he was waiting for me to look up. When I did, he caught my eyes with his.

"Mojo, we could charge you with tampering with evidence," he said sternly. "Do you understand what that means?"

I just stared blankly back at him. I knew it was serious, but it wasn't like I had looked it up or something before I did it, to make sure it wasn't too serious. I didn't say that. Linc was beginning to look pretty furious. Like, so furious, he was just short of sputtering at me.

"Depending upon how the DA wants to pursue it, you're looking at ten to fifty thousand dollars in fines and/or 5 to 20 years in prison."

Oh.

Then Benny chimed in. "I think it's evident that Mojo had no prior knowledge of the crime and isn't involved," he said. "Her involvement stems from her friendship with Caci and Robbie Lynn and her role as a reporter covering the story. It seems evident to me that the location of the phone, in the assistant DA's fiance's closet, bring's the assistant DA's involvement into question here."

Good one, I heard Molly say. *I like him.*

While he was talking, Benny did not look at Linc but instead at the two-way mirror, and I knew that Ty was most likely on the other side.

I looked over at Benny who didn't acknowledge me but continued to stare at the mirror. So I looked at the mirror too and was disappointed to see a dark-haired woman, looking a hot mess, staring back at me. Then the oddest thing happened. I felt Molly surface while I was staring at myself in the two-way mirror. For just a moment, I saw a slightly different face there, mine still, but different, Molly's face. She was there just long enough to wink into the mirror and then she receded, leaving me both astonished and mortified.

Why'd you do that? I thought to her.

I heard her giggle. *Ty is such a jerk. You know he's on the other side of the mirror.*

Despite my horror at seeing her and at what she'd done, I was also oddly pleased at her moxie, wishing I could be that confident.

Benny was staring back at me from his own reflection, his brow slightly furrowed.

"Sorry," I said, looking down at my hands, still tucked into my sleeves, then back up at Linc, who apparently had missed my wink.

Linc looked like he was sorting things out in his mind. Then he blinked, looked down at the folder in front of him and then shut it and picked it up as he stood.

"That's a thought," he finally said, turning toward the door. "Thank you for your time, Mojo. Mr. Self. You're free to go. But please, don't leave town in case we have any more questions."

"Wait!" I said. Linc turned to look at me. He was already halfway out the door and had a distant look on his face.

"What about Caci?"

"They're bringing Caci in, now. I'll question her, and if nothing else comes up, her attorney will likely file for a motion to dismiss." Then he slipped halfway through the door and stopped. He seemed to have a conversation with someone on the other side of the door. When he came back in, he looked angry.

"I've got one last question for you," he said. I glanced at the camera. The red light was still on, and I wondered if he'd left it on purposefully. I looked back at him.

"Where were you the night of February 1?"

That was the night of the murder, I knew. I wondered if Ty had insisted that Linc ask me that question. I looked into the mirror, tried to look through it. "I was at home," I said. "Unpacking."

"Can anyone attest to that?"

"No," I said. "I was alone." It seemed like a silly question, since they had video proof of Memo shooting Mr. Rob. I guessed that Ty was trying to make a point of some kind.

"Thanks," Linc said before slipping through the door.

I turned to Benny, heaving a sigh of relief. "I think I'm going to wait on Caci," I said, aware that the camera was still on and that Ty was still on the other side of the mirror.

"You probably won't be able to talk to her, at least not for long. Unfortunately, the wheels of justice can turn very slowly. I doubt she gets out today."

"But why not? She's innocent. The video proves it."

"Yes," he nodded. "But the judge still has to make a ruling on it."

"And so she has to sit in jail until the judge feels like coming over and banging his gavel?" That really galled me and I glared at the mirror.

He nodded. "Unless somebody bails her out. It could take all week. Depends on how motivated everyone is."

"Motivated? What would motivate them?"

"You'd have to talk to the judge about that. But I doubt he'd let you in his office," he said. He stood and moved toward the door. "Let me know if you need anything else," he said, handing me his card. "These things have a way of getting more complicated."

I nodded, taking the card, and we both left the building. He went toward his car and drove off, while I sat at the fountain in the courtyard which looked out onto the street. I suspected Caci would be escorted through here, and I wanted her to see me.

Sure enough, in just a few minutes, a patrol car pulled up, the deputy got out, helped Caci out and began escorting her toward the sheriff's office. Our eyes met. I winked at her and said, "I'll be here when you're done." Her eyes widened and she gave me a tentative smile.

Within half an hour, Caci and her lawyer came back through the doors of the sheriff's office. This time, there were no handcuffs, and the deputy trailed slightly behind her. I stood up just as she reached me, and she threw her arms around me.

"Oh my God. You're the best friend a person could ever have," she said, sobbing.

"What happened? Tell me what Linc said."

She pulled back from me and held my face in her hands and then pulled me into another embrace. "I love you so much Mojo!"

"Caci! Stop it!" I said, laughing and trying to extricate myself. "Tell me what happened!"

"Okay," she said, pulling away slightly, and glancing up at her lawyer. "Briggs can probably explain it better."

I looked up at her lawyer, who smiled briefly and held out his hand to me. I took it and he gave it a firm squeeze before letting it go. "Mojo, it's nice to meet you." He dove right in before I had a chance to respond.

"Since Caci isn't out on bond, she'll have to go back to jail for now. In the meantime, I'll file a motion to dismiss. I expect she'll be out by this time tomorrow."

23

"I just want to eat some real food," Caci said after another exuberant hug the next day when, true to Briggs' word, she was released. I met her in the parking lot of the jail. Hank had given me the day off to recover, with the promise that the story of Caci's release would be ready before he put the next issue of the paper to bed later in the week.

"Hey, you got it," I said. "My car is over here. We can go to my place. What do you want? Pizza? Burgers? Tacos? You want me to cook? I mean I can, but I'm not that great."

"Tacos sound awesome," she said, as I unlocked the doors and we both got in. I drove us by the Taco Shack where we ordered our favorites, and then she filled me in on what had happened.

"So they told me first thing yesterday morning that I was going back in for questioning. That Linc had some things he needed more information on. That's all they said. Then when it came time, they put me in the car and brought me to the sheriff's office. When I got inside, my lawyer was waiting on me and we went into one of those interrogation rooms, and Linc said you had found my phone and sent it to Monroe or something like that, I'm still not clear on why you did that, and then the DA there sent him this video of Memo killing my dad. Mojo I knew you would come through for me. I can't believe it actually worked. It's like we have a mind meld or something."

"Well it was pretty easy to put together, when you started talking about contraband and made the sign for a smoke," I said.

"I know, but you remembered! I wasn't sure if you would."

She had a point.

"Then Linc wanted to know if I knew Memo's motive for killing my daddy," she said, suddenly getting quiet.

We were waiting for our food in the drive through, so I turned my head to look at her. She was staring down at her lap, avoiding looking at me.

"Do you?"

"I mean, anybody on meth in Bethel knows about Memo," she said. "He's, like, got a monopoly on the meth business. All the dealers report to him." She gave a little snort. "A lot of people report to him."

She paused. "I'd see him when I went out, you know. He was always in the bars. Anyway, that's what I told Linc. He also still came around the restaurant some." she said.

"But there's something else?" I asked. "Is there something you didn't tell Linc?" I was getting a withholding evidence feeling. She still wasn't looking at me, and I knew without her saying it that there was something else.

"Don't you remember that day when we were little, at the restaurant?" she asked. "When the food truck came?"

She had asked me the same question when I visited her in jail. I shook my head, no, and then tentatively, in my mind, *Molly?*

I got nothing, Molly said. *But I'm listening.*

"It's nothing," Caci said. "Don't worry about it." Just then the Taco Shack worker opened the window with our food, and I was busied with taking it and paying and then merging back into traffic. I got the feeling that Caci was relieved for the distraction. But I was worried about it. What had happened? I heard Memo's voice again.

I've always wanted to know where you learned your little tricks.

I felt a cold shiver of fear run through me. He had acted like he knew me. But how?

Molly?

Probably MJ, she said.

MJ?

I'll see what I can find out, she said.

Back at my house, Caci shucked her clothes, which she had been wearing the night she was arrested, the night her father was killed. She stuffed them in the trash after changing into the sweats and tshirt I gave her before we dug into the tacos. After, we relaxed on the couch with some iced tea. Caci refused a beer because she wanted to take advantage of being clean.

"I've got to kick this habit," she said. "I'm all Micah has now."

I nodded, thinking about what Benny had said about triggers and what Caci's were. I wished I was better equipped to help her. I wondered if Dr. Granger could help her. "How are you going to do it?" I asked. "I mean, I know you can, but I hear it's really hard. You have to get a support system in place."

"Brother Emmett told me he would help me," she said.

"Brother Emmett?"

"Yes, he's been coming to see me, praying with me. He's got some suggestions on how to deal with addiction."

"That's great, Caci." I was hopeful for her sake. I was thinking about how that would go for her, when she surprised me with a question.

"Why did you send the phone to Monroe? Why didn't you just give it to Linc?"

"Ohhh," I said. "Well, I wasn't sure I trusted him." I told her about my feelings concerning Edward and Ty being on the case and how I'd seen Ty and Linc glad-handing one day. "It's just suspicious to me," I said. "There are two other judges in this district that could handle the case. And I'm sure there are other assistant DA's. Why would Edward and Ty want to be involved?"

"Well, Dad was really good friends with Ed," Caci began. "And it's a small town."

"That should make him want to recuse himself, not be a part of it. If he was being really honest, he would know he couldn't be objective."

Caci shrugged. "I guess."

"I just think it's suspicious. And I'm not the only one, it turns out." I told her about Hank's suspicions and how he'd hired a lawyer for me and why. I had gone back to the office after leaving the sheriff's office the day before, and Hank had shared some of his suspicions, reminding me of something Linc had said, except Hank had been less vague. He was certain that some Bethel politicians and law enforcement were profiting from the recent spike in the local meth trade. And there was no telling what they'd do to protect their interests, Hank had said.

"I'm not sure who to trust around here anymore," I said.

"Wow, you're like a hard-nosed journalist, Mojo," Caci said, sipping her iced tea.

"No, not really. I hate covering stuff like this. I'd much rather do feel-good feature stories. They're so much easier than trying to navigate all this political intrigue and drug trafficking. Not to mention all the law processes."

She was quiet for a minute, and then broached the subject of Memo again. "Linc said Memo attacked you."

I nodded, uncomfortable, and kept my hands tucked into my shirt sleeves. The scrapes had begun to heal, but I still had no idea how they'd gotten there. I searched for what to say to her. I didn't want Caci to feel anymore obligated than I knew she did. But I also knew she deserved the truth.

"Tell me," she said.

So I did. I told her about how he shot at me and chased me into the woods and how I'd escaped him and been rescued by first Hebert, then Linc and Lear. Then I told her about how he'd gotten to me in my car, leaving out the part about how I had given Linc the slip to go to my psychiatrist appointment. For comic relief I told her he'd made me pee my pants, but it fell flat and she didn't laugh like I'd expected her to. Instead, she got very serious, even a little malevolent.

"God, I hope they find him and shoot him," she said. "Mojo, do you have a gun? You need to get a gun. I need one too, so we can be ready if he ever shows his face again."

I remained quiet, and shook the ice in my tea glass. After a minute, I changed the subject. "What about your mom?"

"What about her?"

"She's got Micah, right? Will she give him back?"

"Maybe. I don't know. I have to cross that bridge when I come to it. I guess I should call her." Then, as an afterthought, she said, "Linc still has my phone."

"You can use mine," I said. "Or I can take you by there. Or both. Just whatever you want to do."

After a few minutes, I finally asked her what had happened the night her father died. This is what I gathered from what she told me:

She had pulled her car into the parking lot of her father's restaurant, Las Paloma's. The parking lot was deserted except for her father's truck. It was Wednesday, almost 7 p.m., such a slow night for a Mexican bar and grill in rural central Louisiana that the restaurant was typically closed in the evening.

But Caci knew her father would be in his office, shuffling papers, smoking a cigar, as he was most Wednesday nights. Maybe drinking a little. She hoped so. He was much easier to talk to when he had a buzz. He also much preferred his office, where he didn't have to take part in any bickering. At home, Caci's mother, Maria, most often won their arguments.

She parked on the far side of her father's truck. She would have had to walk past his truck if she were going in the front door of the restaurant. But she was going in the side door, in the opposite direction, and so missed seeing Memo's Harley. She had woken earlier in the day, following a weekend binge. Right then, her need for a hit was making her throat tight. She couldn't keep herself still. Immediately after coming to she'd hopped in her car and driven to the ATM. The Friday before, she'd bought enough to last herself the weekend, and she'd holed up at her apartment. She couldn't remember what day she fell asleep. She only discovered it was Wednesday later because of the cars parked at the churches. She had just enough in her account for a quarter. She had gotten the money, driven by her dealer's house and smoked a lot of it in his living room.

And now she was coming down again. Didn't have enough to stave off the shakes, which were almost more than she could handle; rage blossomed in her gut as she opened her car door and got out. Rage at her dealer because he had likely cheated her then suggested there were other ways to get what she needed. Rage at her parents for allowing her to be in this mess. When she stepped inside and heard voices, the rage suddenly disintegrated and paranoia seeped in.

Were they talking about her?

Who? She heard her father's voice, raised, and then another voice answered calmly. She peered around the corner and could just see her father standing behind his desk. The other man was dressed in leather, and he stood with his back to Caci.

"I can't possibly do that," she heard her father spit out.

The other man said something Caci couldn't understand. When he turned slightly, her eyes confirmed what her ears already knew. Memo. A puzzle piece clicked into place. And something she'd never thought before, though it had been there all along—if it had been a snake it would have bitten her—slithered through her brain.

Daddy knew he was evil.

She looked down at her hand and saw her phone. She turned the video recorder on and pointed it into her father's office. She was staring into the screen of her phone, zoomed in so her father's face was clear and held her attention; she was fascinated with the emotion playing across his features. Then the gun cracked. She almost dropped the phone. She looked up to see Memo holding a gun. Her father was gone, fallen behind his desk. And Memo was turning toward her. She turned and ran out the door for her car, dove in, started it and peeled out of the parking lot.

Without thought, she whipped off the highway down the first parish road she came to. In her rearview mirror, she saw a Harley, which she knew was his, turn a moment before she lost sight of it in a curve. She floored it, and then whipped into Robbie Lynn's parents' driveway, her tires squealing on the black top. The two-story house was dark; no one was home. She followed the driveway, which branched off from the closed garage and went behind the house where Robbie Lynn's parents had a barn with a tractor in it. The barn couldn't be seen from the front of the house. Caci killed the car lights and cut the engine, straining her ears. She heard the Harley roar past at the end of the driveway. When it was silent again, she got out. She was shaking all over and didn't know if it was from coming down or from terror and shock.

She reached back into the car and grabbed her phone and then went to the back door to find the key to the house. The key was under the ceramic frog holding a cactus next to the door. Caci let herself in. She jogged to the top of the stairs where Robbie Lynn's room was. It was neat, just like Caci remembered from sleepovers in school. She opened the closet and felt for the hiding spot. The place she and Mojo and Robbie Lynn had kept their contraband. She slipped the phone into their hiding spot and then looked around for cash or anything else she could trade for meth. She left, being careful to lock the door behind her. She made one small detour, to the First Baptist Church of Bethel, before heading for her dealer's house.

Two hours later, after she'd left her dealer's house, a state trooper pulled her over. She'd almost made it to Texas. She could see the river on her left from the backseat of the trooper's SUV. Acres of lake glistened in the moonlight on her left. He'd stopped her for a broken tail light. But after running her license plate and discovering she didn't have a driver's license on her, and probably noticing her jittery state of mind, he hauled her to the sheriff's office.

We stayed up into the night talking, moving the conversation to the bedroom as we got ready for bed, much like the times when we were girls, having a sleepover. There was no question that Caci would sleep beside me, just as we had as kids. Neither of us wanted to be alone. And I still had questions. Obviously Caci knew something about Memo. What had Mr. Rob been mixed up in? And then there was Caci's marriage to the Bethel Chief of Police. Hank's suspicions about local law enforcement and politicians, along with what Caci had just told me swirled in my mind, keeping sleep at bay long after Caci drifted off.

24

TUESDAY, FEBRUARY 14, 2017

"All truth is an achievement."

—Thornton T. Munger

When I awoke the next morning, I felt bleary, as if I hadn't slept at all. Caci on the other hand was still sleeping, her hair tangled around her. The scabs on her face had healed, but she was still twitchy, pale and skinny. I wondered how she would overcome the addiction. I knew, as we talked last night, that the thought of her body's need was never far from her mind.

I got up to let Hebert out and to make coffee, feeling like I'd been run over. As the coffee pot sputtered, I checked my phone and realized it was Valentine's Day. I tried not to dwell on the fact that the best I could do probably for a date tonight would be pizza in front of the tv with Caci and Hebert. It could have been worse. Maybe we could share a box of chocolates, too.

There was a text from Dr. Granger asking that I call her. I remembered I had promised to call her. I poured my coffee and went out onto the porch and immediately regretted it. Hebert was snuffling and whining to be let out of the yard. I could only assume it was because of the thick malevolent odor of ammonia that hung in the air.

The hay farmer next door had begun digging into the manure pile. I dragged Hebert back inside and shut the door. The smell was now inescapable. Resolving to breathe through my mouth, I dialed Dr. Granger's office and got the receptionist.

"Hi, this is Moriah Jordan, returning Dr. Granger's call."

"Good morning. Dr. Granger is in a session right now, but she wanted to make sure to get you in as soon as possible. Can you come in some time today?"

"Yes, I can. What time?"

"10?"

I pulled my phone away from my face to look at the time. It was 8:45. "Sure, I can make that. Is there something wrong?"

"No ma'am. She just knew there were some things going on with you and wanted to make sure you were okay."

"Okay, well thank you." I started to hang up, but she stopped.

"And there's one more thing," she said. "Dr. Granger wanted to be sure that you read your journal before you came in."

"Read my journal or write in my journal?" I hadn't written in it in a few days, with all the stuff going on.

"She definitely said 'read' your journal," the receptionist said, adding "We'll see you at 10," before hanging up.

I opened the journal app on my phone and saw immediately that there was an entry I didn't remember writing. What now? I thought. The entry was dated early this morning and I realized why I felt so tired. I started reading.

MJ

My full name is Moriah Elizabeth Jordan. Everyone calls me Mojo. Except the others.

The only reason I'm doing this is because Molly is making me. I didn't mean to tell anyone, but Mya can sometimes see me when I'm in the spot, and she saw me Saturday night. And then Mya told Molly, and Molly can make it so I disappear, so I can't have the spot, ever. She said that I could come out sometimes if I wrote this down, but if I didn't, she wouldn't ever let me out again. I hate her. But there isn't anything I can do about it. So this is what happened. This is how I know Memo, the man in the big, black truck.

When Mojo was four she spent the night with Caci, and they went to work with Caci's dad the next day at the restaurant. Mr. Rob was working in his office, and he told them they could play in the dining room as long as they didn't mess anything up. It was a very big room with lots of tables and

207

chairs all around. Even though the lights were off they could still see because there were lots of windows.

They were playing with dolls, and I liked to pretend I was playing with them. I wished that I had a doll, but I could only come out when Mojo needed me. And she didn't need me to play dolls with Caci. Back then it was just me and Mojo and Moriah, but Mojo didn't know about me and Moriah. And Moriah, well, I guess she was my doll. I had to be watching. I never knew when Mojo would need me to take the spot unless I was watching. But that was okay because I liked to watch her and Caci play because I could pretend that I was a real little girl who liked to do things like play with dolls instead of that other thing. Caci had a new doll that ate real food and needed its diaper changed. Mojo had our doll Milly. Milly was not as real as Caci's doll but we still loved her. And I had Moriah. We were also cutting construction paper because we wanted to make a paper chain. Mojo had brought her little art box that had scissors, colored pencils, markers and crayons in it. Caci had brought a stack of construction paper from her house. Mojo was cutting strips with her scissors when we looked out the window and saw a big box truck drive up and go around to the back door where the kitchen is.

"They're bringing all the food," Caci said. We knew she meant the food for the restaurant.

"It comes in great big cans," she said. "Beans and cheese and chips and lots of tomatoes."

We stared at her for a second. Mojo really wanted to see a big can of cheese. She loves cheese.

"Do you wanna go see?"

Mojo nodded and so we went to the kitchen.

When we got to the kitchen, the back door was open. The truck was backed near the big loading dock, as if it needed to be unloaded. We could hear Mr. Rob talking to someone in his office behind us.

"Come on," Caci said. "Let's see what he brought."

She went through the door to the back of the truck. Standing on the loading dock, we could easily reach the back door of the truck, which had a handle that made the door roll up. Caci grabbed the handle like she was going to push the door up, but it didn't budge. Mojo tried to help her and moved it about an inch; then they both tried extra hard to get the door up. They got it up enough that Caci could stick her head in, if she laid down on the loading dock. Then before Mojo knew what was happening, Caci had disappeared inside the truck.

I knew before she did it that Mojo was going to do the same. It was the sound of a door closing behind us, like maybe the driver was coming back, that caused her to scramble to her knees and crawl through the opening to the inside of the truck.

When she stood up, she blinked in the darkness. The smell was awful. Like somebody had used the bathroom in the truck. Caci was standing beside Mojo with her hand over her mouth and nose when the truck started up and began lurching, like it was leaving the parking lot. We scrambled to get to the door, but the truck tilted and we fell. By the time we got back up, the truck was moving fast. I could feel Mojo's panic, which is always like a slingshot to me, propelling me into the spot where I can see, smell and touch everything so much better than before. A little bit of light came into the truck from an opening near the top. The back door was still up a little, but not much. It was hot and stank so bad in there.

"Where are we going?" I asked. But no one answered me. I thought Caci might be crying, but I couldn't see her face very well. The truck had been moving steadily, but suddenly we felt it slowing down. It had not been a very long time at all. Now it was moving very slowly.

"We have to get out," Caci said, scrambling for the door as if she would roll out. But I was too scared. "Mojo, come ON!" she screamed. But I couldn't move my feet. The truck picked up speed again.

"Mojo, we should have gotten out," Caci said, she was beginning to whimper. "Mojo, he's gonna hurt us."

*"Maybe he'll take us back to your daddy," I said. And I
was right. But so was Caci.*

I stopped reading, knowing what was coming. I was surprised by
the rage that seemed to boil inside me. Rage at Mr. Rob, who surely
knew that something was not right when his little girl and her best
friend disappeared. Did he search for us? How long were we gone?
Long enough, I thought. And then the violation. I had been molested.
Memo had raped me when I was four years old, for surely it was Memo
who had been driving that truck. Had he also raped Caci?

only me

"You betcha sweetheart," he'd said while Caci cried in fear. But he'd
said it to me, with a greasy accent.

I didn't remember it all, but the certainty of it was undeniable,
inescapable. I searched my memory, but had no recollection of it. How
did that even work? Not remembering but knowing it happened was
like a one-two punch to my gut, a molestation of my body and my
mind. Memo had shattered my life, and I hadn't even been aware of it.
Then I remembered that Caci had brought it up, not once but twice.
Caci remembered. Mine was not the only life that had been shattered.
How did she remember, but not I?

25

*"No one escapes the wilderness
on the way to the promised land."*

—Annie Dillard

As if bidden by my thoughts, Caci shuffled in, yawning.

"Hey," she said. "That's probably the best night of sleep I've had in a long time. God, what is that smell?"

I had been so intent on my journal I had stopped noticing. But it suddenly hit me again and the smell combined with what I'd just learned caused nausea to well up.

Then she looked at me. "What happened?"

I didn't know what to say. I knew I was gonna be sick, so I stood quickly and ran to the bathroom.

"Mojo?" I heard Caci call. "It's the smell, isn't it? God it's awful," she said.

I made it to the bathroom and slammed the door behind me just in time before I started retching. I was grateful I hadn't eaten breakfast, but still, coffee coming back up wasn't all that pleasant.

Caci banged on the bathroom door as I was flushing the toilet. "Are you ok? Do you need something?"

"Hold on," I said, and then rinsed my mouth and wet a washcloth to bathe my face with. I reached over and opened the bathroom door. Caci was standing there with a look of concern, her hair wild around her head, like Medusa.

"Tell me about the time I first met Memo," I said. Her face went even more pale.

"You remembered," she said. I just nodded.

"I'm sorry," she said. "I never could figure out which was worse, remembering like I did, or not remembering like you."

"Probably remembering," I said, "because this kind of sucks."

"Yeah," she said. "It does."

"Is that why you never told me?"

"Partly," she said. "What do you remember?"

I wasn't ready to tell her about Molly and now MJ. Telling Benny and Dr. Granger had been different. They were held by confidentiality, and I also didn't have to see them. Telling Caci, or anyone else in my life, would change things in ways I couldn't even imagine, didn't want to imagine. On top of that, what I knew now wasn't even my memory. Well, I guess it was if you wanted to be technical, but I didn't feel like I owned it, if that makes any sense. I knew why Molly had made MJ write it down. It was probably the key to my crazy and Caci's drug addiction. Instinctively, I knew we each would have to face what happened in order to move beyond it. But I did not want to go down that road. Not by myself and not with Caci and not with Dr. Granger.

So I shrugged in answer to Caci's question. I both wanted her to tell me what I didn't know because I knew that was the path toward healing and I wanted her to keep her mouth shut because I'd have to go through all kinds of crap and hell first to get to the healing. And I was just too tired. I moved past her back into the kitchen, and I heard her as she followed behind.

In the kitchen, I took down another cup and handed it to her then motioned to the coffee pot. I pulled out the sugar and cream as she poured her coffee. "On second thought, don't tell me," I said. I knew I sounded cavalier, but I couldn't help it. "I have an appointment in a little while that I can't miss," I said. "I'm not sure I can handle knowing more right this minute."

She pursed her lips and nodded as she stirred first sugar and then cream into her coffee. "Believe me, I understand. It's not something you want in your brain unless you're prepared to deal with it. I'm living proof. I mean look at what it's done to me." She let out a bitter laugh, but I could tell she was near tears. She turned and leaned against the counter, cradling her cup in her hands. "It's like, I'm so tired of carrying it by myself, but I don't want to burden anybody else with it either, especially not you. After everything you've done for me." She put her cup down and then swiped violently at the wet tracks on her cheeks and buried the heels of her hands in her eyes. "God, it was so awful, what he did. What I let him do. How can you ever forgive me?"

"Forgive you? Caci, we were only four. I'm sure you didn't have anything to do with what he did."

She dropped her hands and looked at me intently. "You don't remember all of it, do you?"

"I really don't know," I said, avoiding her eyes. "Look, let me go to this appointment. I'd rather not talk about this right now. Can we just agree to talk when I get back? I'll have the rest of the day." I looked up and saw that she was nodding.

She picked up her coffee cup again. "Is it ok if I stay here while you're gone?"

"Of course you can if you can stand the smell," I said, realizing how awkward she must feel. "You're always welcome." I reached out to her, and she put her cup down again and closed the distance between us, wrapping her arms around me.

"I'm so sorry," she said.

I didn't understand why she was apologizing, but I felt the familiar need to protect her well up in me. It felt savage, brutal. I hugged her back and told her it would be okay, that everything would work out. She released me then and, wiping her eyes, said, "Okay. I'm so sick to death of crying. Go get ready for your appointment. I'll cook breakfast or something."

And even though eating was the last thing on mind, I did as she said. As I left the room, I turned back for just a second. "Guess what today is?" I said, immediately regretting it, but realizing I wanted someone to share the misery with me. She looked at me with an eyebrow cocked, tear tracks still on her face, and held her coffee cup up as if in a toast.

"Happy Valentine's Day to us," she said.

"What a crappy day," I said.

I arrived early for my appointment, mostly because I didn't want to be in the house anymore with Caci and the knowledge that she knew more than she was telling me and more than I wanted to know about what had happened when we were four. Part of me knew she was protecting me, and I was grateful for that. But another part of me was resentful. What if she had told me years ago? Would I be crazy now if I'd had a chance to deal with it? Maybe not. But then again, maybe I would have become a drug addict too. As soon as Dr. Granger came into the room, I asked her the question that was most on my mind.

"What am I supposed to do with this information?"

"What do you want to do with it?" she countered, plopping down into her chair as was her custom and hooking the ottoman with her toe.

"I want to forget it," I said, without hesitation.

She didn't respond. Instead she just peered at me and blinked. After a few seconds, she took a deep breath and let it out.

"Why don't we go back a little bit. Tell me what has happened over the weekend. Detective Matthews called me this morning and filled me in on what happened after you left my office. I can't tell you how sorry I am that happened to you in my parking lot."

"It's not your fault," I said, and I meant it. That was the furthest thing from my mind, that Dr. Granger somehow had responsibility in my being attacked.

"Still," she said. "I'm looking into better security. Your detective seemed to know someone. I've already called him."

I nodded. "Yeah. He worked on my place too," I sighed. Jimbo was getting a lot of business because of me, I thought. Maybe I should ask for a discount.

"Anyway," Dr. Granger said, "I understand you were also questioned. Did you tell them about the phone?"

I nodded, filling her in on the phone, the video, my job status and Benny being called as well as Caci being released and staying with me.

"My, a lot has happened," she said. "Plus your unfortunate meeting with Memo and the journal entry."

"Yeah," I said. "Plus all that. Caci came into the room just as I was finishing reading it. It made me physically sick to think that that man raped us. We were little girls. How does something like that happen?"

Dr. Granger was silent for a moment. Then she seemed to choose her words very carefully. "It does happen, Mojo, more than you would think. Children, in some ways, make the perfect victim for vicious crimes like that. Fear can be a very powerful motivator for kids to stay silent and so can wanting to please adults or others who have power. In addition, in my practice I've learned that some children are quite proficient at blocking unpleasant things out and avoiding thinking about them and thus talking about them. It's a coping mechanism. But unfortunately, that trait also makes it easier for the perpetrators to get away with it."

"Is that what you think I did? Block it out?"

"I do," she said. I let that sink in.

"So, if I hadn't blocked it out, he probably wouldn't have gotten away with it."

"I wouldn't go that far with it," she said. "I don't want you lose sight of where the evil lies in your situation. Nothing you or Caci did excuses what he did. You are not to blame here. None of it is your fault. We all make our own choices. You and Caci were the children. He was the adult. He bears all the responsibility for what he chose to do."

"Why does Caci remember it and I don't?"

"That's an excellent question. You and Caci are two different people, with different experiences, different abilities, different talents, different gifts. And on the flipside, different weaknesses and different inabilities. All of those things, I believe, come together to create infinite possibilities in the ways people learn to cope, in the way they grow emotionally, cognitively, even physically. In a way, you are the result of your environment." Here she paused and tilted her head, as if she were herself absorbing her words. "But you are also a result of your genetics." She smiled. "I don't want to get into a debate about nature versus nurture, but suffice it to say that I personally think both play a vital role in shaping who we are, who we become."

"I don't know what to do."

"Why must you do anything?"

"I feel like I have to do something. Tell somebody, find out more. Go to the police. Something," I shrugged.

"What will any of that accomplish?"

"Well, if I told the police, maybe they could stop him from doing it to somebody else."

"Raping girls," she said. "Do you think that telling the police these added details about this man's depravity will help them find him any sooner?"

"I guess not. I didn't think of it like that. But isn't me not telling the police sort of like obstructing justice?"

"It certainly isn't worse than mailing that phone to your friend," she said. "At this point, I don't think giving yourself a few days, at the very least, to absorb it all is going to make that big of a difference. Don't mistake me. I am by no means telling you that when the time comes you don't have a responsibility to justice and to other people. What I am saying is that given the current circumstances, the fact that this Memo character is already on the run for other crimes that are just as serious, gives you a space to breathe for just a moment. And there is nothing wrong with that. You and Caci have lived with this for 24 years. I don't think a few more days is going to make a big difference, other than giving the both of you the time and space to recover a little before subjecting yourselves to more invasion. And you can be sure that an investigation of this sort can be just as invasive as the act that is being investigated. It is not for the faint of heart and it changes everything for some people."

"Okay," I said, suddenly relieved that I had permission to not do anything yet.

"And besides all of that, let's take a closer look at what you actually know."

"What do you mean? I know he molested me."

"How do you know that?"

I blinked at her. "Because the journal..."

"Yes, the journal," she said. She glanced down at the papers on her lap and began reading: 'Mojo, we should have jumped," Caci said. "Mojo, he's gonna hurt us."

"Maybe he'll take us back to your daddy," I said. And I was right. But so was Caci.'"

I realized what words were missing from the journal, what words I had filled in.

"I don't really want to know what Caci knows," I said.

"I can understand that," she said. "Knowing seems to make you feel responsible somehow."

"Yes," I agreed. "I would have to do something about it. And I'm all out of ideas on what to do," I paused. "But it's not just that. I don't want to lose anymore of myself."

"You sound conflicted, as if you feel you must know."

I nodded.

"What do you think would be accomplished by knowing what Caci knows?"

"I think it would help her. She pretty much told me this morning that it was a burden, that it was probably why she was an addict, knowing what she knows. She said something like she felt responsible. She even asked for my forgiveness. Plus, it happened to me. It's part of me. I should know about everything that's happened to me."

"I see."

I suddenly lost my patience. "What does that mean? Just tell me what I need to do!"

"Mojo, I can't do that. I can only listen and offer you insight," she said, unrattled, her voice still calm, still soft.

I let out my breath. "I just need guidance."

"How about this," she said. "Concerning the matter of helping Caci: have you ever been on a plane?"

"Yes," I said, not knowing where she was going.

"You know the speech the flight attendants give, about the oxygen in the event that the cabin loses pressure?"

"Yes," I said, aware of the point she was going to make. "You can't help someone else until you've helped yourself."

"Yes," she said. "It's my professional opinion that you are in no position to take on other people's psychological burdens, even if you are under the impression, wrongly or rightly, that you may be the cause of those burdens. I believe that Caci needs professional help, as evidenced by her drug addiction. You are not equipped to help her. Be her friend, yes, but you don't have to take on all of her baggage when you can barely carry your own."

"That sounds kind of harsh," I said.

She shrugged. "Reality can be harsh sometimes. I'm not advocating you being callous toward her at all. I'm suggesting that you encourage her to look elsewhere for the help she needs, much like you have sought help from me. As if you knew your friends, your loved ones, were not equipped to give you the help you need."

"So I should tell her to make an appointment with you?"

"Meh," she said. "Probably not me. But someone. I can make some recommendations."

"Why not you?"

"I'm tied up with you," she said, shrugging. "It's not really a conflict of interest, but I'm not sure I can handle the both of you. And besides, another professional opinion certainly wouldn't hurt."

I thought about the suggestion for a minute, and the more I examined it, the more I liked it.

"So you're saying I don't have to hear what Caci remembers, but she can get relief by telling someone else, someone like you?"

Another nod.

"So I don't ever have to face it?"

"Not immediately. When you're both ready." she said. "And that brings us to the point you made about knowing yourself and the things that have happened to you. The human psyche, your psyche, Mojo, is very creative, bent on survival. Don't you think there is a reason your mind has blocked this incident from your memory? Mya, Molly, MJ, you created them to protect yourself.

"I think it would be wise for us to first create an environment between the two of us, in which you feel safe and secure before we start tearing down the walls that are hiding the secrets you're keeping from yourself."

I did a quick calculation in my head. "You mean the five of us."

Her head jerked a bit, but then she smiled. "Yes, the five of us," she agreed, a little smile on her face.

I nodded, feeling relieved that I didn't have to tackle any more hard stuff immediately. But then she changed the subject back to Memo.

"So tell me about Saturday, after you left the office and Memo held you at knife point. I only have the details from Linc." She was watching my face.

I took a deep breath and let it out. "I was hoping you wouldn't ask that," I said. She gave another small smile. "I know, dear."

"Well, it scared the pee out of me," I said, trying the joke out again and not surprised at all when it bombed with her too. She looked at me expectantly, so I told her what had happened. This time, I included the black out at the end, my sore muscles, my scraped knuckles, which she examined closely.

"Linc said it looked like I had gotten into a fight," I said.

"So it does," she said. "What do you think?"

"I must have fallen or something. Or he did something to me. I mean who would I have fought? Memo? He scares me to death."

"Are your knees scraped?" she asked.

I reached for them and felt but already knew they weren't. "No," I said, shrugging. "What do you think?"

"I honestly don't know. You're a little thing to be getting into fights, that's for sure. Maybe you can talk to Molly about it."

"I did, but she doesn't know either."

26

"...we become just by doing just acts, temperate by doing temperate acts, brave by doing brave acts..."

—Aristotle

On the way home, I did try to talk to Molly, but Molly was not communicating. Was she sleeping? Did other personalities sleep? What did they do when they weren't occupying the body? Did they stop existing for those moments? No that wasn't right, because I could communicate with Molly sometimes, and obviously she could communicate with MJ and Mya. I wondered about those two and why I couldn't feel them, communicate with them, my mind spinning like a crystal suspended by a chain, set to twirling in the sunlight by some random passerby, enamored with the colors shooting through me.

When I opened the front door it was to the welcome distraction that Caci had picked up the remaining mess left over from the break-in, given Hebert a bath, washed the rental car, scrubbed both my kitchen and bathroom and made us a lunch of tuna salad sandwiches, chips and iced tea.

"Caci, you didn't have to do all of that," I told her.

"I absolutely did," she said, crunching a chip. "I have to keep busy or my mind goes places it ought not go, and then I get upset and then I do stupid things."

"Speaking of which," I said.

"Yeah."

"Look, you may as well know, I've been seeing a psychiatrist," I said.

Her expression was fearful surprise. "I wasn't expecting that," she said. "Is something else going on?"

"Yes," I said. "But I'm not ready to talk about it." Her look of hurt bothered me. This wasn't going the way I wanted it to.

"No, no, don't be hurt. She's helping me deal with my memory problems. That's actually where I had to go today. And we talked about this," I indicated her and me with my chip. "Her name is Dr. Granger. I really like her. She helps me to see things differently."

I took a breath and dove right in. I was afraid I would hurt her feelings, but I had concluded this was the right thing to do.

"You've got too much going on to take on my crap, too, Caci. I mean one day I'll tell you about it, once I learn to deal with it. But you shouldn't have to deal with it too when you've got so much else going on."

Caci shrugged. "I thought that's what friends did," she said, not convinced.

"Psychologically stable friends, maybe," I said. "But neither one of us are that."

She barked out a laugh. "You've got that right."

I smiled at her. "We're messed up."

She held up her tea glass to bump against mine. "Basket cases," she said.

"You said that Brother Emmett was gonna help you some," I said, trying to create an opening for suggesting she also seek counseling.

"Yes," she nodded, crunching another chip.

"What if you got counseling, too?" I asked. She stopped chewing and looked at me, then shrugged.

"It's worth looking into," she said. "If I can afford it."

I nodded, knowing that my own insurance offered a limited number of sessions. How would someone unemployed pull it off? I slipped a piece of paper with names and numbers on them. "Dr. Granger wanted me to give you this. It's a list of doctors she recommends."

"Thanks," Caci said, studying the list. I could tell she thought I was blowing her off.

"Caci?"

She looked up. "Yeah?"

"I don't think I'm ready to hear what he did to us. There's a reason I blocked it out. There's a reason I don't remember." She stared at me for a long minute and then nodded and looked away.

"I don't blame you," she said.

"But I think you need to tell somebody," I said. "Tell somebody that will help you deal with it, like one of these people or Brother Emmett."

She nodded slowly. "I will, Mojo," she said. "But if you remember one day, before I've had a chance to ask your forgiveness, please promise me that you won't hate me."

I promised.

That afternoon, we drove over to Caci's mom's house. Caci had spoken with her briefly on the phone and gotten permission to come and see Micah. I went with her because Caci insisted she needed back up.

Mrs. Maria still lived in the same house that Caci had grown up in. A modest, well-kept one-story ranch house in a section of town that had aged well and not far from the restaurant. The lawns, though small, were kept clipped neatly; the streets were quiet, with higher end vehicles parked in the driveways. She answered the door, and we followed her to the kitchen. She didn't hug Caci, simply gave us each a once over, as if to make sure we weren't bringing anything distasteful with us, and then stepped back with a gruff, "Come in" before turning toward the kitchen.

Her coldness had always puzzled me. I knew she loved her family and would have fought a circle saw for any one of them, but she had also been very gruff, never demonstrative with emotion, and I knew that her relationship with Caci's dad had always been rocky, as if she didn't approve of him.

I also didn't understand her refusal to visit Caci in jail, to attend the bond hearing, and now, to pull her daughter into her arms in gratitude that Caci was not going to spend the rest of her life in prison. I thought back to that day at Robbie Lynn's house when we were kids. She had been cold that day as well, but her coldness had been directed toward Mr. Rob. Not for the first time, I wondered why. My own feelings for Mr. Rob had changed significantly over the past 12 hours. He had been a weak man. Why had he not protected us better?

I shut the front door and followed behind Caci.

"Sit down," she told us, pointing toward the breakfast table. "Do you want something to drink?" It wasn't an invitation, so we both shook our heads no.

"Micah will be home from preschool in a few minutes," she said.

"He rides the bus?"

"Yes," Maria said. "It's good for him. So he doesn't get too big for his britches," she added, as if she thought that might be Caci's problem. I thought of the pool party. Mr. Ed had said the same thing about the thug they had been discussing. Caci's mouth tightened, but she didn't say anything. Then she took a breath.

"Mama," she said, her voice tight. Maria looked straight ahead. "Mama, I'm sorry."

"What are you sorry for?"

"For being such a terrible daughter," Caci said.

"Well, make up for it by being a good mother," she said stiffly.

Caci nodded, tears falling. She swiped at her face. "I'll try," she said. Maria raised a brow, but didn't comment.

"Mama, how did this happen?"

I knew she was talking about Memo, asking her mother about his motive for killing Mr. Rob.

The silence that followed was almost offensive.

"You know your father was mixed up in things. Where do you think all the money came from Caci, the restaurant? Don't keep hiding from the truth. Don't be stupid." She laughed derisively. "I told him this would happen."

I couldn't help but feel my own bitterness. If Memo, the local meth dealer, had been at the restaurant when we were little, then there was little doubt in my mind that Mr. Rob had been involved in something for a very long time, and that his involvement had widened until it affected his wife and child, then me, and who knows who else. I was battling anger at him myself, but I felt Maria was just as guilty for not insisting on putting a stop to it earlier. It seemed that she had known.

Caci looked down at her hands. "I'm sorry, Mama," she said, but I didn't know why she was apologizing.

Maria shrugged. "I knew it was coming. He kept saying that they would kill his mother if he didn't go along with it."

My spine tingled, and the conversation I'd overheard at the pool party surfaced again.

"But I knew it would eventually be both of them. There was no way around it. When your grandmother died, he tried to stop, so they killed him."

"Who are they?" I asked. But she just looked at me.

"Rob never told me names. He said it was too dangerous, but I have my suspicions," she finally said. "The police are investigating."

"Did you tell them about his fear? That his mother was in danger?"

"Yes," she said, simply. "The night he was killed they questioned me." I hoped she meant Linc was investigating. Again his words, and Hank's, came back to me. It felt like my ideas about my hometown were falling apart, just as the details concerning Mr. Rob's murder were falling into place. The silence grew unbearable, so I rushed to fill it.

"Will there be a service?" I had not seen Mr. Rob's obituary come through the newspaper, even though I'd been waiting on it.

"He wanted to be cremated," she said, indicating an urn that stood on a shelf near the window. Caci took a ragged breath, her hand to her mouth, as if she could hold in the tears.

"I'll go to Mexico when it gets warmer and spread his ashes on his parents' property. It's what he wanted. We'll do a memorial service here, now that everything is cleared up with you," she said to Caci. Her voice had softened toward her daughter when she saw the way Caci was struggling with her grief.

"Thank you Mama," she said. "Thank you for waiting on me. I didn't think you believed me." Caci put her head down and really did start crying.

"I don't believe you about a lot of things, Caci, but I know you loved your daddy. I knew you didn't do it. But I had Micah to think of."

Caci nodded, wiping her eyes. I stood up to get a paper towel for her just as the front door slammed.

"Abuela!" we heard Micah call from the front door. "Abuela! I'm hungry!"

"Stop slamming my door and come and get your snack!" Maria shouted. "And come see who is here."

By the evening, Maria had convinced, no, it was more like demanded, that Caci move back in with her and Micah.

"You be the one to wake him up for school and make sure he takes a bath," she said. "I'm old. I need my sleep."

Caci was ecstatic, having thought that her mother would shut her out. Inwardly I was relieved, as I didn't see how Caci could be my roommate and either of us resist the temptation of talking about what had happened when we were four. Eventually we would talk about it, but doing so now, I was coming to believe more firmly, would be a mistake for both of us. We needed to take baby steps toward psychological health. I also was ill-equipped to deal with Caci's other issues, including her drug addiction.

27

"'I charge you, O daughters of Jerusalem, That ye stir not up, nor awake my love, Until he please.'"

—Song of Solomon 8:4 KJV

That evening, I was alone again, with Hebert and musing that Valentine's Day was turning out worse than I had expected. Caci, at least, was spending hers with her little boy. I, on the other hand, had my dog, and the pungent aroma from the pasture. Warm temps during the day had baked the chicken manure in the field behind my house into its most fragrant state. But it had turned chilly again, and I was building a fire when there was a knock on the door.

I wasn't surprised to see Linc. He had knocked and then turned his back to the door to look out toward the road. When I opened it, he turned back toward me. He was wearing his sheriff's jacket, with jeans and boots. I imagined he had a tshirt underneath the jacket.

"Hey girl," he said. His face looked bleak, so I braced myself for more bad news.

"What's up?"

"Man it stinks out here," he said. "Can I come in?"

"Sure," I said, stepping back and letting him in. "It's not much better in here, though. I was just building a fire. Come in. Have a seat." I was glad that the house was put back in order. But the smell.

I went back to the woodstove to finish building the fire, which was doing little more than make a bunch of smoke that hovered in the stove. Maybe it would smoke up the house and cover up the manure smell. He was still standing at the edge of the room.

"How do you stand it?" he said.

"What?" I asked, pretending.

"The smell! It's terrible. I think it's worse inside!"

"Breathe through your mouth," I said, sagely. "After a while your nose hairs get singed and you lose your sense of smell." I smiled, but he was still lingering near the door.

"Linc, just come in," I said, exasperated.

"Okay," he said, holding up his hands. He sat down on the couch.

"You want some coffee? Iced tea?"

He shook his head, looking at his hands. "No. It would smell like chicken crap," he said sadly.

"What is it?" I asked, giving him my full attention.

"We lost Memo," he said.

"You lost him?"

"How did it happen?"

"No one cares who goes into Mexico," he said, shrugging.

I let that sink in for a minute.

I had turned back to my fire, which was taking a long time to get started and was, in fact, getting smokier by the minute.

"There's no doubt he messed up somebody's money-making system," Linc said.

"Do you have any leads on that?" I shut the door on the little glimmer of fire, knowing that the smoke would suffocate it, and turned back to Linc. He was watching me with an odd look on his face.

"What is it?" I asked.

"I can't tell you," he said.

"You can't tell me what? You can't tell me what's wrong or you can't tell me if you have any leads?"

"I can't tell you if I have any leads. And that's what's wrong."

"Why can't you tell me and why does it bother you?"

"I can't tell you because you're a reporter," he said, standing up.

I was taken aback. "Well why does that bother you?"

"Because I want to tell you."

I was confused. "So, you want me to not be a reporter so you can tell me?"

"Could you do that? Could you not be a reporter for a few minutes, and then forget what I've told you when you go back to being a reporter?" He had taken the few steps between us so that he was standing right in front of me. Only an inch or two of space separated us. For just a short second, I got a whiff of his cologne.

"Well, everybody knows I'm great at forgetting."

He seemed to take that in, one eyebrow raised for just a millisecond, as if he'd forgotten that himself. "There is that," he said, reaching out to put his hand on my hip. I wanted him to pull me closer, but he nudged me aside. "Let me look at this fire," he said. "You're terrible at this."

He bent over and opened the wood stove door, letting a cloud of smoke into the house.

"I was gonna let the smoke dissipate before I started over. You're gonna smoke the whole house up."

"It'll be fine," he said, poking around. "Maybe it will cover up the chicken crap smell." He reached for a bottle of lighter fluid, which had come with the house, and that I made a point of never using. He sprayed the wood with lighter fluid and then lit it. A whoosh erupted from the stove, and in two seconds, the fire was crackling merrily.

"Cheater," I said.

He shut the door of the stove, and turned to warm his backside. "I had to do something before I froze to death."

I flopped down on the couch. "Who do you think Memo was working for?"

"Seriously, Mojo, I can't tell you."

"Then why did you even bring it up?" I crossed my arms over my chest. Then I had an idea. "I'll let you speak off the record! I won't quote you at all. I'll just say something like 'a source close to the investigation.'"

He rolled his eyes. "Everybody in Bethel would know that's me," he said. "And besides, how do I know you won't forget it was off the record?" His eyes were wide, as if daring me to tell him he could trust me not to forget.

I looked away and didn't answer. He was beginning to tick me off. "Did you come by just to tell me about Memo and tease me with the rest?"

"No," he said quietly. "I came to tell you about Memo and to check on you."

I held my hands out as if to prove how ok I was, but also not willing to let him off the hook. "I'm perfectly fine."

His eyes landed on my scraped knuckles and his eyebrows crinkled for a second. He glanced up at me and took a breath as if he would say something, and then let it go. I pulled my hands back, tucking them into my sleeves.

"What has your doctor been telling you about your memory issues?"

"I'm sorry, that's privileged information. Your security clearance isn't high enough," I spouted at him.

"Come on, Mojo. You know I really can't tell you. What if you let something slip? It would put you in danger. I've had about enough of that I can stand." I finally looked at him, and I could see that he was serious and that he really did feel regret. "I shouldn't have even brought it up. I'm sorry."

I shrugged, understanding that he had a job to do. And honestly, I didn't want to know. That was the part of being a reporter I hated, all the corruption and ugliness that I suspected was out there. I didn't want to be the one to uncover it. That meant I'd have to fight it.

"It's no biggie." I stood and went to the kitchen. "You're not the only one with investigative skills, you know," I said with false bravado. "You sure you don't want something to drink?" I tossed behind me, offering again.

"Sure," he said, following me into the kitchen, where I pulled out the iced tea, glasses and ice. He filled the glasses and poured the tea, while I refilled the ice trays and put them back in the freezer. We took our glasses back to the living and sat on the couch, each on our own end.

"So, you won't tell me anything about what the doctor is telling you?"

I took a deep breath. "You're kind of taking me off guard, here. I haven't thought about what to tell people. I didn't really want anyone to know I was seeing a psychiatrist."

"I'm not going to tell anyone. It would be unprofessional for anyone else who found out during the course of the investigation to spread it around, but I can't promise it won't get out there. All I can promise is that it won't come from me."

I nodded, knowing he was telling the truth.

"So…?" he said.

"Why do you want to know?" I asked, stalling for time, stalling for something to tell him that was both truthful and not too revealing.

He shrugged. "You worry me," he sighed. "You've always worried me, from the day I met you. It's kind of a big deal not to remember things. I mean, I've never stopped caring about you. I can't just turn it off." I looked over at him. "Plus, I think it's kind of obvious that Memo must have done something else, maybe when you were little. And you just don't remember."

He was so close to the truth it put a lump in my throat.

"You know," he added, seemingly out of nowhere. "We've spent a goodly amount of our relationship on different ends of the same couch."

"What?" I had been caught off guard by his comment about Memo and was searching for something to tell him. His odd comment about the couch caught me by surprise. "What the heck are you talking about?" I thought for a wild second that he was telling me that he was also seeing a psychiatrist.

"When you were recovering from the accident in high school. We spent a lot of time on the couch in your mom's house. You don't remember." He wasn't asking, only confirming what he already knew.

I shook my head tentatively, not sure if his feelings were hurt.

"That's so bizarre, Mojo." He paused, and I thought he was dropping it, but he continued. "Anyway, every time I came over, I sat at one end of the couch and you were at the other."

"I'm sorry I'm bizarre and that I don't remember," I said, realizing that not being able to share memories with someone must be difficult. "I can tell you that Dr. Granger says it's a coping mechanism."

"Oh yeah?" He smiled and put his hand to his chest. "Are you saying that my presence in high school was so overwhelming, so stunning and blindingly amazing that you had to forget about it in order to cope with it?" He turned wide eyes on me, his look so guileless I had to laugh.

"Yes, that's exactly what I'm saying," I said, knowing that he was letting me off the hook.

"I knew it," he nodded, as if I was confirming a long-held suspicion. Then he winked at me and smiled. "It took me a long time to get over you Mojo."

His sudden seriousness, his words, took my breath away.

"In fact, I'm not sure I ever did."

The room got very bright and very still. *He's talking to me,* Molly said. But she didn't push me out of the way. Things did not go black. I was still very much present. Me. Mojo. And then she did push forward to speak.

"What am I supposed to do with that?" she asked, the words were forceful, disdainful, almost a challenge.

Linc shrugged. "I don't know. Just let it be, I guess. I don't think we should do anything. It's a terrible idea, us getting together. You've got a lot going on. You've always had a lot going on. And our jobs don't really jive with one another. I get it. It was a bad idea in high school. And it's a bad idea now."

"You're assuming I'm into you, Linc," she said, with so much derision I cringed. I wanted to shout, "I'm into you! I'm so into you! We can figure it out!" but Molly kept me down.

"There she is," he said, in a low growl.

"What?" Molly and I both said it together. I think both of us thought for just a second that he'd actually seen Molly, the way I had in the interrogation room, recognized her and realized that we were two different people.

"That snarky girl from high school," he said. "I'd thought you had changed, but I was wrong. You can be just as snarky now as you were then. But you're more now, too."

"Is that supposed to hurt my feelings?"

"No, Mojo. I'm not trying to hurt your feelings. I'm just trying to be honest."

Molly was quiet, and I didn't know what to say.

"Well, I'm glad to know that you're doing something about your memory issues," he said, standing up and taking his glass to the kitchen. "I really hope you get to the bottom of it." When he came back in the living room, Molly had receded, and I was still dumbfounded at his words, at Molly's reaction to them, and a little bereft that the opportunity to get closer to Linc had both appeared and disappeared all in one blinding second, like a shooting star.

"Yeah," I said. He moved toward the door, and I followed him.

"It's also good to know where we are with each other," he said, his hand on the doorknob. He was looking back at me.

"Where exactly are we, Linc?" I felt like I had missed something. I didn't remember deciding where we were, but I knew I also hadn't blacked out. He had arrived there all on his own, and was making me go with him. Even though I knew it was probably the wise thing to do, I didn't want to be wise. I wanted to be a stupid reckless idiot and launch myself at him. I held on to the back of the couch to keep from doing it.

"We're old friends from high school," he said. "We see each other professionally and help each other in our jobs." He paused, as if searching for something more to say. I found myself hoping he would find it.

"We might run into each other at church or somewhere else," he continued. "And if something happens, if we need each other, if we need to talk or something or just want to share what's going on, we can call each other."

He was looking at me intently, and I knew he was telling me that if things changed, if I suddenly found a solution to what was going on inside me, that he would want to know about it. That he would want to do something about this thing that was still between us.

He reached out and ran a finger down my jaw and it felt like an electric shock.

"We can always call each other." Then he stepped out and shut the door behind him, leaving me feeling more shattered than before and seeming to take with him all prospects for joy I might have ever had.

THE END

Epilogue

"Life is given for wisdom, and yet we are not wise; for goodness, and we are not good; for overcoming evil, and evil remains; for patience and sympathy and love, and yet we are fretful and hard and weak and selfish. We are keyed not to attainment, but to the struggle toward it."

— Thornton T. Munger

"Do you know what your name means?"

Memo drew back, like a snake, as if the words were sharp and had nicked him.

"It means 'idiot,'" Mojo said, taking a step toward him.

Caci's bladder relaxed. As the heat left her body and ran down her legs to puddle on the floor, blood roared into her head. Deafening, suffocating, blinding, sickening waves of it washed over her. Yet she saw Mojo's words drive Memo back, further into the dark storage room.

"You are an idiot, Memo."

The air crackled with Caci's terror. She could not pull enough into her lungs. She was drowning in thin air. Her kitten's full, dark eyes swam before her own. She wanted to run, but she could not leave Mojo, because Mojo would never leave her. Caci expected a blow from Memo. But none came, because Mojo stood between them.

It seemed to Caci, years later, as she pondered it from the safety of her jail cell, that Mojo must have decided to and then grown from her ten-year-old stance as she spoke to Memo that day. She became larger, older, stronger. Even more clever than before. She believed and became.

Memo's face had flushed, but not as it usually did above her, and while this flushing didn't bring an end to her current terror, as it usually did, she could feel the end coming. She dared not hope for it, though it felt like it could be wonderful. His face seemed to slowly swell until she thought it might burst. His fists clenched, and Caci braced herself, looked around the storage room blindly, her head moving wildly from side to side as she cast about for anything that might save them from Memo's coming wrath.

But there was only Mojo. Tiny Mojo, who had seemed somehow to grow before her very eyes. Mojo did not care that Memo was posing to strike back; she moved closer to him, as if she might embrace him, receive him, even cradle or curse him. She stood on tiptoe and whispered close to his face, like Caci had seen lovers do on tv. As she'd seen her parents do before they hated each other.

"Do you think I'm afraid of an idiot like you, Memo?" she whispered. "You aren't smart enough to scare us anymore."

Caci's body quivered. Memo would kill them and dump their bodies in the lake as he'd promised so many times before. She thought about the cot, about trying to distract him, the same way Mojo had saved her. But Memo didn't want Caci. He only wanted Mojo. His only use for Caci was to lure Mojo, telling Caci he would make her watch when he killed Mojo if she ever told. Mojo had always allowed Memo to do what he wished to her, as long as he left Caci alone.

But it had been Memo's lie. And it became Caci's lie, as well.

She hadn't meant to. She had meant to protect Mojo, as Mojo had protected Caci. But somehow, Memo had turned it on her and clever Mojo had figured it out. When it dawned on Mojo what was happening, she went immediately to confront Memo. Caci had trailed behind begging Mojo to stop. But Mojo was determined to stop Memo. "He will kill us," Caci had hissed at her.

"I want to die," Mojo had said without looking around as she walked back to the restaurant. And Caci hadn't known what to say because she, also, at times, wanted to die. But at other times, when her mother or father was cuddling her or singing to her, or when she was at the table in the restaurant and it was just the three of them and no one was angry, Caci wanted to live. Caci wanted to live when she and Mojo were playing together, or drawing, or lying on their backs in the backyard playing in the clouds. And sometimes she still wanted to live even when she thought of Memo.

Caci followed Mojo, silent and resolute, until they were standing in the storage room where they knew Memo would be. It was his job to keep the storage room neat, all the cans of beans and cheese in their places, the bags of rice stacked like hunched guards beside the shelf in the back of the room that hid a cubby hole where Memo, everyone knew, came sometimes.

Mojo had thrown open the door and without any warning strode into a room where they had just barely escaped moments before, Caci had thought then, slinking out like wounded cats. The door bounced off the wall and almost closed in Caci's face, except that she had her two hands in front of her, as if she were warding off something evil. The door swung back away and Caci also stepped into the storage room. She didn't notice that the door closed behind her; they were back, this time willingly, where all their pain started.

Caci, in her cell, wondered how painful it had been for Mojo.

It was something Memo had said to Mojo while Caci had tried not to watch the two of them together on the cot in the cubby less than an hour before. He always made Caci stand nearby, to watch. She could hear them whispering, but she never knew what they said. It was another way he punished her. After, when Memo was gone, Mojo had cleaned herself up, almost as if nothing had happened, and they had walked back to Caci's house down the street, as they always did. Silent.

But then, out of nowhere, Mojo spoke. Caci actually jumped, so unexpected was the sound.

"What did Memo mean when he said to me, '"You're better'?"

They had reached the empty driveway. The sun was shining. It was a Saturday. Early afternoon. Everyone was at the restaurant getting ready for the coming night. Caci and Mojo, who had spent the night with her (and now Caci wondered why. Why had she willingly come, weekly, sometimes twice a week, for six years?), had been summoned by Caci's parents to help Memo unload the food truck and bring things to the kitchen from storage. They had known what would happen when they got there. Memo would be waiting on them.

Caci, having borne the secret, the shame, and the guilt for so long, dissolved into tears at Mojo's question, confirming that Memo preferred Mojo in all things, and knowing they were going to die now and it would be her fault for not finding a way to stop it. He was going to kill them both, and she would have to watch her best friend, who thought she'd been saving Caci all this time, be murdered.

They had turned right around and gone straight back to the restaurant.

Now, Mojo seemed to be towering over Memo, who, at twenty-five, was much larger. He had told them he would stab them to death and dump their bodies in the lake if they did not keep the secret, if they did not continue to participate in the awful messy, as Caci had come to call it. That was when they were four, after they first met Memo in the back of that truck. He'd come all the way from Mexico to work for his uncle, Caci's father. Later, he'd made them watch as he twisted the neck of Caci's kitten as proof that he would do what he said.

Her parents thought the kitten had disappeared, so they had gotten her another one. And it too disappeared, her parents thought. But Memo had made her hold her hand out when no one was looking and whispered, "Don't tell."

Then he'd put something soft in her hand. She'd been so terrified she would say something she wasn't supposed to that she'd not even looked at what was in her hand until she was in the bathroom. There, she'd opened her fist and lying on her palm was the tip of her new kitten's tail, no bigger than her thumb, but recognizable by the distinctive pattern in the fur.

"Do you know what else your name means?"

Mojo was still up close to Memo. If he wanted, Memo could slip his hand around Mojo's back, pull her into him, against him. But his fists were still clenched.

'A note to remember.' You're just a stupid note you're stupid father wrote to himself so he wouldn't forget to stop having kids."

Memo's face lost its color, and his fists relaxed. He hunched, like an impotent bag of rice, against the shelf that hid the cot. Mojo stood still in front of him, watching while he slumped lower and lower, so that she had to duck her head to see into his face. She studied him.

"We're gonna leave, Memo. And you're gonna stay here til we're gone. And you're never gonna bother me or Caci again. If you even act like you want to touch us, we will tell. Do you hear me?

"We will tell. And you will go to jail. Your father will be glad to get rid of you."

"Caci, go," Mojo had said. And Caci left the storage room, where the beans, the cheese, the tomatoes, napkins, extra silverware, cot, and now the awful messy were stored. The cot her father hadn't used in years, everyone knew. It was just a cot, no blankets or pillows, shoved against the far wall, behind the shelf of beans, easily missed if you didn't know it was there or you weren't looking for the person who might have been using it. But no one ever did. Except Memo.

If Caci understood correctly, the awful messy had just come to a wonderful end. She was baffled, holding the ecstatic relief at bay until she had better understanding, but it was there, knocking furiously on her heart as she stood just outside the door, waiting for Mojo. In less than a minute, Mojo had joined her. The door snicked shut behind her, with Memo still on the inside.

Mojo was little again. She had shrunk somehow, and when she spoke, her voice had gone back to normal as well. Caci didn't hear what Mojo said so transfixed was she by the transformation. Then they joined hands and were running together out of the back room into the bright sun, for it was still early afternoon, though it felt as if an eternity had passed. They burst out into the sun where it baked the empty parking lot, preheating it, her father liked to joke. They didn't stop running until they were in Caci's room, and by then they were laughing, thinking they had won, that they had escaped, ecstatic relief washing over them in waves of hysteria.

The memory of how they had finally escaped Memo and why they had needed to would fade, but only slightly for Caci, unless she had some other substance on which to rely. And like the memory, Memo himself seemed to fade, but only slightly, after that. He still worked for her father, but they didn't see him as much. Occasionally, as the years passed and everyone grew, he would come into the restaurant when the girls were there, as if to test them. But they always ignored him, never made eye contact, and slipped out of the room as soon as possible. Without discussing it, they had decided to pretend he didn't exist anymore. Except for that one time when he came in and Mojo attacked him. Caci knew it was because she herself had suddenly frozen in fear. She had begged her parents to not get her another pet. She could bear no more sacrifice. But they had. And Memo had never really left Caci alone. He still tortured her whenever he could.

As they grew, Caci came to understand she and Mojo were not the same. Caci was trying to pretend Memo didn't exist, but Mojo was not pretending. Mojo had folded her memory of the whole thing neatly into itself, a sealed packet, never to be opened. Caci had thought this trick of Mojo's, of not remembering, was even more clever than the trick of becoming a smart grownup who could scare off the likes of Memo. Except for the time in seventh grade, when Mojo bit Memo, they never spoke of it again. Even then, they didn't speak of it, but Caci knew why Mojo had attacked Memo, even if Mojo did not herself know.

Though Mojo somehow, miraculously forgot, neither Caci, and especially not Memo, ever forgot the time leading up to that moment in the storage room, when Mojo, a little pipsqueak girl, had told Memo, a big man, that he was an idiot. The worst part for both Caci and Memo was that they both had believed her.

And that's how Caci had ended up in jail, she knew.

If only she could have forgotten it all, like Mojo. She had tried. She'd tried every trick she knew to forget. By the time they were in eighth grade, Caci was on the fast track to becoming an alcoholic, sneaking liquor from the restaurant. Mojo drank some, but only enough to make it seem like she was having a good time. She was always looking out for Caci, always protecting her, could never let loose because something might happen to Caci. Somehow, when it all started when they were four, Mojo had decided then it was her job to protect Caci.

Caci didn't mind, until that last day in the storage closet when she saw Mojo whisper to Memo one last time. She'd tried to be friends with Mojo after, but when Caci started drinking and Mojo didn't follow suit, Caci blew up at her. Mojo just stood there blinking, like she didn't understand what was going on. And Caci, sick of looking into the face of her own shame, pushed Mojo away. After the accident with Linc, it was easy for Caci to stop inviting her over or answering the phone or even looking at her. Even when Mojo was in the hospital in high school, Caci had not relented, except for that one time they went to the lake, that one time that Mojo had needed Caci. Besides then, she had never wanted to look at Mojo's face again.

But Mojo had come to her hearing. Seeing her there, Caci's first thought was that Mojo would help her. Mojo had always helped her. Mojo would know what to do. And now she was here, as if summoned. The guard had just told her she had a visitor, and Caci knew it was Mojo. Who else could it be? Caci couldn't remember a single other soul it could be.

ACKNOWLEDGEMENTS

In no certain order, but rather as it comes to me, I have to thank my family, close and extended, friends, teachers, and students. No one is an island. We are shaped and shape each other, and I've been blessed with scores of kind, thoughtful, helpful, insightful people in my life.

There are also those who worked alongside me specifically on this project, with consideration, careful eyes, kind words, and other sacrifices, even when it wasn't easy, my first readers: Kenny Sharp, Connie Hale, Donna Rambo, Lori Smith and Michelle Gentry.

The ones I'd be lost without, the kin God gave me first, just to name a few: Homer. Mama, Daddy, Donna, Aunt Beck, my brothers, my cousins, nieces, and nephews. There are so many I lose count. They showed me right from wrong and how to treat the snakes I might meet out there.

Then there's the kin God gave me next, and I'm only naming the giants in the crowd that surrounds me: Granny-bo and Papa Dick. Kenny, Matt, Brea, Devyn, my Zaya, and all the grands. They all show me how best to love.

Then there's God Himself. Just look at what He does. He leaves me speechless with gratitude time and again.

CONTACT

I hope you enjoyed my debut novel, *A Fortunate Murder*, the first book in the Shattered murder series. Please do let me know what you think! I would love to hear from you at **mojonovel@gmail.com.**

You can also interact with me (the author) here:
https://www.facebook.com/Tammy.Hale.Sharp/
or with Moriah Jordan (the character) here:
https://www.facebook.com/mojonovel/

If you're part of a book club, I would be honored if you recommended *A Fortunate Murder* to your group. I'd also be happy to consider visiting with your group or at your local library. Shoot me an email or message me on social media, and we'll talk about it!

You can also sign up for my newsletter and be the first to know when the second book in the Shattered murder series becomes available:

https://forms.gle/JAuJ71DcHjcL9x4m6

Thank you again for reading my novel.

An Essential Murder Excerpt

—from book 2 of the SHATTERED series

FRIDAY, MAY 19, 2017

*"An inconvenience is only an adventure wrongly considered;
an adventure is an inconvenience rightly considered."*

—G.K. Chesterton

Mojo's hand flew to her phone on the table beside the bed. She was sprawled on top of the covers, fully dressed, and she couldn't remember why.

remind her

She turned the phone on to see the date and time, but her eyes were too groggy, her mouth too dry. She had been sweating, face down, mouth open. Creases on her left cheek, like gashes, and an angry splotch, told the story of deep sleep. She tried to wipe her cheek, but her hair, thick, long and dark, got in her way. She swiped at it; her hand tangled. She brought it around to see what the tangle was about. Purple hair tinsel sparkled at her, its texture slick.

not a lot

too much

She got up to look in the mirror and stumbled on a pair of boots which had been kicked off and left where they fell beside her bed. They were cute but impractical. Some would call them cowgirl boots, but the fancy kind no one would wear in a barn except with a dress at a wedding. The heel was too high, the footbed too narrow. Not good for walking or running. But they were lusciously beautiful: a nude suede, with turquoise trim.

not good for anything

a white dress

throw them out

into the room

like a rhinestone cowgirl

Remorseful and a little outraged at herself, she made it to the bathroom mirror to peer at her reflection. She flipped the tinsel back and forth in disgust.

Medusa

my turn

I want to be

She tried to see how the tinsel was attached, but it was at the back of her head, and no matter which way she turned, she couldn't see it. It would take multiple mirrors close up.

a friend

She couldn't take the tinsel out by herself without making a bigger mess, so she tried to conceal it with a ponytail, which only accentuated the sparkle. Then she tried a messy bun, which seemed to work, though a thread of purple ran through the back where she couldn't see and forgot to check because her hands, as they worked on her hair caught her attention. She switched from looking in the mirror to looking directly at her hands. It was the blood that had come into focus—*when I see the blood*—and which caused her to rip her hair down, give it and her whole body a vigorous scrub in a scalding hot shower. After, she twisted her wet hair back up into a tight bun. The tinsel sparkled in the back, but she couldn't see it. Before the shower, she'd gone back to her bed for a closer inspection of the sheets. The amount of blood alarmed her.

"Whose blood is this?" she asked out loud in a strangled voice. There was no answer. She thought she was alone.

She had no scratches or injuries, and it was not her time of the month. She stripped the sheets, checked for more bloody towels or clothes and, finding none, stuffed it all, including the clothes she had on, in the washer to run while she showered. Words escaped her mouth as she performed the tasks in front of her.

I will pass, I will pass over you.

When she was ready to leave for work, she stored the boots in her closet for further consideration. Looking for her keys, she wondered if she'd left them in her truck and peeked out the window to her driveway as if she might see her keys waving at her from the driver's seat. But her truck was not there. Instead, there was a teal Chevy truck waiting. It was an older model, with chrome fenders, a curvy body.

three on the tree

I will pass, I will pass over you

She went outside to see, and there was more blood on the truck's chrome, but no denting. The truck had killed something.

murderer

I will pass over you

Gore and hair were mixed in the blood which had dried on the silver chrome and was smeared on the beautiful paint on the left fender. She stood staring at the blood for a long minute before pulling out her phone and calling someone who answered as if expecting her.

"You told me to call if something happened."

Mojo nodded in agreement while the person on the other end of the line responded.

"I'm on my way," she said, ending the call, and checking the GPS on her phone.

She drove the truck to an upscale automatic car wash. The keys had been in the ignition. The attendant noticed the mess on the fenders, but didn't say anything as he sprayed it, unblinking, until the water pressure dislodged it all, washing it away down the drain as if it never existed. Then she drove to the Desperada bar where her own truck, a new, red Dodge Rebel, was parked. She had found her keys in the Chevy's glove compartment, where she also found papers belonging to Preston Miller. She put his keys in with the papers and left one of the Chevy's doors unlocked for him before getting into her own truck.

It was 7 a.m. She texted her boss.

"Will be late this morning"

Dr. Granger, a short pudgy woman who looked like Mrs. Claus was just getting out of her car in the back parking lot. She waited on Mojo to hop down out of her truck, gave her a once over.

"Mojo?" she seemed to ask.

Mojo nodded.

"Well, come in." Dr. Granger fiddled with her security system, trying to unlock the back door to her clinic, a renovated ranch house in an older neighborhood next to the hospital. Her security system had recently been upgraded from nonexistent to hidden cameras and coded entrances to the parking lot and all the doors.

because of me

Memo

I will pass

I will pass

Suddenly cracking the code, Dr. Granger was in and moving like an efficient machine, flipping on lights as she made her way through the building to the small room where she and Mojo had their bi-weekly sessions.

"Coffee," she said, nodding to the Keurig which sat on a nearby table.

Mojo obediently went to the machine to get coffee going. While the Keurig huffed, squealed and poured its insides out, Granger continued to prep the building for opening. When the blubbering stopped, Mojo set it up again, topping it off with a tank of cold water. She doctored the first steaming mug with half and half and lots of sugar before folding herself on the low sofa in the room to wait. She eyed the familiar books in the case nearby, but left them unmolested as she sipped her breakfast. In a moment, Dr. Granger came in, picked up her own cup of coffee, black no sugar like a grownup, and sat in the only chair. Hooking the toes of her right foot under a stool, she dragged it near to rest her feet on.

It was a problem no one talked about. But it dogged women everywhere they went; couldn't be avoided, she thought, and not for the first time. Most chairs did not allow people like Dr. Granger or Mojo to reach the floor. Short women adjusted themselves to the discomfort of most chairs with stools or by folding or crossing their legs or by staying seated for only short periods of time.

Mojo had half folded herself, tucking her left ankle under her bottom. She had draped her left arm along the back of the sofa, letting her right leg, alone, dangle to the floor. It would fall asleep eventually, if she didn't change positions. Left too long would it fall off? But before then, if she needed to, she could rise in a fluid motion, no struggling.

"What happened?" Dr. Granger asked, noting Mojo's disarray, her wide eyes, the way she sat, as if ready to bolt.

"I don't know. I woke up hung over. I think. I don't remember what happened. But there was blood."

Dr. Granger turned pale. "Tell me." When Mojo finished telling about the unfamiliar truck, the blood and car wash and retrieving her own truck, Dr. Granger wanted to know if she had checked her GPS.

"Yes."

"What did it say?" She tried not to sound impatient with Mojo's reticence.

"I went to the Desperada last night, at least until 10."

"Did you go somewhere else?"

"I'm sure I did, but the phone was turned off until I turned it back on this morning."

Dr. Granger absorbed this information. "You outsmarted yourself."

"Looks like it."

"Who does the truck belong to?"

"Preston Miller."

They were both quiet until Mojo, almost strident, said, "I really think it was an animal I hit." She looked at Dr. Granger with pleading eyes.

"Let's pray so," the doctor said. "But we still have to tell someone."

"Who?"

The doctor didn't answer because they both knew she was talking about the police. One policeman in particular.

"He'll take my keys."

"Of course he will," Granger said. "And if he doesn't, I'm obligated to find a way to do it myself."

"How will I get to work? How will I get here? What about Mama? I can't afford not to work or drive. I may as well be a deadbeat." Granger remained silent, but stoic. After several minutes of silence, she relented, but not much.

"You cannot continue to drive if you think you are losing control of good sense or getting drunk and getting behind the wheel. It's reckless. It would be very difficult for anyone to forgive you if you hurt someone. It would be irrevocable and hurt many people."

Mojo bowed her head.

"You also have to make sure you haven't already hurt someone."

"Tell me what to do." And Dr. Granger did, eventually, but not before she talked to whomever had been in the driver's seat. Mojo tried to listen but could only hear the sound of a familiar grief all around her.

When the emergency session was over, Mojo washed her face in the bathroom, wondering what she'd been crying about. But Granger wouldn't tell her. It would break a confidence she said.

She stood at the door to leave.

"So next week?"

Granger nodded.

Mojo took a few deep breaths before leaving. For all she knew, she was about to turn herself in for murder.

The doctor gave her an encouraging smile, as if to say it would be ok. Mojo didn't believe her, believing instead the doctor was distancing herself, like any good doctor would do, but she left anyway, to do the right thing. The tinsel, which Granger had declined to cut from her hair at Mojo's outraged request, snaked through the messy bun on top of her head like a strand of royal angel hair.

About the Author

Tammy Sharp, a native of Vernon Parish, Louisiana is an award-winning poet, journalist and teacher. She and her husband, Kenny, also own and operate Hobo Holler Farm in Sabine Parish, Louisiana, where they live with two sons, two dogs, two cats, three cows, two pigs, three ducks, 13 chickens and a dizzying procession of bunny rabbits.

www.ingramcontent.com/pod-product-compliance
Lightning Source LLC
Chambersburg PA
CBHW022159170626
46807CB00005B/2268